THE

TIMEKEEPER'S

SON

MIKE E. MILLER

For Cassy

You are a one-of-a-kind woman,
and I cherish you with my whole heart.

Table of Contents

ONE

"Come on, Andy. It's time to get up." The voice was far away and muffled as though I were under water. "Rise and shine." It was louder that time as I emerged from the depths of sleep. My eyes fluttered open and I strained against the fogginess that enveloped my consciousness.

"Mom?" I squinted at her as I pushed up onto an elbow. "Is everything okay?" I reached across the bed to wake my wife, but I hit empty air. She was gone. In fact, her whole side of the bed was missing. I was in a twin bed.

"Everything's fine, hon. It's time to get up for school." She leaned against the doorjamb, an amused smile crossing her lips.

"School?" I blinked my eyes, trying to coax them into focusing. The room wasn't my own, but it was strangely familiar. And my mom wasn't really my mom; she couldn't be. The woman standing in the doorway couldn't be any older than I was. But she was also undeniably familiar. I knew her, but I couldn't quite place how or where. Where was I?

I surveyed the room around me and felt my heart rate rise as the sense of familiarity became recognition. Luke Skywalker and Darth Vader were on my blanket, fighting an eternal, lightsaber duel. An old, beaten up, puke-green dresser stood in one corner. On the wall next to it, there was a poster of the U.S.S. Enterprise emblazoned across a backdrop of stars. It felt like I had been here before because I had. It looked just like the room I grew up in.

I sucked in my breath as I shot up into a sitting position, pushing myself backward toward the corner of the bed. This bedroom was not the

1

only replica from my past. I looked again at the woman in the doorway and she did look like my mother after all, only not in this decade. That was why I could recognize her. She could be my mother's twin, only the gray was gone from her hair and the coarse lines that framed the corners of her mouth and eyes were smooth. She was an impossibly young version of herself.

I was in my old bedroom. My mom looked like she stepped straight out of the past. I thought through the implications and lifted the blanket that covered me, terrified of what I might see. My terror became real as I saw that my feet were only about half as far away from my body as they should have been. They were the short, skinny legs of a child. I jumped backward again, only there was nowhere else to go. I ran out of bed and I fell off the edge, landing in the space between it and the wall.

My mom started to laugh as she watched the spectacle. "What in the world was that about?"

I righted myself and looked up at her from my cubbyhole, still unable to believe what I was seeing. She was looking back at me with a grin and I was at a complete loss. To her, the only odd thing was that I had fallen off the bed. The fact that I was a child seemed to be perfectly normal.

Realizing that she was still waiting for a response, I said the first thing that came into my head: "Spider! There was spider on my bed!"

That made her laugh even more. "Babe, that spider is more afraid of you than you are of it. It thinks you're a great, big giant." As her giggles trailed off, she added, "I'll bet you're plenty awake now, though."

"Yes," I said. "Yes, I am." The past several seconds had definitely ripped away any leftover remnants of sleep.

My mother threw me a wink and turned, walking out my room and down the hall. She left me to my predicament, only I didn't know what to do with it. What I wanted to do was climb back into bed. I wanted to pull the covers over my head and go back to sleep. I wanted to wake up normally. Instead, I looked down at the miniature version of myself, my heart thumping in my chest as my brain still tried to comprehend what my eyes were seeing. Everything – my room, my mom, me – was as though the past twenty-five or thirty years had never happened, except for the fact that I knew things. My child-sized brain contained my entire life and I knew things. I *knew* things. I remembered graduating high school; I remembered my father's death. I remembered marrying Sarah. I knew how to drive, how to cook, how to… be a man. I knew things that this body could not possibly have experienced.

I climbed up and across the bed, dropping off the other side. As I swept back the curtains, I stood in amazement as I saw my old neighborhood below me. The Johnston's house was across the street, untouched by the flames that caused them to rebuild when I was a teenager. Next door, the Mitchell's Toyota truck was in the driveway, a sticker across the back window that read, "A man's gotta have a Toy." A white dog named Cat lay under the large oak in their front yard.

"This can't happen. This can't be real." But as I looked down on the neighborhood, I knew it had to be. I could feel the carpet between my toes. The rough texture of the curtain's underside was a scratchy contrast to the velvety surface of the front. This was too real to be a dream. I had somehow stepped directly into my own past; I had walked headlong into the impossible.

I let the curtain go and turned back to face the insanity that was my childhood bedroom. I felt completely stunned as I tried to take it all in. It took most of my energy just to keep myself from hyperventilating. None of this made sense. This kind of thing didn't happen in real life. It just didn't.

I sat down on the bed and put my head into my hands. "What am I going to do?" I asked the walls around me. They didn't answer. There was only a silence that reflected my own feelings of hopelessness. I wanted to run away, but there was nowhere to go. I wanted to scream for help, but who would help me? I was alone without even a clue about what to do next.

All I could think of was that it had to be some big, cosmic joke. In my imagination, I could see God having a huge belly laugh at my expense. And He didn't even have the common decency to let me wake up on my own. No, my mom had to be standing in the doorway, increasing my freak-out factor by ten. But that was assuming God even had a part in it. As I sat there with my head in my hands, I knew nothing. I didn't understand what happened or why. I didn't know what was going on or what to do next.

The only thing I did know was that my mom was going to come back to my room soon to check on me. I didn't want to be sitting on my bed in my miniature tighty-whiteys with my head in my hands when she did. I had to get some form of control over myself so I wasn't a babbling idiot.

"Okay, Andy. You've got to get up," I told myself, surprised at the sound of my own prepubescent voice. It was alien to me. It was high pitched and it sounded nothing like the voice I remembered. But still, I pushed myself off the bed. I had to get dressed. I had to play along and hope things would start to make sense. I could only pray that something would reveal itself. There was nothing else to do.

I slid open one of my drawers and the clothes inside were, without a doubt, from my childhood. There were corduroy pants and there were stiff, dark, blue jeans. There were mesh t-shirts and Izod knockoffs. I saw white tube socks with big, red or yellow stripes at the top. I let out a sigh as I sorted through them. I thought these clothes were so cool when I was a kid. Now, I wanted nothing to do with them.

I settled for a pair of jeans and a white and red shirt. After taking care of my morning business, I braced myself for the trip downstairs. I knew it was going to be an equally shocking reflection of my past. And I was right. The carpet, the pictures on the walls, even the ugly, white couch with the gold, embroidered vines were straight from my memories. They were simultaneously stressful and comforting.

My father's old chair sat on the far side of the room. It was a gigantic thing compared to my small form. The tan, corduroy fabric was old and worn. I hadn't seen that chair in decades. It was one of the first things to go after my dad died. Looking at it now, I could see myself climbing up into my dad's lap. We would watch *The A-Team* or *The Fall Guy*. Many of my memories from this time were vague, but I could remember loving the excitement of the shows and the closeness of my dad.

My eyes began to tear up as I saw his coffee cup sitting on the small table beside it. The morning paper sat alongside the cup, opened to the daily crossword puzzle. "He's still alive," I whispered as I ran my hand along the fabric of the chair. He used to sit here in the mornings, sipping his coffee as he worked through the puzzles. I picked up the cup, cradling it in my hands. I had hoped that there would still be some warmth to it, that there would be an additional confirmation that he had been right here. It was cold.

As I sat the cup back in its place, I started to wonder what else might be different. I thought about my mom. She was nothing like the woman I remembered. And it wasn't just her age. Almost everything about her was different. She had been smiling and laughing. She actually winked at me. She was waking me up.

Thinking back, I could only remember the times I had to wake her up. Pounding on her door almost never worked, so I would have to make myself walk through her door. I would often find her lying uncovered on her bed, sometimes still in her clothes from the night before, sometimes not clothed at all. There would be an empty bottle lying next to her on the bed or maybe on the nightstand. I would shake her; I would yell at her that I needed to go to school and that she needed to get up.

She would eventually stir, but it was often a long and painful process. And when she did wake up, she would always look embarrassed – as though she wanted to climb inside a deep hole and hide. She would sit there for a moment, not speaking and not moving except to pull the sheet over her nakedness. She would stare off into nothingness, telling me to get some breakfast.

Then she would come downstairs and do her best to pretend nothing had happened. She would try to be upbeat and she would make herself smile and laugh in spite of the incessant pounding in her skull. I could always tell it wasn't genuine, though. Even with my child's eyes, I could see. We both knew it wasn't right and we knew it was no way to raise me. But we would go about pretending until the next time it happened. It might be the next morning or the morning after that. Sometimes it was a few days or maybe a week. On very rare occasions, she might even go a month before she shattered the illusion that things were getting back to normal. But she always did.

Shaking off the memory, I hurried to the kitchen and grabbed one of the barstools, pulling it behind me as I crossed the linoleum. I slid it up against the cabinet and clambered up, reaching out a hand to steady myself as the seat tried to spin beneath my weight. I had to see. I had to see if she really was as different as she seemed.

There was an old tea set in the cabinet above the stove. There was a turkey platter and a deviled egg tray, too. What wasn't there was the assortment of booze. There was no rum, whiskey, bourbon, or any of her other vices, which usually included anything she could get cheap. In my memories, she would stock up on as much as she could afford, sticking them in this cabinet where she thought I wouldn't see them.

Back down on the floor, I swung open the pantry door. The trashcan inside held some papers and a used bologna wrapper, but no empty bottles. The couch cushions weren't hiding any bottles either: none were stashed in the recesses beneath and behind them. I breathed out in relief each time I came up empty, but I was almost afraid to believe it. Dad wasn't dead; Mom hadn't fallen into her pit.

Maybe it was my pessimistic nature, or maybe it was too many years of watching her drink away her pain, but a new question formed in my mind. It threatened to vanquish the spark of hope before it had a chance to ignite. How old was I? Where in my past did I land? I thought of my dad's newspaper on the table and I scooped it up, looking at the date. April 23, 1983. A feeling of dread replaced any hope as I realized how close it was to another date that was branded into my mind forever. It was only four days before the date inscribed on my father's tombstone.

"Oh, man," I said. The paper fell from my hands, doing a half turn and then flopping over as it hit the carpet at my feet. My dad was alive and my mom was carefree because it hadn't happened yet. I was standing on the precipice of my own living hell. Things just kept getting better and better.

From upstairs, I heard the sound of my mom's bedroom door opening. "Hey babe, did you get something to eat? I'll be down in just a couple minutes." Great. She was going to come back down and I would have to appear normal. I couldn't be babbling about time travel, being married, and my father dying. She would think I was nuts.

"Getting it now," I said, barely able to get the words out. I didn't want to eat. I didn't want to talk to my mom. I just wanted some time to myself so I could figure something out. I had no idea what I was going to figure out, but it couldn't be too hard to know more than I did right then. As it was, I knew absolutely nothing. Zero, zilch, and nada.

I fixed a bowl of cereal anyway. Conflict didn't seem like a good idea in my current state of mind. I was already stressed out enough. So, instead risking confrontation, I sat down to a bowl of Cookie Crisp.

I actually started to relax as I ate and I added that to my mental list of things I couldn't believe. And, before long, my mind started to wander. Almost everything around me brought back some kind of memory. Even turning my world upside down couldn't change that. I was practically swimming in nostalgia. The cereal itself, even the ceramic bowl with its multi-colored, concentric rings brought back scenes from my youth. To my right, I could see the burn marks covering the cabinet by the sink. The whole side was black as a permanent reminder of my independent nature.

When I was maybe five or so, I had gotten up one morning to a quiet house. I was hungry and I decided to make some toast. The only problem was that I had never actually done it before, but I wasn't going to let a thing like that stop me. So, I grabbed the bread and climbed up, sitting cross-legged on the countertop in front of the toaster.

I couldn't remember for sure, but I must have put butter on the bread before I put it in the toaster. I dropped the bread into the bread slots, pushing down the levers to activate the toaster. Everything was as it should have been for a minute. The wires inside glowed a bright red and the bread started to turn a golden brown. But then, everything went horribly wrong. Little flames started to flicker up from inside the toaster.

The little flames became big flames and those flames became what seemed to be a raging inferno. I flipped backward off the countertop, falling onto and off of the stool behind me. I lay there on my back looking up at the flames as they shot up the side of the cabinet, scorching it. I jumped to my feet, watching with wide eyes, terrified that the whole house was going up. It must have been luck, but I hit the toaster on the side and knocked it into the sink. It managed it to land upside down and the fire went out as it lost its oxygen.

"Lanie should be here soon," my mom said, startling me out of the memory. I hadn't heard her come down the stairs. I didn't remember the house being this quiet.

Lanie. That was a name from the past. What was her last name? Parker, I think. Lanie Parker. I hadn't thought of her in years. She was a couple years older than I was and she lived just up the street. We had started the tradition of walking to school together when we were younger and the habit just stuck. My mom walked us to school and Lanie and I walked home. I couldn't be sure, but I thought I would hang out at her house in the afternoons until my dad got home. That was a long time ago.

My mom pulled a cup from the small mug tree on the counter and poured herself some coffee. She lifted the cup so that it was just under her nose, taking time to inhale the scent of the dark brew. She was not the woman I remembered. I knew she was still this way because my dad was alive, but I just couldn't remember this side of her. Her future self was distant and morose. She was only a shell of the woman standing in front of me and it only grew worse over the years. Once I moved out and there was no one to take care of, she no longer had to pretend that things were okay.

The woman in front of me was vibrant. She was alive. Most of the differences were subtle and dramatic all at the same time. The facial expressions she made when she talked, the way she was smiling now as she enjoyed her coffee. I had only been around this new version of her for a few minutes, but she was so different that I almost couldn't fathom how it could really be her.

We sat in silence for a while as we waited for Lanie. I imagined her thoughts were filled with the tasks of the day. I couldn't remember what she did for a living back then. So many of those subtle details were lost in the years that had passed. They were distant tidbits that lay just beyond my grasp.

Three quick knocks floated in from the living room. Lanie was here. I followed my mom into the living room and another memory from the past took me by surprise. I couldn't get away from them. Only this time wasn't like the others. Not really. This memory overtook my vision in a flood, immersing me in the vision. The doorbell had rung and I was standing here as my mom went to answer. She opened the door, but it wasn't Lanie outside. No, it was no one as pleasant as Lanie. It was one of the many ghosts from my past that still haunted my dreams from time to time, even as an adult.

My mom swung open the door, revealing a policeman standing on our stoop. He somehow managed to look disheveled even though the creases in his pressed uniform looked sharp enough to cut like a knife. He was holding his hat, looking grateful that he had something in his hands because he didn't look like he quite knew what to do with them. He was stiff. He was nervous, awkward.

She opened the screen door a few inches, hesitating before she spoke. "Yes, officer?"

"Mrs. Myers?" he asked. There was a mask of seriousness over his anxiety that said he was not here to sell us tickets to the Policeman's Ball.

"May I help you?"

"You are Donna Myers?"

"Yes. What's this about?" Her look of concern was quickly transforming into one of fear. It was never good when a policeman comes to your door asking for you by name.

The officer looked at me, but quickly lowered his eyes. He lifted his gaze back to my mom and asked, "Could you come outside for a moment?" He looked like he didn't really want her to come outside. He looked like he wanted to climb back inside his cruiser and drive away. He ran his fingers around the perimeter of his hat as he waited for her to respond.

My mom pushed the screen door open enough to squeeze through and then stepped outside. She let it fall closed behind her, but she forgot to close the actual door.

"Ma'am, I..." He paused for a moment as he gathered his resolve. My mom stood tensely, leaning slightly forward onto the balls of her feet. I thought she just might come out of her skin in that brief moment. "I don't know how to say this, but there's been an accident. Your husband. He... He didn't make it. I'm so sorry."

I did believe the officer when he said he was sorry. He was sorry he had to be the one to deliver the news. He was sorry that she had to hear it. And he was sorry that she would be without a husband and I would be without a father. My mom could only look at him as he stood there holding his hat. She was frozen in place as though she had forgotten how to move, how to speak. It was only a moment, but it seemed to be a minute or maybe an hour. Maybe a week.

Finally, she spoke in a flurry. All of her words spilled out in a rush of desperation. "No, that can't be. He was just here this morning. He dropped me off and left. It was only an hour ago. There's a mistake. You must have made a mistake." The terror in her eyes gave way to a fiery anger as she fought to believe her own deception. "How could you do this? Scaring a person this way without checking. Without knowing for sure. I'm... I'm calling your superior."

"Ma'am-"

"Look at him!" she yelled, pivoting at the waist and flinging the screen door open, pinning it behind her leg. Her eyes were wild. They were feral. His eyes, in contrast, said that he had seen this reaction countless times before. They were full of pity. "You should be ashamed, coming here and telling me that his father is dead!"

"Ma'am, I'm sorry, I really am. But, there is no mistake. He had his identification on him. I'm so sorry."

"He can't be. You don't understand. He... he can't be." Her voice was starting to break. She couldn't hold back the truth. She was starting to believe. She was starting to believe what she didn't want to believe, what she couldn't believe. If she believed that he was dead, her entire world could collapse. And it did collapse. In that moment, everything changed.

"Earth to Andy. Come in, Andy." Slowly, I blinked back into the reality of the moment. Lanie was standing in the doorway, a silly grin pasted on her face. "It looked like you were on Mars or something. Or maybe Pluto, dog breath," she laughed. I think she was quite pleased with herself, coming up with that Pluto bit.

"Shut up, Lanie." It was the best nine-year-old comeback I could think of. I wanted to tell her that Pluto wasn't even a planet anymore.

"All right, you two. Be nice," my mom said. "Ready to go?"

We stepped out the door and into the bright, morning sunshine. Spring was in full bloom, but the mornings were still a bit crisp. Lanie's blonde hair flew out behind her as the breeze picked up into a stronger wind. As we started the short trek to school, the idea of sitting in a classroom all day was about the most unappealing idea I could come up with. The bright side, if there was one, was that it would only be fourth grade material. Maybe I could actually spend some time trying to figure out what to do.

"So, anything big happening at school today?" my mom asked.

"Not that I know of." I really had no idea, of course.

"Didn't you say you had a spelling test? What words are on it?"

"Um..." I had to think for a second. Not to remember, but to make something up. "Tornado, electric, principal, I can't remember all of them, but I know how to spell them."

"How about dork?" Lanie chided. "Is that on your list?"

"Very funny, Lanie. How about annoying? I'll bet that's on your list."

"I don't have lists anymore," she smiled. "My teacher said I was too smart. I get to sit and watch all the other kids do the work. I just have to go because it's the law."

"Okay, you guys. How about stinker? That's got to be on both your lists."

TWO

As I stepped up to the doors of Crestfield Elementary, I was overcome again by how real this all was. It still didn't make any sense, but it was certainly real. There were children all around me and I fit right in. I wasn't the adult who was out of place among a sea of children. No one was wondering why I was here. I was just another fourth grader taking part in the institution of American education.

But, to me, it was all wrong. I had already spent kindergarten through sixth grade in these halls. I had gone on to high school, to college, and into the military. I had gotten married and Sarah and I had built a life together. Now, I was a child and there was no Sarah in my life. I was stuck revisiting a painful past, dropping into my youth mere days before my father was supposed to die. I had no idea why I was here, what I was supposed to do, or how I was going to get back where I belonged. I only knew I didn't want to do this again. I didn't want to re-experience my father's death and I didn't want to watch my mother deteriorate into her own hell. And I really didn't want to throw in lower elementary studies on top of it.

My gut reaction was to turn around and walk away. I wanted to go down to the creek or into the crawlspace under my house or just about anywhere but here. I wanted to get away from all of it and be alone with my thoughts. The only thing that kept me from it was all the drama that would ensue if I did. I was going to see my dad again tonight. I was going to see him for the first time in twenty-five years. I didn't want to cloud that reunion with my having skipped school.

So, instead of walking away, I walked inside. The building was enormous to me. The ceilings seemed to be fifteen feet high and the teachers looked like giants. Of course, the ceilings weren't that high and the teachers really weren't giants, but they sure looked that way. Somewhere between yesterday and today, I had lost a couple of feet in height.

I was in fourth grade. That meant my teacher was Mrs. Leach. Where was her room? I started to feel a twinge of panic, but I reminded myself that there were only two main hallways. I had a fifty-fifty shot of picking the right one. I made my way down the corridor in front of me, looking at the nameplates next to each door as I went. Mrs. Thompson, Mr. James, and Ms. Abramowitz were on my left, the restrooms and a janitor closet were to my right. Artwork created by the student body covered portions of the sea-foam green cinderblocks: chalk drawings of the moon and stars on black paper; blue, green, and purple kites were cut from construction paper.

Farther along, I saw Mrs. Leach's name printed next to a door on my right. I turned in and was surprised again by the familiarity of it all. I hadn't been in this room for decades and yet I still felt as though I knew the place. It was as though the memories had sat just below the surface this whole time, just waiting for the right trigger to bring them out. I didn't have all the details, like where I was supposed to sit, but the classroom was unmistakably familiar.

I breathed a sigh of relief as I looked down at the desks. Mrs. Leach had put stickers on each one, identifying the assigned student. "Thank God," I whispered under my breath as I saw the word "Andy" printed in neat, block letters. Staying under the radar was one of my prime objectives this morning. Sitting in the wrong seat probably wouldn't help me achieve that goal. I slid into my seat to wait for the final bell to ring.

As I waited, I lifted up the top of the desk to see the jumble of textbooks inside: Social Studies and Math, Reading and Science. It occurred to me how much was missing or even incorrect in some of those books. Technology and society had come a long way. Back then, there were no cellphones, tablet computers, or GPS navigation. NASA wouldn't launch the Hubble Space Telescope for another seven years, and HIV had only been discovered two years before: the worst of the AIDS scare was yet to come. It was sobering to think about how much of what I took as history was still the future. None of these people had experienced the world I had taken for granted.

"Get out of my stuff, Andy," I heard from above me. Lowering the top of the desk, I realized my mistake as I saw the boy standing with his arms crossed. It turns out that one of the details I was missing was that there was more than one Andy in the class. Evidently, Mrs. Leach hadn't thought to put the first initial of our last names. So much for not wanting to draw attention by sitting in the wrong seat.

"It's not your stuff. It says 'Andy' right there. My name is Andy, isn't it?" I said, tapping the block letters with my finger. I smiled up at him, hoping at least to salvage the situation with some laughs, but the best I got from the kids around us was a couple of snickers.

"Mrs. Leach, Andy's in my seat and he won't get up."

Crap. Tattletale. "All right, Andy, don't get all worked up. I'm going, I'm going." Thankfully, Mrs. Leach only shook her head as I got up and found the correct seat. That at least saved it from becoming a bigger deal.

As the bell rang and we got started, the morning lessons were pretty much as I expected them to be. We talked about states and capitals. We did some basic multiplication and division. Thankfully, recess wasn't that long of a wait.

I spent most of the break hanging back, keeping to myself. That actually surprised me. I had the energy of youth, but no will to exercise it. I must have said a dozen times or more how much fun it would be to be a kid again. I thought it would be awesome to have the vigor of youth along with the appreciation for life that you don't get until much later. But, being a kid with an adult's brain meant that I brought all my troubles with me.

So, instead of engaging with the kids around me, I just wandered around, acting out the introverted nature that I didn't pick up until the years following my dad's death. I watched the kids I had known in another life. It was strange, seeing them in their youth. I knew more about some of them than they did and I could see those things reflected in their younger selves.

Alicia Brower and a girl named Tonya, I think, were playing on the swings. They swung back and forth, pigtails swaying as they moved. They looked as though they didn't have a care in the world. If I remembered right, Alicia grew up to start a web company and made out pretty well for herself. Tonya's story wasn't as happy. I think she got pregnant at sixteen and ended up dropping out of school.

Behind them, Tommy Helms was kicking a ball back and forth with a boy I didn't know. They were grinning and laughing, talking trash whenever one of them would miss. Tommy eventually took his own life. He slammed his car into a rock wall at the bottom of the Y-Highway exit ramp off of 71. I didn't remember all the details, but I did remember that about a hundred kids held a candlelight vigil the night before his funeral.

As I walked further, a weird set of monkey bars sat off to my left. I still couldn't quite figure out what it was supposed to be. It looked like a worm, only it had big ladders that extended off its trunk like legs. The paint was peeling and bits of rust showed from underneath as the elements took their toll. I drove by here a couple summers ago, reminiscing about the past, and they had ripped all this stuff out and replaced it with newer, safer equipment. There were actually wood chips under each piece instead of the hard asphalt that was there now.

At the base of one of the insect's legs, there was a small group of fourth and fifth graders gathered around another boy. As soon as I saw him, I knew exactly who he was. His name was Aaron Rogers. Kind of like my dad's tombstone, some things burn into your memory so permanently that you might never forget them – even if you lived two lifetimes. He was one of those.

To the casual observer, it looked like they were having a great time, joking and laughing. The unfortunate truth was that they weren't. Or at least Aaron wasn't. He was a target for the other kids. Torturing that poor boy was almost a sport.

Aaron was an overweight kid with a shock of bright, orange hair. It was almost the color of a carrot. His clothes were always too small and it was common for his shirt to pull up, exposing his belly button as his generous gut spilled over the top of his pants. And I'll never forget the smell that came off him. The distinctive smell of body odor constantly emanated from him like steam rolling off a pot of cabbage. Sometimes, it was so bad that he would leave his scent behind in an invisible cloud that hovered in his wake for several minutes after he departed.

I adjusted my course, moving to bring myself within earshot of the group. If I was going to be trapped in this rehash of my youth, I may as well try to correct some of the sins of my past. As I drew closer, it looked like two of them were the main antagonists. The others stood by in the same way people slow down to watch a traffic accident unfold.

"Man, Aaron, you stink!" one of them said. I couldn't remember the boy's name. I thought he was a fifth grader, but he looked like he might even be in sixth grade. He towered over the other kids.

"Yeah, you smell like butt. Don't you ever wash?" another chimed in. I think his name was Ernie Hammett.

Aaron didn't say much and he certainly wasn't trying to defend himself. He just laughed as though he thought they were funny. He was likely hoping they would get bored and move on, but they didn't. They almost never did. Instead, they continued to throw insults at him. They worked to chip away at his resolve, and they wouldn't stop until recess ended or they reduced him to tears.

"Hey guys, what's going on?" I asked as I walked up. Of course, I already knew. I had been one of the kids who had laughed when they made fun of him. Maybe not in this particular circumstance, but there were others. I still get pangs of regret when I think back to this time. I wasn't one of the instigators, but I always felt like I may as well have been.

"Hey, Andy!" The kid whose name I couldn't remember lit up as he saw me. He lifted his arm and pointed in my direction, bouncing up and down on his toes. "Maybe you can help us. We're trying to figure out how Aaron can love smelling like donkey crap."

He looked like he was having the time of his life. He shifted his body back toward Aaron and folded his arms across his chest. He still had that same, smug smile. Everything about him seemed to be daring the boy to fight back.

Aaron, however, was not smiling and he certainly wasn't fighting back. He had been trying everything he could to keep them from knowing how much they were getting to him. He waited for me to respond, but the smile was gone. There was a mix of sadness and fear in his eyes as he looked at me. I imagined that it wasn't me he was seeing. Instead, he saw another lion that had come to clamp down on his neck as he tried desperately to escape.

Bobby Richardson. That was the big one's name. Suddenly and out of nowhere, the memories popped back into my consciousness. He was never a nice kid. In fact, he had gone well beyond not being nice. He was a bully. Even at such a young age, he seemed to have mastered the art of sniffing out weakness and exploiting it for his own pleasure. He preyed on the weak as if he actually was a lion, waiting for a member of the herd to separate and leave himself open for attack.

His mean streak had gotten worse over the years. He eventually ended up in juvenile hall because he beat a nine-year-old girl unconscious, leaving her for dead. It wasn't until he went away that we understood how badly he had it at home. Rumors had spread like wildfire about the abuse he endured. His father would come home drunk and take his frustrations out on the boy. He would often invent reasons to punish Bobby just to satiate his own need for control and retribution.

I took a step closer to them and made a point to look Aaron in the eye. "What makes you think he likes it?" I asked Bobby without looking back at him. There was a moment of relative silence as I locked eyes with Aaron. All around us were the sounds of children playing, but that spot on the playground was completely without sound. I could hear the girls on the swings and a group of kids playing kickball. There was a crow crying out in the far trees. But the children around me were silent.

Finally breaking the silence, Bobby said, "He's that way all the time. He's got to like it."

"Oh?" I asked, still not turning to face him. "Do you think he has more control over his life than you do?"

Bobby stood silently, not sure what to say. I didn't think he was used to people standing up to him, particularly people who were so much smaller than he was.

"How much control do you have when your daddy comes home drunk? When he takes the belt to you or locks you in your room for hours at a time, why don't you do something about it? Why not rip the hinges off the doors when you have to pee instead of soaking it up with dirty laundry?"

I had no idea why, but I could see a clear picture of Bobby in his room, sitting on the floor with his knees pulled up to his chest as he sobbed into his arms; his urine soaked clothes lying next to him in a pile. There was no way the image could be of a real situation, but I had an odd confidence that it was. Impossibly, it seemed to be more than just the benefits of age and hindsight. Little snippets of his life were floating across my mind like photographs flipped about in a breeze.

When I finally turned to face him, every boy in the group was staring at me. Not one of them was moving. None were speaking. "I'll tell you why, Bobby. You don't fight back because you are just a boy. What happens to you isn't your fault just like what happens to Aaron isn't his."

"You shut up, Andy. You just shut up. You shut up or I'll make you!" he said. He wasn't smiling anymore. Instead, the anger and hurt in his eyes were boring a hole through me.

"I know plenty about you and your daddy, Bobby. I know that both of you like to pick on people you think are weaker than you. I know that you feel powerless and you look for ways to feel powerful –to feel strong and unafraid. What your father does to you isn't your fault, but what you choose to do is."

"I said shut up!" Bobby raised his fists and ran towards me like a bull charging a matador. As he came, I suddenly found myself hoping that I had better hand-eye coordination than a normal nine-year-old. I was willing to take a beating, but I really preferred not to.

As he approached, I managed to sidestep out of his way. He ran a little past where I was standing and he tried his best to come to a quick stop, bending over a bit in the process. I turned toward him and kicked him in the backside as he was still fighting his forward momentum. This sent him toppling and he didn't have enough warning to be able to soften his descent with his hands. Instead, his face half smacked and half slid across the asphalt.

Bobby rolled over and sat up, looking up at me. He had small bits of gravel stuck to his face and blood was flowing freely from his nose. Tears streamed down his face. He started to get up, maneuvering an arm and one of his legs under himself to push up. Surprisingly, two of the boys in the group stepped toward him, silently telling him that further aggression was a bad idea. Bobby clambered to his feet as he watched them, brushing the rocks and sand from his hands.

"You need to go the nurse," I said. "Tell her you fell. And you might tell Mr. Paterson about your dad. There are people who can help you." Dropping his head to look down at his feet, he just walked away. He reminded me of a whipped dog as he went. All the fire seemed to have gone out of him.

"You... you talk like a grownup," Aaron said as I turned back to face him.

"I know I do. Aaron, I want you to know that there is nothing wrong with you. When kids like Bobby pick on you, it's because they think making others feel badly will make them feel better."

I don't think he knew what to say. I didn't know if it was because he was shocked that I was trying to help him or if it was because I didn't sound anything like a fourth grader. What was clear was that the pretense of laughter was gone now; tears were openly rolling down his cheeks, creating blotchy red marks around his eyes and on his cheeks. Off in the distance, the teacher's whistle blew indicating it was time to line up. Recess was over. Aaron used both hands to wipe the tears from his face and then turned to go find his place in line.

The rest of the school day was a challenge to get through. In part, it was because of the lack of stimulation from fourth grade material. Mostly, though, it was because I couldn't stop thinking. I thought about Bobby and Aaron. I thought about my dad. I thought about the mess I was in and I wondered whether I would ever see Sarah again. I was torn between the desire to see my dad again and the need to go home to my normal life. I had only been in this time, this reality, for less than a day and it was already lonely.

After school, I made my way out to the base of the flagpole where Lanie and I met to walk home every day. Lanie was already there waiting, squinting at me as the afternoon sun shone into her eyes.

"Hey, squirt. How's it hanging?" she asked, raising her hand to block the sun.

"Pretty well. How about you?" I asked as I stepped onto the sidewalk, looking back at her to follow.

Instead of following, she cocked her head to the side a bit and looked at me for a moment before she responded. "I'll bet you're feeling good. I heard about Bobby Richardson."

"Oh?" I replied, trying to feign ignorance. Evidently, news of the incident travelled quickly. I didn't end up in the principal's office, so it must not have made it back to the teachers yet, at least in a way they could corroborate. Maybe Bobby really did say he fell. I could only hope.

"Don't be a dork. I heard you beat him up pretty good. I didn't know you were a fighter. And he's even in fifth grade."

Oh, that. Well, he was picking on Aaron Rogers. I told him to stop and he wouldn't."

"My hero," she said in her best imitation of Darla from *The Little Rascals,* holding both hands up to her cheek and pretending to swoon.

"Oh my gosh. Now who's being the dork?" I asked, rolling my eyes. I reached over and gave her arm a light shove. "Race you to the stop sign!"

I got the head start, making it ten or fifteen feet before she recovered and got her body into motion. "No fair, Myers. I'll get you," she yelled, pumping her legs to catch up.

I ran as fast as I could, but she was faster. Lanie had just over two years on me and her legs were a lot longer. Looking back over my shoulder, I could see that she was closing the gap quickly. Seeing her approach pushed me to move my legs even faster and I was surprised at how great it felt. There was a freedom to running I hadn't felt in a long time. None of the normal aches and pains or tight muscles associated with age were weighing me down. I felt like I could run forever. She managed to catch me just as I was crossing the stop sign, but I still won, even if it was barely.

"Ha, I won! You suck!" I said, bending over and placing my hands on my knees to catch my breath.

"Only 'cause you cheated," she replied, breathing just as hard.

We started walking again, this time more quietly as we worked to get our breathing back under control. As we reached our street, Lanie looked over at me and asked, "So, is that why you seem so much happier than you were this morning? Because you beat up Bobby and saved the day?"

I didn't know that happy was the word I would have used to describe me. Although, I guess I did feel better than I had that morning. The situation with Aaron showed that I really could change things. I hoped that meant that I wasn't constrained by what happened the first time around.

"I don't know," I said. "I didn't really beat him up though. I just made him stop."

"Not what I heard."

We reached her house and made the turn into the driveway. A Bradford pear sat in the front yard, covered by the white blossoms that marked springtime. Their sweet smell wafted over to us, whispering to our senses.

Lanie bounded up the steps and poked her head inside the door, calling out, "Mom, we're here. We're going to play outside for a bit."

I heard her mom's muffled assent from inside as Lanie let the storm door fall closed, clanging loudly as it bounced off the frame. She came down the steps in short, quick hops from one step to the next, allowing herself to fall back on her hands and butt as she reached the last step.

"What time is your dad getting home?" she asked, looking up at me.

"Pretty soon, I think." My dad's restaurant was only open for breakfast and lunch, so he got home a lot earlier than my mom did. I didn't remember it being that long of a wait after school.

I stepped up to the porch and turned around, dropping down beside her. As I did, Jimmy Thomas and a friend emerged from the house across the street. They descended the steps and Jimmy vaulted the porch railing, swinging his legs over with ease. As he landed, the other boy threw a soccer ball at him, smacking him in the forehead. Now with Jimmy cursing and the other boy laughing, they crossed into the street. They started juggling the ball between them, bouncing it off their knees, chests and foreheads.

I looked over at Lanie to find her gaze fixed on me. "You beating up Bobby isn't the only thing I heard today," she said.

"Oh." I said, holding back the sigh I wanted to let out. "What else did you hear?"

"I heard you sounded like a grownup. When you talked to Bobby and Aaron, you talked like you were twenty or something."

"Who said that?" I asked. I knew it had seemed odd to them, but I hadn't thought that part of it would spread. I guess I had been hoping they would dismiss that part as just being weird.

"Julie Reeves told me."

"Who?"

"Ernie Hammett told Julie Reeves in Special Ed. She told me at second recess."

As we sat, a black Camaro turned onto the street. Its paint was like glass, reflecting the leaves from the trees above. A distinctive lightning bolt was painted across the side. The boys stopped passing the ball back and forth and stepped out of its path only to watch it pull over to the curb a few houses down.

"She said you were talking about Bobby's dad and how what he did didn't give Bobby a reason to be mean to other people. She said you told Aaron that he picked on him because he felt bad about himself. It did seem pretty smart for a rug rat like you," she said, giving a nudge to my ribs with her elbow.

"Well, that's what my mom and dad tell me sometimes. When I talk about someone being mean at school, that's what they say."

"Yeah, that's what my mom says too. But it isn't just that. You seem different today. I don't know how, but different."

Before I could respond, my dad appeared from behind the hedgerow that separated Lanie's yard from her neighbor's. Seeing him walk up to the end of Lanie's driveway was like seeing a ghost. I hadn't even seen a picture of him for years, but he was just like I remembered him. Most everything I saw today fought a strange battle between the real and the unreal, but this took it to another level. He had been dead for twenty-five years and yet there he was, standing at the foot of the driveway waiting for me to walk over to him. Seeing him like this made me want to believe that we could walk off into the sunset, live happily ever after, or do whatever it was people did in storybook endings.

Except I knew that wasn't the ending that was planned. Everything was in place for him to be taken away from me all over again. Intervening with Aaron had planted a seed that said things could be different, but seeing my father challenged the idea. I felt the conflict between seeing him and remembering life without him. In that moment, I felt both the enormity of my loss and the joy of seeing him again. But in that moment, joy won out.

I launched myself off the step and ran as fast as I could to the end of the driveway. I caught him off guard, jumping up and grabbing his neck. I was a smiling, incoherent mess and I was trying as hard as I could to hold back the tears that wanted to come. He reached around my middle, helping to support the weight and returning the hug.

"Wow, bud. I'm happy to see you, too," he said as he set me back down on the concrete. "You act like I haven't been home for a month."

Try years, decades even. I couldn't say that, so I kept it simple. "I just missed you today."

"Well, I missed you too. Ready to go home?"

"Yeah, sure." I turned toward Lanie and waved. "Bye, Lanie. See you tomorrow."

"See you," she said. She had stood up and was resting her hands on her hips. She turned, pulled open the screen door, and disappeared inside as it closed behind her.

THREE

The short walk home was almost like a dream. We talked about my day at school; we talked about his day at the restaurant. It was chitchat, but it was nice. And I was glad he was initiating the conversation. Events that were recent memories to the people around me were ancient history to me. I had no idea what we had for dinner the night before or what we were doing that weekend. I knew none of the details of my new present and that made conversation difficult. I didn't know what to say.

At the same time, I had a million questions that I didn't know how to ask. There were so many things that I wanted to know, that I wanted to hear about. I wanted to know more about who he was and where he came from. I wanted to know him in ways I never got to the first time around. I had so few memories about him. And getting my mom to talk about him was next to impossible. If I brought him up, she would usually start crying if she didn't shut me down immediately. Sometimes she would try to be clever and redirect the conversation. Other times she would just tell me she didn't want to talk about it. The few times we did end up talking about him almost came with a guarantee that I would find her passed out the next morning. I eventually stopped asking.

I knew almost nothing about him as a result. All the pictures were gone or locked away and she had sold off or given away most anything that served as a reminder. It was as though she tried to remove everything that triggered her memories in a vain attempt to silence them, to silence the pain associated with them. And, when that didn't work, there was always help in the bottom of a bottle.

We walked inside the house and the sharp contrast between the bright sunshine and the dim room made it difficult to see. We usually kept the drapes closed during the day, so only a thin sliver of the sun's rays penetrated into the room. Stepping over to his chair, my dad picked up his leftover coffee cup and the paper.

"How do cheeseburgers sound?" he asked as he started toward the kitchen.

"Oh yeah," I said. His cheeseburgers stood out in my mind as almost being a delicacy.

"Well, good. I'll call you when your mom gets home if you want to go play."

"Maybe I could help you?"

"Sure you can," he said, a look of surprise on his face. I don't think I showed much interest in helping him cook at this age.

He got the ingredients out of the fridge and I grabbed the stepstool. When they were home, I went through the effort of getting out the stepstool. When they weren't around, the barstools were easier.

We had a great time making the burgers, or at least I did. Part of it was the time together, but a lot of it was that I could see so many things about him for the first time. The way he laughed, the way he talked, all the mannerisms I recognized in myself. Even the way he could only take cutting onions for a couple minutes at a time before he had to leave the room to get away from the fumes. It was uncanny how many ways we were alike.

He let me help form the patties and even flip the burgers a time or two. I tried to act as if I had never done it before and I think I did pretty well at faking it. I tried to ask questions and even messed up a little. As we were working, it occurred to me that I was about the same age as him. But, he was still my dad. Helping him in the kitchen and letting him teach me was awesome, even if what he was teaching me had nothing to do with making burgers.

We had just put pieces of cheese on to melt when my mom walked in. Closing the door behind her, she slung her purse down on the table by the door. It always made a meaty thump as she dropped it. My mom did like big purses. Her purse always reminded me of Mary Poppins' magic bag. If you needed something, it was probably in there somewhere.

"Long day," she said, coming into the kitchen. My dad wiped his hands on a towel and stepped in to give her a peck on the mouth.

"Well, go sit down. We've got this covered. I *am* a professional after all."

"Whatever. You had just as long of a day. What can I do to help?"

"No talking you out of it is there?" my dad asked, smirking. Funny that I never pictured my mom as strong willed. "Set the table?"

She walked past me, pausing to run her hands through my hair, and grabbed a short stack of plates from the cabinet. My dad piled the burgers on a plate and took them along with the fries to the dining room while my mom couriered the plates and other fixings. I don't think I remember ever seeing that table cleaned off. Bills, books, and other assorted clutter always covered it. After my dad died, we usually ate dinner in front of the TV. There were a lot of TV dinners, potpies, and frozen entrees in my youth.

After dinner, we sat around together, talked for a bit, and then had TV time. We watched some shows and just hung out. The evening was very much like what I would expect normal to be – almost too normal, in fact. It reminded me of something you would see on a cheesy TV show: everyone is happy and laughing, there is lots of hair tousling and winking, and everyone is nice to everyone else. It was almost too normal to be real, but I wasn't going to complain. Not today.

"All right, bud, it's nine o'clock. Time to hit the hay," my mom said, tapping her wrist where a watch would have been if she were wearing one. Bed did feel like a good idea. The day had been a long one and I was ready for sleep. She didn't get any argument from me as I walked over to give her a hug and a kiss. Besides, maybe I would wake up in my adult body. I woke up in the wrong body this morning. Who's to say I couldn't wake up in the right one tomorrow?

"Good night, babe," she said, pulling me into a hug. "Don't forget to brush your teeth."

In the bathroom, I noticed a yellow slip of paper stuck to the glass of the mirror. As I stepped closer, I could see it was a sticky note that you might use to leave yourself reminders. It was crisp and new and the corners rested flat against the mirror. It contained only three words written in sharp, block letters: LET IT HAPPEN.

That was an odd thing to leave on a note. There was no context, no signature, nothing. Just those three words. I reached out and lifted the edge of the note, pulling it off into my hand. As I held it, I had the distinct sensation that the note was for me and that my parents didn't write it. I didn't know how I knew, but it wasn't a note with good intentions. I believed that nothing good was going to come from it. I folded the yellow square in half, dropping it into the trashcan. Just holding it had given me the willies.

Back in my room, I slid into bed and pulled the covers up to my chin. I was exhausted from stress, but I had the feeling sleep was not going to come. My brain was in overdrive, turning over the events of the day. I thought about how different my mom was. I thought about seeing my dad for the first time in twenty-five years. That was insane. And the note. I didn't even know what to think about the note except that my gut told me it was bad news.

Then there was Sarah. As I lay there in the dark and stared at the ceiling, I kept seeing her face in front of me. Her soft, auburn hair and the way her curls rested on her shoulders. The way her bright, green eyes seemed to get even more intense when she was excited or angry. I thought about her gentle spirit, how she was always trying to help those who needed it.

Little fragments of time were like shards of glass penetrating the surface of my consciousness. I thought about the time I talked her into riding that ride at the amusement park that shoots you straight up into the air. I think it was called the Xscream. It was this big column with seats all the way around it and they would strap you in. The whole section of seats would shoot upward at some crazy speed. Sarah was terrified of heights.

When the ride shot up, her eyes were huge as the shock set in. She gripped the handles on the seat as tightly as she could, afraid to look, but also afraid not to. When the ride came to a stop, she looked at me for a moment and tears practically burst from her eyes. She was so mad at me that day. She yelled, "Don't you ever ask me to do that again. Never, ever, ever!"

Each memory only made me miss her more. They made me wish she were here with me. I wished she were lying next to me so that I could hold her. If only she were with me, I think I would be okay. I could share how I was feeling and she would help me work through all this. But the truth was that she was not here. She was not with me. She was somewhere else in the city right now, but she had no idea I even existed. Her child self didn't know me, didn't love me.

And, as I walked this new version of the past, I didn't know what would happen. Would we even meet? Would we fall in love? Would my knowledge of the future cause me to push too hard when I did meet her and push her away? I had no way of knowing these things. I had no way to know if the future would bring her back to me or if she was lost forever.

In that moment, I felt like I had lost her. I had lost everything I knew, trading it for what was old. I had exchanged it for a childhood that I didn't want. If the future was as I remembered it, if this wasn't some alternate future where fathers don't die and mothers don't withdraw into a protective shell made of liquor, then there was hope that I would one day be reunited with my love. But I was torn. I didn't want to reenact the pain of my childhood, but it felt like the only way to go where I wanted to go. If it were instead some parallel version, then there was the chance that Sarah and I would never come together.

Eventually, I did find sleep. But it was a fitful sleep, and my dreams were full of things that were lost. And they were filled with things I did not want to find.

FOUR

The next morning, I couldn't help but feel a sense of disappointment as I came into consciousness. I was still a kid and I was still in my room on Henry Street. Everything was still as it used to be. Some part of me had hoped that it was just a dream and that I would wake up into normalcy. My intellect told me that was a foolish idea, but that hadn't kept me from hoping.

I wanted to go home. I wanted to be with Sarah. I was thrilled to see my dad, and last night was like a dream come true, but it just wasn't right. He had been dead for a very long time. Things were what they were and I had dealt with them as much as I could. I didn't want to pretend to be nine anymore. I didn't want to go to fourth grade. I didn't want my dad to die again. I didn't want any of it. Even if I had the power to change things, I still would have chosen to go back to my old life right then if I could have.

Sitting up, I tried to blink my eyes against the grainy feeling that comes from too little sleep. That never worked, not really, but I was hopeful. I guess there are some days where you just don't get what you want, no matter how much you hope. There are some days where life comes at you whether you are ready for it or not, whether you like it or not.

As I sat there bemoaning my predicament, I realized that I had woken up on my own. Today was Friday. I had school today. What time was it? Why hadn't my mom come in to wake me up? I felt a familiar feeling of dread as I was reminded of the events of my childhood. It was a bit of a mixed feeling because I hadn't found any alcohol; there were no bottles, no whiskey glasses with traces of her fearful escape. All of the evidence said that she wasn't drinking or that she was hiding it very well.

I forced my body to get out of the bed, but I didn't want to take the short walk to her bedroom. The lack of bottles from the day before wasn't enough to untangle the knot that had formed in my stomach. I thought about leaving her be and, instead, going down the stairs and waiting for Lanie on my own. I was an adult, at least in intellect and experience, and I would be just fine getting myself off to school.

But as I reached the top of the stairs and placed my hand on the railing, I knew I couldn't do that. A curiosity had formed in my head that was battling with the dread in my heart. I had to know. I turned away from the stairs, forcing my legs to carry me toward her door.

The door was slightly open and the light from her windows came through, cutting into the dimness of the hallway. I could see her through the crack in her door. She was lying on her side and she clasped a crumpled corner of her blanket tightly up against her chest. She purred softly as she slept.

I raised my hand and rapped twice on the door. Immediately, she lifted up, turning toward the source of the sound.

"Honey? What's wrong? What time is it?" she asked, squinting in my direction as she tried to focus on me through the slightly open door. She pushed herself up, turning to look at the clock. The broken, red lines of the digital display read 7:40. My mom threw the blankets back, swinging her legs out to meet the floor. "I overslept. I'm so sorry." She brought a hand up to her face, using her pinky to dig the sleep from the corner of one eye.

"That's okay," I answered, feeling a sense of relief. There were no signs of her having drunk the night before. There were no bottles, no empty glasses. She woke up easily and was immediately coherent. She had just simply overslept.

Still, there was something wrong. I couldn't put my finger on it, but something was off. Maybe the feeling was stemming from the note on the mirror with its cryptic message: *Let it happen.* Or maybe it was just a holdover feeling from the old memories triggered by waking up on my own on a school day. Maybe it was just from not sleeping well; a bad night's sleep can play havoc on my mood. Maybe it was all three things combined. I couldn't be sure, but the feeling was definitely real. It was almost palpable.

"Come on, babe, you've got to get dressed; Lanie's going to be here in half an hour." She pushed herself up off the bed. She tugged on her nightgown to make sure it fell into place as she stood. "Thank you for waking me up," she said as she headed for the bathroom.

Back in my room, I started to get dressed, but I realized I had no idea when I had last bathed. For all I knew, yesterday could have been the second or third day since a bath. I was guessing that it wasn't, but I had no idea. I lifted my arms and did a quick sniff-check on my pits. I didn't detect anything that was likely to knock anyone over, but I also wasn't old enough for odor trapping hair.

I decided it was better to be safe than sorry, so I grabbed my clothes and headed to the bathroom for a quick shower. As I stripped off my clothes, I caught my reflection in the mirror over the sink. I still couldn't get used to the sight of myself. Two days ago, I had been shaving and looking for gray hairs and I was probably despairing about my receding hairline while I was at it.

In the current version of me, my hairline was back where it was supposed to be and I wasn't showing even a hint of facial hair. There were no crow's feet, no lines, freckles, or any of the other signs of age. Looking into the mirror and seeing a different face looking back was unlike any experience I have ever had. It really brought the whole thing into perspective in a way nothing else could. Seeing my mom or the kids at school, even seeing my dad upright was amazing. But having my younger version look back at me was like seeing an animal talk or something. I couldn't believe my eyes no matter how many times I looked.

I took my shower, dressed and then headed down to see if there was still time for breakfast. It was 8:00, so I had about ten minutes. I wolfed down a bowl of Cap'n Crunch and was just rinsing my bowl as the doorbell rang.

"Mom, Lanie's here," I yelled. I opened the door and she was standing on the porch, hands stuffed in her pockets. Her long, blonde hair splayed out over her shoulders, looking much more flat than normal, thanks to the gray, morning light. I stepped outside and the bright sunshine from the day before was just another memory. Cooler air had crept in overnight and had brought along clouds that threatened rain. They were fitting, considering my mood.

"Morning, Lanie," I said as I stepped out the door. "My mom's coming." I had no more than said it when she came through behind me, pulling the door closed.

"Andy, did you run the shower this morning? It sounded like I heard it while I was getting ready."

"Yeah," I answered. "I felt dirty."

"Wow. I'm impressed. My little boy is becoming not so little, I guess."

Lanie turned to look at me, letting her gaze move from my feet to my head. "Nah, he's still a twerp, but thanks for playing." She grinned, delivering a jab to my upper arm.

I hadn't really thought about her hearing the shower. Taking a shower at nine wasn't a huge deal, maybe just out of the ordinary. It was all the other stuff I wasn't supposed to know how to do yet that could cause me problems if I forgot. Things like cooking an egg or sounding too smart. Those things could draw a lot of attention to me. They would look suspicious. But, then again, so what if they did?

What if I stopped trying so hard to convince everyone? It was as though I thought people were actually going to guess that I was a thirty-five year old man in a nine-year-old body. That seemed silly now that I thought about it. They might think I'm a prodigy or a genius, but there was no way they were ever going to think I was an adult trapped in a kid's body – at least in the literal sense.

I did still need to be careful because a nine-year-old with the full intellect and wisdom of a thirty-five-year-old could end up being quite the spectacle. I could see myself performing feats of what seemed like genius for entertainment or, even worse, being put under a microscope for scientific study. Maybe that was an exaggeration, but, regardless, I did need to try to keep things subtle. But maybe too much control was only serving to stress me out. Every time I turned around it seemed I was making a mistake and doing something odd for a kid my age.

"Well, don't you look like someone peed in your Cheerios," Lanie said. I guess my lack of sleep gave me a bit of a sourpuss expression.

"Sorry, I didn't sleep very well last night."

"You feeling okay?" my mom asked, pressing her palm against my forehead. "You don't feel like you're running a fever."

"Nah, I'm fine, Mom. I just had a hard time falling asleep."

I found myself wishing I had worn a heavier jacket as we walked up the hill. The one I had on was light and it let the wind through easily. It really was quite a bit cooler than the day before. That's the funny thing about the Midwest in the spring and fall: the temperature can shift twenty degrees from one day to the next.

As we reached the top of our street, a dog started barking off to our right. As we kept walking, the sound seemed to draw closer. I looked over and saw it was coming from a large dog that had appeared from behind the house. It barreled toward us, lifting its legs in great strides as it ran.

It was a monster of a thing with splotches of black, brown, and white. Its hair was matted and unkempt and, even though it was so large, it didn't look like it had been fed nearly enough. It was simultaneously extremely powerful looking and waif thin. At first, it appeared to be a stray, but it had a faded, blue collar around its neck with a thin, metal chain dragging along behind him. The dog had broken its chain and it looked like it wanted vengeance.

It charged up to the edge of the yard, stopping just short of the curb. The dog lowered its head, staring up at us with a guttural growl. It began darting back and forth along the curb as it switched from growling to a tirade of menacing barks. As impossible as it seemed, that dog looked as though it had hate in its eyes. It looked like it was hoping for a reason, any reason, to attack.

We froze where we stood. The dog had come from nowhere and it caught us off guard, although I don't know that we would have done anything differently even if we had seen it coming. There was nowhere to go, so we just looked at it as it looked back. It continued its warning barks, telling us in its animalistic way that it was in charge.

I looked behind me and saw my mom standing there just as transfixed as we were. The look on her face was one of sheer terror. Her body was tense as she leaned forward with her weight on the fronts of her feet. Her arms were outstretched slightly with her hands balled into tight fists; her knuckles were nearly white with the force she was exerting against her own flesh. She had locked eyes with the dog and it seemed that everything else in the world had disappeared. It seemed that, in her mind, she was alone with her horror.

As I looked at her, the feeling of dread, the feeling that something was wrong, came back in full force. I had been here before. This was not the first time I had experienced this. The dog had charged and stopped just short of the street. We had stood still, afraid to move. My mom had the same look of paralyzing fear that she had right then. The whole scene came back in an instant, playing before my eyes as it had happened so long ago:

It was a showdown and the dog was not going to back down. We had frozen in fear until Lanie, in her panic, dropped her bag and began to run. No one stopped her, neither of us even had the presence of mind to try. We were terrified. I have often heard of the fight, flight, or freeze response and now I saw it in action: my mom and I froze, but Lanie flew. None of us fought.

She stretched her legs out in a sprint and that was all that the mutt needed. Her movement kicked in the dog's prey instinct and it attacked. It leaned back on its haunches and propelled itself out into the street in a dead run. Lanie didn't even make it ten feet before the dog caught up to her.

It leaped into the air, catching Lanie by her arm. Its teeth sank into her as its weight knocked her tiny frame forward. They fell to the street in a jumbled mess. The dog maneuvered around, biting at her face and head, tearing at her arms and legs. It was attacking any part of her it could fit in its mouth, all the while waiting for a clear shot at her throat.

She was lying on the ground, screaming and thrashing, trying desperately to protect herself. She was helpless against the raw power of the beast. I was so small and I didn't know what to do. Looking back at my mom, she was still frozen in her fear with a mix of panic and horror in her eyes. Her fear made her as helpless as I was.

The attack had only gone on for mere seconds, but it felt like hours. The door to the house in front of us flew open and a man leapt through. He ran across the yard, letting out a primal scream to get the dog's attention away from Lanie, but it was no use. The dog had focused in on its prey and it had only one goal: to kill.

The man finally reached the dog and kicked out with his leg as hard as he could, making solid contact with the animal's side. The impact made a distinctive cracking sound as the dog's ribs broke. With a wild yelp, the dog separated from Lanie, sliding several feet across the asphalt. Her arm, which the dog had held in a ferocious embrace, fell limply to the street. Blood flowed from the flesh beneath the shredded skin on her arms, face, and body.

The dog gained its feet almost as quickly as it lost them and it charged the man, jumping to bring him down as it had Lanie. The man reached out with both hands and caught the dog by its collar. He twisted it down to the street, pinching and pulling with all his might, cutting off the dog's air supply. It was a literal battle to the death. The dog was not going to stop until it killed or was killed. Finally, after several moments without air, the dog's breathing ceased. The panicked dog's struggle slowed and then stopped. Finally, he lowered the animal's lifeless body to the ground.

Lanie lay on the street, curled into a ball and weeping. The dog lay alongside her and was no longer a threat, but she continued burying her head and neck to protect them from harm. It looked as though she had withdrawn into herself, trying to find comfort and peace within.

My mind returned to the crisis of the present and I knew we were on the precipice of history repeating itself. My mom was just as helpless as she was in my memory and I knew I had to be the one to react if Lanie was to be saved. In the original past, Lanie's downfall was her flight. I needed to keep her from running.

As I reached out to grab her arm, three words found the surface of my consciousness like a small ball floating to the top of a pool. LET IT HAPPEN. I saw the yellow sticky note in my mind's eye and I suddenly knew what it meant. I didn't know where the note came from or who wrote it, but they were telling me not to intervene. They were telling me to let the future take its course just as it had so many years ago.

I held my hands just inches from Lanie's arm. They hovered in indecision as I weighed the meaning of the block letters inscribed on the note. I didn't have long to consider the idea as Lanie lifted her leg to break out in a sprint. The dog was still snarling. My mom was still paralyzed. Everything was happening just as it had before and Lanie's fate would be out of reach in an instant.

In my mind's eye, I saw Lanie's crumpled form with her blood pooling around her. I saw the raw flesh beneath her skin and I saw the way her pretty, blonde hair had been soaked and matted with her own blood. I remembered the reconstructive surgeries. I remembered the teasing she endured all through junior high until her mother finally moved her away from her hell. I couldn't let it happen, note or no note. I could not let this torture be the result of my conscious inaction.

Making my decision, I closed my hands around her arm and pulled her into me with all of my force. Her center of balance had shifted as she was preparing to take off and we nearly went down in a heap. As we stumbled backward, I managed to use my leg to keep us from collapsing. We remained upright, watching the dog bark and growl its fury.

I wrapped my arms around her, saying only two words: "Don't run."

Then, just as in the events from years ago, the front door of the house burst open. The man from my memory ran out, yelling at the dog. "Boomer, No! Here!" The dog paid no attention. He only kept barking and snarling. It lowered its head nearly to the ground and growled.

"Boomer, No!" There was still no reaction from the dog. The man approached and reached out for the dog's collar. He missed. His fingers only scratched across the surface of the fabric and the dog turned and bit, piercing the flesh of the man's forearm. The man screamed and pulled back, dragging the dog along with him. The dog's jaw closed and released several times, trying to gain better purchase into his muscle and bone.

The man was clearly in agony, but he still had the presence of mind to reach around with his other arm. This time, he hit the mark, grabbing the collar and twisting the dog down to the ground. The dog still had its teeth clamped down on the man's arm in a deathly vise. He brought his knee down onto the dog's chest and pushed with all his weight until the dog released his arm with a squeal of pain. Free of the dog's mouth, the man jerked his bloodied, mangled arm away from the dog and then brought it to bear on the collar for more leverage.

He twisted and pulled the collar just as he had decades before. The dog writhed and squirmed on the ground, trying desperately to escape. The man held firm until, finally, the dog breathed its last breath. Satisfied that the dog was no longer a threat, he let go, allowing it to sink into a heap. He stood up with his blood running freely down his arm, dripping onto grass and leaves under his feet in tiny, circular droplets.

I looked up from the dog to the man. Behind him, a flash of light caught my eye. The brake lights of a black car, a Camaro, shone briefly as the driver braked to put the car into gear. Only a moment passed before the lights went dark and it pulled away from the curb, rolling slowly away. I could only see it for a moment, but I saw the lightning bolt painted on the back of the car. It was the same car that had parked near Lanie's house yesterday.

"I'm sorry, I'm so sorry," the man said as I returned my attention to him. "His chain broke." He cradled his wounded arm, holding it in close to his body. "I'm so sorry."

At the sound of his voice, the fear finally broke its paralytic hold over my mom. She looked at the man and all of her fear transformed into rage. She ran over to the man, screaming, "What is wrong with you? What was wrong with that dog? What did you do? Why was it so mean? So, so... so evil?"

She took her anger out on him, hitting him on his shoulders and chest. The man only stood there, holding his arm in close as he tried to protect it. But he did not stop her. He did not pull away. He only looked down at the ground, refusing to defend himself from the onslaught. He was filled with remorse and my mother with rage. Both of them seemed to have forgotten that he saved us, even if the dog's state was his doing.

"I'm sorry. I knew he was mean, but I didn't know that this would happen. I'm so sorry. He could have killed you and I'm so sorry." The horror on his face was real as he looked from the torn flesh of his arm to Lanie and then to me. He knew that it could had have been us. What he didn't know is that it had been one of us once, long ago. Lanie's whole body had looked just like his arm did. The fear that had paralyzed my mom in an instant had caused a lifetime of pain. Thankfully, we had avoided the pain this time around. I didn't know what that meant to whoever wrote the note, but I was glad.

My mom stayed still for a moment longer. She had spent her anger, but she could not look up at the man. She turned away and came back to us, placing her hands on our shoulders: one hand on mine and one on Lanie's. Gently, she nudged us toward the school, leaving the man to nurse his wounds and to bury his dog.

FIVE

Lanie and I sat on her porch as I waited for my dad to get home from work. The clouds from that morning had blown over and the rays of afternoon sun warmed our faces. Looking over at her, I noticed the smoothness of her face; her delicate features were untouched by the events of our alternate past.

She was quiet this afternoon. She sat on the steps with her knees pulled up into a makeshift table. Her arms were folded around them as she stared at a young maple across the street; its leaves fluttered in the light breeze like bits of tissue paper.

"You okay?" I asked. She tilted her head up and down in a few, short nods, still not looking away from the tree. I couldn't blame her for being quiet. Even if the events with the dog were just a close call in her mind, she had still been terrified. She still had to watch as the man's arm was shredded like beef, which was traumatic all by itself. Even more so with the realization that it could have been, should have been, her. She knew what would have happened had she ran, but fear has a way of short-circuiting our brains when we are in the moment.

We both had plenty to think about. I kept turning the note over in my mind. How could someone have known? It couldn't just be a coincidence. The note had to be for me, it had to be about Lanie. It seemed impossible, but whoever wrote that note knew what was supposed to happen. They knew the dog would get loose; they knew she was supposed to run. She was supposed to be attacked and she was supposed to suffer through years of therapy and plastic surgeries. She was supposed to experience years of torment at the hands of her classmates.

I glanced over at Lanie and she was looking at me again as though she wanted to say something. "What?" I asked.

She sat for a moment longer, still studying my face. She turned her body toward me, her hand reaching out to rest on the stair above her. She seemed to search my eyes before she spoke. "Do you think you're psychic, Andy?" she asked.

The question caught me off guard. "No. Not that I know of. Why?"

"I was just wondering," she answered. Her gaze moved to follow a calico cat as it sauntered across the neighbor's yard, flopping down in a sunny spot and rolling onto its back. As I followed her gaze, I noticed that the black car from this morning and yesterday afternoon sat down the street a bit. It wasn't in the same place as yesterday, though. I thought it was one house farther down.

"My aunt Bonnie says her friend is a psychic," she said, still watching the cat. "Says she can talk to dead people. She said they had a..." she paused for a moment, trying to find the word. "I can't remember what she called it. It's where people gather around a table and ask a dead person questions. It sounded like science, I think."

"A séance?" I asked.

"Yeah," she said, snapping her head around to look at me. "That's it."

I was so not good at acting like a kid.

"They had a séance and her friend was talking to someone's dead mom or grandma or something. She was able to tell them things that happened a long time ago. My aunt said that her friend knew things she shouldn't have known."

"So, what are you saying?" I asked, knowing full well what she was going to say.

"You knew I was going to run. You knew I was scared and I was going to run. The dog would have done to me what it did to that guy's arm. Did you see the way his skin was hanging in little flaps? There were holes in his arm everywhere. There was so much blood. How did you know, Andy? How did you know I was going to run?"

"I can't talk to dead people, Lanie," I said.

"You know that isn't what I meant. I just don't get how you knew what was going to happen."

"I didn't know," I lied. "It just looked like you were. You were all tensed up and it looked like you were about to take off." Technically, that part was true.

"Lucky for me you were watching." She looked into my eyes and I could tell she wasn't convinced. She didn't know what the answer was, but she could tell there were pieces that didn't fit together. She knew there was more to the story than I was telling her.

And the truth was that I found myself wanting to tell her. I sat on that step looking into her eyes and I realized that I wanted to talk. I wanted to get it out of my head and into the air. So much had happened over the past two days and I was all alone in it. I had lost my wife; I was at a real risk to lose my dad if I didn't figure out what to do about it. And if I did, I would still have to watch my mom descend into her alcohol-laced depression. I was stuck in a world I didn't want to be in and I was without a path home.

If that wasn't enough, my entire life was starting to feel like a lie. At that moment, no one knew who I really was. When the people around me looked at me, they saw a nine-year-old. They saw a child's face, a child's smile. They could not see the mind that occupied this small body. And, because of that, I could not be the authentic me. I was constantly acting, constantly pretending to be someone I wasn't, even if I had decided not to try quite so hard. And it was starting to wear on me.

I had known something was bothering me. There was the obvious stress, but it wasn't until she started asking the questions that I realized how it had all piled up like a big snowball that was bearing down on me. Yet I still couldn't bring myself to speak the words and I wasn't sure why. Not really. I knew there was a part of me that believed she would think I was crazy. That she would run inside and tell her mom that I must have been down the street with Billy Mancini smoking the wacky weed because I had lost my marbles.

But it was more than that. The note scared me. I could not shake the feeling that whomever left it knew I was here. What was worse than anything was that I didn't know who they were or what they wanted. I didn't know if they were only intent on influencing that one event or if they had more plans. And I didn't know what they were going to do about me ignoring their note. Something told me they wouldn't have gone through the effort if it wasn't important to them. Sometimes people do bad things when they don't get what they want.

The black car down the street started to move. It had looked unoccupied, but someone must have been inside the whole time. It turned into the adjacent driveway and then backed out again, turning so that it was facing the opposite direction. It sat that way for just a moment. Then, the brake lights went dark and the car drove away.

Something about that car bothered me. The way it parked in different places, the way it just sat there this morning watching as the man on the corner strangled his dog. The way no one got in, but it drove away – as though whoever was inside was just sitting there, waiting, and watching. It hadn't done anything that was specifically threatening, but my intuition said that something was wrong. My gut said that they were the writers of the note.

From up the street, I heard the sound of a car door closing. It was my dad, more than likely. "I think my dad's home." In truth, I was glad to be able to get away. I knew it was probably inevitable that I was going to tell someone my predicament, but I didn't feel ready. A part of me wanted to get away from the temptation.

"Okay," she said as I got up. "I know there is something you're not saying, but thank you for stopping me."

"You're welcome."

I walked down the drive and turned out into the street. It had been my dad – his Nova was sitting in the driveway. The blue paint was faded from years of sitting out in the sun. There were small dots of rust where a piece of decorative, chrome trim, having long since fallen off, used to attach to the body.

That night at dinner, we sat down to heaping plates of spaghetti. The piles of pasta were covered in a rich marinara sauce and topped with meatballs the size of my fist. Granted, I had a little fist, but my stomach was also a lot smaller than it used to be. The smell of garlic, tomatoes, and oregano was tantalizing. My dad's time spent running a restaurant had definitely paid off, at least in his ability to prepare a meal.

As my mom slid into her seat, she said, "Honey, you should let me make dinner more often. You cook all day long and then come home and cook some more. I wouldn't even want to look at food after doing it all day."

"But I enjoy doing it." He reached for the container of parmesan cheese, its green metallic cover reflecting the light from the chandelier, and sprinkled some of the contents across the top of his spaghetti. He pointed the container toward me, shaking the end for emphasis, "Son, if there is one thing you should remember when you grow up, do something you love. You have to spend a whole lot of years working to put food on the table. Make sure you enjoy it."

That was good advice. I had spent too many years doing things I didn't like to do, including working as a short order cook while I was in college. I was okay at it, but I definitely didn't have the passion for it that my dad did.

"Okay," my mom said. "But don't say I didn't offer. Oh! I forgot about the wine." She slid back out of her seat and stepped into the kitchen. "Did you want a glass?" she asked.

"Sure," I said. I really did want one.

"Not you, you goofball. Joe?"

"Maybe half a glass." She uncorked the bottle and poured two glasses, returning to her place at the table.

"So, how was your day?" my dad asked before delivering a forkful of spaghetti to his mouth.

"It was kind of a crazy day, Dad."

"Oh?"

"We almost got attacked by a killer dog on the way to school."

"Yeah, he was quite the brave, young man," my mom said.

"Well, I don't doubt that. What happened?"

I finished chewing a mouthful of pasta, resting the end of my fork on the table. "You know the house up on the corner? The green one?"

"Yeah, the one with the dog that's always tied out? White and brown, I think."

"Yeah," I said, although I didn't remember it being tied out all the time. "And black. Well, it broke its chain this morning. It came charging at us and it was barking and growling and the whole bit. And the guy that lives there came out and tried to get the dog, but it attacked him."

"Whoa. It attacked him?" He held his fork in the air, a loose strip of unwound spaghetti dangling from the end.

"Yeah, it tore his arm to shreds. Bad. The guy had to strangle the dog to death."

"Oh, wow. To death? He killed it? You guys are all okay, though? No one got hurt?"

"Just the dog," my mom said. "But that's not all. Andy thought Lanie was going to run, so he grabbed her arm and told her not to. I was impressed."

I spun my fork on my plate, twirling a couple strands of spaghetti for another bite. I looked up and both my mom and dad were staring at my fork. Evidently, that is something else I didn't know how to do two days ago. Too late now, I thought to myself. I raised the fork and shoved it into my mouth, slurping a stray noodle.

"Wow. Way to go, Andy!" my dad said. "What about the guy? Did he go to the hospital? What did the police do?"

My mom drained the last of her glass, getting up for another. "I don't know. We didn't wait to find out. I needed to get the kids to school."

I wasn't sure what to think about the wine. One glass became two and two became three. She started to open a new bottle for a fourth, but my dad suggested that she save some for another night. I thought it was a pretty tactful way of saying she had enough. I knew it was just one night and she wasn't completely drunk yet, but it still bothered me. I'm sure it had everything to do with her history.

I went to bed earlier than I had to, partly because I didn't sleep well the night before and partly because I didn't want to see her drunk, even if she was just a bit tipsy. I had hit a point some ten or twelve years before where I would not tolerate her if she was drinking. I didn't want to be around it. There were too many painful memories associated with it. That and I got tired of watching her run away from life.

Unfortunately, I lay in bed staring at the ceiling just as I had the night before. Tonight, it wasn't so much that my brain wouldn't stop working as it was the sound of my parents' voices carrying up the stairs. They had gone back into the living room and my dad was asking about the events with the dog.

"So, what happened today?" my dad asked. "Something tells me that I didn't get the whole story at dinner."

"What do you mean? We told you what happened. The dog broke his chain and went crazy. The guy came out, tried to stop the dog, and got bit. He had to kill the dog to get it to stop. There really isn't any more to tell."

I snuck out to the hallway and crept over to the top of the stairs. I couldn't see much; I could see most of my dad as he sat in his chair. It looked like she was sitting on the couch, but I couldn't actually see her.

"Babe, you downed three glasses of wine and wanted to open another bottle."

"So? I felt like having some wine. That's okay every now and again, isn't it?"

"Yes," my dad said. "Of course it is. But I know it's more than that. Maybe we aren't old, married fogies yet, but I've known you for fifteen years and we've been married for ten of them. I'd like to think I know you pretty well."

My mom got up from her place on the couch and walked over to the piano. She loved that thing. My dad had bought it for her once the restaurant started bringing in some money. They didn't splurge on many big-ticket items, but that was one thing my mom had always wanted. She ran her hand across the top, looking at her fingertips for dust.

She turned around, putting her hand on the top of the piano as she leaned into it. "I froze," she said, looking down at the floor. She stood there for a moment, not speaking. Not moving. "I saw that stupid dog and I was terrified. I was eight years old all over again and it wasn't a white, brown, and black mutt, it was a Doberman; black and brown. In my eyes, it was like I was back in time and that stupid dog was right there."

"Oh, honey," my dad said as he pushed up out of the chair. He walked over to her, but she held up her hand, stopping him. She was still looking at the floor.

"I was eight years old and it wasn't Andy and Lanie standing there, it was Katherine. Katherine was there and I was there and that dog was there. And I froze. I couldn't move. I was standing there just like I did when it happened. If Lanie had run, that dog would have gotten her just like Katherine. It would have torn her to bits and there was nothing I could do. Nothing I *would* do. I froze and she would have paid for it. It would have been my fault. Again."

"Donna," was all he could say. He didn't say anything else for a few moments. I'm not sure he knew what to say. I'm not sure I would have known what to say. This story was new to me. My mom had never spoken of it. I knew she had a sister named Katherine and I knew she died, but that's about all I knew. She never talked about her; she never said what happened. It was just one of those forbidden subjects. Kind of like my dad.

"It wasn't your fault. You were a kid. What could an eight-year-old do to protect someone from a dog? The only thing that would have happened is that it would have come after you. Then you would have both been dead-"

"Maybe that would have been better!" My mom was raising her voice now. "Then I wouldn't have to carry around this guilt all the time. Maybe I would have died and she could have gotten away!"

"You know better than that. It wasn't your fault. You were both little girls. There was nothing you could have done."

"Andy is just a boy and he told her not to run. He knew! Why did he know and I didn't? Why did he have the sense to keep her from running? Why didn't I? I was frozen. I was a coward and it killed Katherine. Today was just the same. Lanie could have died because of me. Because of me!"

Instantly, I could see that sticky note again and the block letters printed on it: Let it happen. Did I mess up? Did I make things worse? Is that why they put that note on my mirror, why they tried to intervene? No. No, it couldn't be. She has regret tonight because of what could have happened. Not what did happen.

"But she didn't, Donna. She didn't. Lanie is safe. She is at home right now, probably in her bed, and she is fine. You can't blame yourself for what could have happened. And you can't blame yourself for what did happen when you were eight years old. No more than you would blame Andy if Lanie weren't okay. You know that you would never blame him and you shouldn't blame yourself either."

He stepped up to my mom and pulled her into him. She raised her hands, pushing away, but he pulled her anyway. She didn't say anything more. She just lowered her head into his chest and cried. Her chest heaved as she was overcome by her grief over what was lost long ago and over what could have been lost today.

Leaving them to their embrace, I crept back to my room and climbed into bed. All of this was new to me, but I couldn't see things the same way anymore. I had always been so angry with my mom for her alcoholism. I saw her as weak. I thought it had everything to do with my dad dying and her inability to cope, but it didn't. Not completely, anyway. It was the double whammy of Lanie getting mauled and losing her husband just a few days later. She saw Lanie as her fault and Katherine as her fault and then she lost my dad. And she shattered.

My one hope in that moment was that I had somehow averted her depression. I had a seed of faith that she would not succumb to the temptation to numb her existence with alcohol. Even if my dad still died, maybe she would be able to overcome the certain grief that would follow. Maybe all was not lost. There was no way to know for certain, but I could hope.

I had a feeling that it was going to be another sleepless night. This was so much to take in and my brain was having a hard time processing it all. Not to mention that I still had no idea how I might keep my dad from dying. I couldn't even really remember it very clearly. It was so long ago and the details had become fuzzy. I did have the power to change the future, it seemed, but I had to know what was coming in order to do that. I could only remember that he died in a car accident. The rest was infuriatingly hazy, lying just out of reach.

So, I looked up at the ceiling just as I had the night before. I lay there and waited, settling in for another long night. But, I had evidently had enough and my body could not resist sleep. It was only a few minutes before I slipped into a deep slumber, leaving the chaotic world of the past behind, even if only for a few hours.

SIX

When I woke, the house was silent. The early morning sun came through my window, cutting a swath of light across the carpet. A million particles of dust hovered as tiny specks suspended throughout the bright light. As I slipped out of bed and entered the hallway, I could see that my parents' door was mostly closed and I could hear my mom breathing softly from within. It was still early and my father must have already gone to work for the Saturday shift.

I padded down the stairs, thinking I might watch some Saturday morning cartoons. Bugs Bunny and Roadrunner, Pac-Man, Super Friends, shows I hadn't seen for years. As a kid, I always looked forward to dragging my blanket downstairs on Saturday mornings, curling up on the couch, and allowing the glow from the TV to wash over me as I watched. No school, no responsibilities, just cartoons.

I flipped on the TV to the familiar sound of the Looney Tunes theme song. I settled back and watched as Bugs Bunny gave the giant, orange Gossamer a haircut, trimming him down to nothing. Next was the egghead chicken creating contraptions designed to terrorize the gabby Foghorn Leghorn. As I sat and watched the episodes unfold, I found it hard to keep my mind from wandering. No matter how hard I tried, it became impossible to just relax and enjoy my childhood vice.

I finally gave up and pressed the button on the TV, plunging the screen into darkness. Instead, I would get some breakfast and then maybe get out of the house for a bit. I walked into the kitchen and paused, giving some serious thought to making some eggs and bacon before my mom woke up for the morning. The nostalgia of the sugary cereals was good for a couple days, but my grownup palate was looking for bigger and better things – probably because it was another thing that my nine-year-old self wasn't supposed to do on his own.

Instead, I spied the coffee maker sitting with a nearly full pot. It was silently beckoning me to indulge in a mug of liquid bliss. I turned my ear to the stairs, listening for any sign of movement. The house was completely quiet, so I climbed up and pulled a coffee cup from the mug tree on the counter. I filled the cup halfway with the rich, dark brew. I dumped in a spoonful of sugar and carried the cup over to what had once been my normal place at the bar.

As I sat there sipping my coffee, I actually felt like my old self, even if it was only for a moment. I was no longer a child sitting in the kitchen of my childhood home. I was enjoying one of my longstanding morning traditions and I was able to focus on the aroma and on the warmth of the coffee on my tongue. It wasn't quite enough to make me forget where I was, but it helped.

It wasn't long though before my mind turned back to Sarah. We had often sat in the kitchen sipping coffee before we began our preparations for the day ahead. We would talk about life, bills, or our futures as we sat. It was a moment of quality time before the chaos of the day began. On weekends, we would sometimes sit there for hours, just enjoying the time together.

This morning wasn't one of those mornings. I sat by myself in the quietness, my too-small hands wrapped around the mug in front of me. I had been around people almost constantly for the past few days, but I could not escape the feeling of being alone. I was alone in my dilemma. All my conversational energy went into maintaining the illusion that I was a child. There was no one to talk with about the turmoil that was constantly present just below the surface.

I couldn't tell my parents. How could they believe me? Even if they did, I wasn't sure what to say to them. Hey, Dad, you're going to die in a couple days. Mom, my only memories of you are as a raging drunk who could barely hold down a job, let alone take care of a family. No, I couldn't see how talking to them would work out well.

Lanie was another option, but she was just a kid. I looked like a kid, but she and I might as well be from two different worlds. She was a smart girl and I didn't want to be too quick to discount her, but I was still afraid that the best she could offer was an ear to listen. Then again, that's really all I wanted. I didn't expect anyone to have the answers. Things like this don't happen. No one else was going to have any more answers than she would. I knew I didn't.

I thought about some of my friends I had growing up, but my mind kept going back to Lanie. She was already suspecting something. I wondered if that meant she might be more open to the absurd. I found myself hopeful that she might actually be able to accept what had happened to me. Convincing someone I was telling the truth was going to be a whole other challenge all by itself.

"Are you drinking coffee, Andy?" My mom's voice startled me. I hadn't heard her come down. She was standing in the doorway, her bathrobe fastened tightly around her. Her dark hair was sticking up in a hundred different directions, giving the impression that she had a rough night.

"Um... yeah." I wasn't quite sure what to say. I hadn't even considered that she might catch me off guard, so I hadn't preplanned a response. Thinking as quickly as I could, I said, "I wanted to try it. You and dad drink it every morning."

"And? What do you think?" she asked, a smile spreading across her face. From her look, she seemed sure I would twist my face in disgust. She looked to be in a much better mood, even if she didn't look like she got the greatest night of sleep.

"It's good. I put some sugar in it though. I remember Mrs. Leach saying she likes hers with sugar," I lied. I had no idea how Mrs. Leach drank her coffee or even if she drank it.

"Oh, really? And just how much sugar did you put in it?" She crossed the kitchen, selecting her own cup from the tree. The mug tree held an eclectic collection: one of them was black, one was green, and there were a couple other varieties as well. She picked a pink and white one that sported a teddy bear sitting in front of a giant heart.

"Just a spoonful."

"Wow. Just one? And you like it?" she asked, turning toward me, the cup dangling from her fingers by the handle. You do know that'll stunt your growth, don't you?" she asked as she pointed the cup at me.

"How come?" I asked.

"Um. That's a good question. It's just what I've always heard, I guess. Maybe because of the caffeine?" Turning back, she lifted the pot from the coffee maker, pouring her own serving.

"Doesn't pop have caffeine too? Kids drink that all the time." I wasn't going to give up my coffee without a fight.

"Hmm. Good point. Still, let's not drink too much, okay? Besides, you'll be bouncing off the walls. Oh, hey, I have to go into work for a while this afternoon. I was thinking that maybe we'd do lunch at the restaurant and then you can hang out with your dad until he gets done."

"Sure. Can Lanie come?"

"I guess so. I'm surprised how well you guys are getting along these days. Just last week you were complaining that you had to go. Makes me wonder if you're starting to think girls don't have cooties anymore."

"No!" I said, drawing the word out for emphasis. "She's just nicer than I thought she was. She's growing on me." I had to suppress my instinct to say I was married. After ten years, it was automatic.

"Andy has a girlfriend! Andy has a girlfriend!" my mom teased in a singsong voice.

"That's not funny, mom. Not even a little bit," I said, taking a sip of my coffee. "Care if I run down there for a while? I'll ask if she can go."

"Not at all. Just be back by 12:30, okay?"

Dressed and teeth brushed, I stepped out the front door. The Midwestern weather still couldn't make up its mind what it wanted to do. I was glad I had picked a short sleeve shirt because the sun felt hot as it covered my face and hair. It had that quality that said the day was going to be very warm, at least relative to the season.

I stepped out to the street and looked left and right. The black car that had made an appearance the past couple days was nowhere to be seen. Mr.

Johnston was across the street, fiddling with his mower. He had the top of the carburetor taken off and was holding the gas can above it, trying to tease a couple of drops in to help get the mower started.

The Penningtons were sitting in lawn chairs in their normal spot on their driveway. They were an older couple and had long since retired. As a younger boy, I remember sitting over there for hours, watching Mr. Pennington make knickknacks on the collection of woodworking tools in his garage.

"Hey, Andy," Mr. Pennington called out from his seat. "Gonna be a warm one today. Bet it's going to be a blistering summer."

"I bet you're right," I said, waving. It almost seemed odd that I knew all the neighbors' names. Back then, it seemed like that was just the way of things, at least in my neighborhood. Everybody knew everybody. When I was eight or so, we had a block party and the police had set up barriers with orange flashing lights on the top to keep cars from entering the street. We had set up tables in Melissa's mom's driveway because she was the only person who had a driveway that was two cars wide. We played music and people danced and we ate tons of food. Burgers, dogs, potato salad, and all sorts of other things.

Back in my normal life, I don't think I know more than a couple folks' names from my neighborhood. It made me wonder whether it was my age or if it was a sign of the times. We did have a sort of block party once in my neighborhood a couple years ago, but everyone seemed like they were only there because they didn't want the neighbors to see them as snobs. It could be that the only difference was the age lens I saw the parties through, but it just seemed different back then.

I climbed the steps to Lanie's door, knocking a couple times. At first, there didn't seem to be an answer; there was only silence. But then, the curtains pulled aside and I saw the top of Lanie's head as she peered out at me. The curtain dropped and she pulled open the door, but she stood off to the side, only letting her head poke out.

"Hi, Andy," she said, a crinkle forming between her eyebrows as she scrunched up her nose. "It's Saturday, you know? No school."

"I know." Her greeting caught me off guard and actually made me feel a tad nervous. I hadn't thought about the fact that she and I didn't spend much time with each other except for after school. I rubbed my hands together, trying to wipe away the thin sheen that had developed. "I just thought I'd come down and hang out."

"Oh. Okay. Hold on a sec? I'm in my PJs. I'll be out in a minute." She stepped away from the door, leaving it slightly ajar.

The sudden feeling of nervousness surprised me. I had planned to come down and let the truth out if the opportunity presented itself. What I hadn't thought about was the fact that I looked like a child to her. In her eyes, I was the little kid from up the street who probably had a crush on her. She could be up in her room right now trying to figure out a way to get rid of me without hurting my feelings.

As I plopped down onto the top step, I thought about the irony of it. Here I was, nervous that a twelve-year-old girl wasn't going to want to talk to me because she thought of me as a kid. And I didn't like the feeling.

Behind me, the screen door opened and Lanie stepped out into the sunshine wearing denim shorts, a bright pink shirt, and pink KangaROOS shoes to match. "Bright out here," she said, lifting a hand to shield her eyes. She dropped down onto the step beside me. "What's up?" she asked.

The newly formed knot in my stomach made it challenging to find words. "I don't know. I didn't feel like watching cartoons this morning. I thought I'd come down and see what's going on."

"Oh. I was just watching TV."

We sat in silence for several moments. When I came down, I had been ready to spill my guts and tell her all about my situation. Feeling nervous had taken away some of my steam. "Hey, you want to go down to the creek? We can catch crawdads or something." I felt a little silly as soon as it was out of my mouth. I had just asked a twelve-year-old girl if she wanted to look for crawdads.

"Crawdads? Oh my gosh. You're such a boy. But, yeah, we can go. Let me check with my mom." She stood and disappeared inside the door.

After a moment, she came back out, letting the screen door slam against its frame. "Ready?"

We went around the side of the house and went through the chain link gate that led into the back yard. The houses on our side of the street overlooked a small stream that caught a lot of the water runoff from the neighborhood. It was one of my favorite places to hang out as a kid. It sat at the bottom of a deep valley with trees and thick foliage on either side that made it easy to pretend you were an explorer, blazing a trail through the untamed wilderness.

I spent many summer afternoons in that small strip of woods when I was a boy. Sometimes, Mike Bennett and I would sneak some bacon out of his refrigerator and we would try our best to catch crawdads. We would sit on the bank or wade in the ankle deep water, trying to use the bacon to lure them out from rocks. To this day, I'm not sure whether the bacon helped or if they even liked bacon for that matter, but we tried anyway. Most times, we would get tired of waiting and would start lifting up the rocks to see if there were any of the elusive creatures hiding underneath.

Sometimes we'd get lucky and find one and we'd do our best to catch them. We would have to do it just right, using our index finger and thumb to grab them right behind their pinchers. We'd pull them out of the water, setting them aside to play with once we caught a few. I remember he'd always try to get them to fight, even making a miniature boxing-ring once from a shoebox lid.

Reaching the fence at the back of her yard, I asked, "You okay jumping the fence?"

She rolled her eyes at me. "Andy, just because I'm a girl, doesn't mean I'm a wimp." She placed her hands at the top of the fence, launching her body up. She lifted her legs and swung them over with the grace of a gymnast.

As I started to do the same, I realized I hadn't hurdled a fence in fifteen or twenty years. I hesitated as I put my hands on the top of the fence. I could see myself catching my foot on the top of the fence and falling over onto my face or, even worse, hanging upside down by my shoelace or something. I launched myself up, using one leg on the top to support myself while I brought the other over.

"You look scared, Andy," Lanie said, crossing her arms with a grin on her face. "Don't tell me you just got bested by a girl."

"I'm short. Shut up."

Over the fence, we crossed a small field and walked into the miniature wilderness. It felt great stepping back into those woods after so many years. The area wasn't huge, but it was just big enough that you could drop over the crest of the hill and not be able to see any houses. There were no power lines, no roads, no people except for the occasional kid with the same goal to escape and explore. It gave the illusion that you were alone and had the world to yourself.

A small creek ran along the bottom of the valley. On either side were elms, oaks, cottonwoods, and hedge trees. To my left, there was one of those trees with thorns as big as a finger. To this day, when I see one of those trees I have visions of how terrible it would be like to fall into the thorns. I've never fallen into them, but they've always creeped me out.

We made our way down the slope, being careful to watch for loose rocks and dirt. Parts of it were steep enough that you could take quite a tumble if you missed a step. As we clambered down, we scared up two deer from where they had been sleeping on the other side of the stream. They rose to their feet, lifting their noses to sniff the air as they looked for potential threats.

"Shhh." I pointed to the deer. Lanie stood still as a smile crept across her face.

"They're beautiful," she whispered. The deer were a picture of grace as they approached the creek, each of them dropping their heads to take a small drink. Then, like a flash, they took off, following a trail along the stream.

A large, fallen tree lay at the stream's edge. A large rock supported one end of the tree so that it ran in a slight angle toward the ground. I walked up to the log and lifted a leg over, pulling myself on top to straddle it. She leaned up against it a few feet down from me. I noticed her legs, bare from the top down, and then noticed my own. I hadn't thought about the fact that we should have worn pants. Chiggers were probably going to eat us alive.

"I love coming down here," I said. I looked over at the water as a small fish took an insect off the top. Small, concentric rings spread away from the spot where the fish broke the surface.

"It's so peaceful. It's quiet. I've never been down here."

"I like it. You can just get away from everything. There's usually no one but me and I can watch the animals, play in the water. Do whatever I want to do. I love it."

We sat in silence for a moment, soaking in our environment. Gone was the manufactured scent of suburbia, replaced by the deep, earthy smell of nature. As we watched, two young squirrels played at the base of a large oak and, somewhere nearby, a turkey hen clucked, maybe trying to attract a mate. The sun rained down on the tops of the trees, but could not penetrate to the floor. We were cast in shadow and a soft breeze disguised the rising warmth of the day.

"Andy," she said, bracing her arms on the top of the log and lifting herself to sit on it. "What didn't you want to tell me yesterday?" She turned to face me, pulling a leg over to straddle the log as I was. "How did you know I was going to run?"

As I looked into her eyes, I could see that I probably wasn't going to get away with pushing her off again and this was, after all, what I came down here to do. But, I still felt all the same feelings of conflict. I wanted to tell her, I wanted to stop living a lie – even if it were only with one person. But now that we were sitting here and the moment had come to talk or not talk, I was suddenly worried.

I didn't want her to think I was insane. And I was afraid of the possibility that she might tell. If she told the kids at school I thought I was from the future, they would label either her or me as crazy. I didn't connect with the kids at school, there was no way I could, but I didn't necessarily want to brand myself as a loony bird either.

And then there was the note. Whoever had written it knew I was here and it was getting harder to deny the possibility that they were watching me – that the note writers were in the car and they were monitoring me. I didn't want to put Lanie in danger. I didn't want my need to share to put her at risk.

I lowered my eyes to the log, using my fingernails to pry up a loose piece of dead bark. "I told you, I don't know how."

She swung her leg back over the log, dropping onto the ground. She stood there for a moment, her anger becoming visible. "Andy, I'm not stupid." She turned and started pacing back and forth in front of me. Her hair drew out around her as she spun at the end of each pace. "Don't lie to me. I know that something's not right and I know you're lying to me."

She stopped, turning to face me again. "Tell me how you knew what to say to Bobby and Aaron. Tell me why you haven't mentioned Darth Vader or Spock or guns or Donkey Kong or any of the other stuff you normally don't shut up about." Her blue eyes were like lasers, piercing into mine.

"Tell me why you have been hanging out with me after school instead of veg'ing out on the couch watching stupid cartoons. Tell me why you came over this morning. You've never come over to hang out unless you had to, not once! Ever! I want to know why you don't sound like any nine-year-old I know. I want to know why I feel like the kid when I'm talking to you. Talking to you is like talking to my uncle or my dad or something."

I sat on the log and she stood; our eyes locked in battle. I was in battle with myself and she was in battle with me. I knew I had to tell her something. I had to tell her because she wasn't going to accept any other option. I had to tell her because I wanted to be honest with someone. I looked back down at the log and started prying up another piece of bark.

"Andy," Lanie said. "Are you going to answer me?"

"Yes, but I don't think you're going to believe me." I looked up at her, making eye contact. "Can you promise me that you won't repeat a word of what I tell you to anyone? Not anyone. Not your mom, not your dad, no one at school. No one."

"Yes, Andy. Now tell me before I punch you." She came back to the log, pushing herself back up to straddle it.

I took a breath. How exactly do you tell someone something you don't understand yourself? Something that is completely unbelievable. Even to you.

"Yesterday, when the dog came out barking, I knew what was going to happen because it wasn't the first time it happened. It happened once before, except that it was different."

She sucked in her breath in surprise. "That dog has attacked somebody before?"

"No, Lanie. I mean you. It attacked you."

"I've never had a dog attack me before and definitely not that dog. Oh, wait. You mean like, what's it called," she paused for a moment, recalling the word. "Déjà vu? Where you feel like something has happened before?"

"Not exactly. I am different than you think I am. I was a grown up and I was… I *am* married to a woman named Sarah. All of this has already happened for me. To me, all of this happened almost thirty years ago. I don't know how, but I woke up as a kid Thursday morning."

Lanie let out a heavy breath. "If you don't want to tell me the truth, just say so. Tell me to go jump in a lake or whatever, but don't say you're going to tell me and then make up some stupid story." It was her turn to play with the dead bark from the tree. "I told you already; I'm not stupid."

"What were you expecting the answer to be? You asked me how I knew you were going to run. Were you just expecting me to say that I'm like your aunt and I can see things I shouldn't be able to see?"

"I don't know what I thought," was all she said for a moment. "It was my aunt's friend, not my aunt."

"Think about it Lanie, think about what you asked me. You asked why I'm suddenly different, why I'm not talking about Star Wars or video games or whatever. You asked why I was suddenly hanging out with you. You asked why I don't sound like any nine-year-old you know. Why did you ask those things?"

"Because you are different, but people don't travel back in time. I don't know what I was expecting, but it wasn't that." Again, she was quiet as she gathered her thoughts. "This isn't the Twilight Zone. This is stupid. Just tell me the truth or tell me to screw off. You know what, never mind. I don't want to know." She lifted her leg over the log and dropped back down to the ground. "I'm going home, Andy. I'll see you Monday."

"Lanie, wait. You asked why talking to me was like talking to your uncle or your dad. Why would it seem that way? Why would it seem like I am older? Could it be because I am older?" I paused for a moment, but she only continued looking at me. At least she didn't walk off. "I'm telling you the truth. I don't know how it happened. I don't know what happened. I just know that I woke up Thursday morning and I was in this puny little body. I almost crapped myself, Lanie. I couldn't believe it and it happened to me, so I can only imagine how hard it is for you to believe."

She actually laughed. I didn't know if I was any closer to convincing her, but at least she laughed. "Okay," she said. "I'm not saying I believe you, but what happened yesterday, then? What happened the first time with the dog?"

"You ran. You ran and the dog chased you. It wasn't good, Lanie. It was really bad. You almost died. You were in the hospital for a couple weeks at least. I don't remember if they had you in intensive care or just the regular hospital, but I remember they did a bunch of surgeries those first few days trying to stitch you back together."

As I thought about it, the memory was again replaying in my mind. "I remember my mom was at the hospital constantly. She felt so guilty. No one could even talk to her. She sat by your bed almost twenty-four hours a day. I think she ended up losing her job because she was there so much."

"Why did she feel guilty?"

"Because she didn't stop you from running. She was terrified and she froze. You ran and there was nothing she could do, nothing she did to stop you. So she stayed at the hospital and was afraid to leave. My dad tried to stay there with her, but someone had to be here with me."

The more I talked about it, the more the details started taking shape, as though they were emerging from a thick fog. "I remember my dad sat with her as much as he could. Sometimes he would take me with him and sometimes I would stay with a sitter. I remember that he made my mom come home and get some sleep but he was going to go back to sit with you. He..."

The memory came back in a rush. He had fallen asleep at the wheel as he drove back to the hospital. He fell asleep and went off the road, hitting a semi head on. He never even knew what hit him.

"What, Andy?" she asked.

"Oh, my God. He died while driving to sit with you. He died because he was so tired trying to work while sitting with my mom as much as he could. He fell asleep and he crossed the median." I felt as though someone had kicked me in the chest. I could hear my own heart pounding in my ears and I got that distinct tingly feeling on the back of my neck as the realization swept over me. "If you didn't get attacked, my mom wouldn't be at the hospital. That means my dad wouldn't have anywhere to go. He wouldn't be too tired to drive. He wouldn't have fallen asleep at the wheel. Lanie! My dad isn't going to die. My dad doesn't have to die!"

"Your dad is going to die?" she asked.

"No!" I ran forward took her hands in mine. "He isn't!"

It was just like one of those old movies where the main character is so overcome by joy that he just wants to kiss someone. It was cheesy, but it was real. Tears were streaming down my face as I began to understand how things had changed. That one instant in time, the decision to act or not had so many ramifications. Everything was different. My life was different; my mom's life was different. My dad would actually have a life where it had been extinguished before. And Lanie, of course Lanie. She wouldn't have the scars her whole life and she wouldn't have to move away because the kids picked on her so much.

"Whoa," I said. I hadn't thought about the impact to Lanie.

"What?" I could tell she felt left out. She couldn't hear what was going on in my head. "I changed your entire life that day too."

"What do you mean?"

"When you got attacked, you had to have so many surgeries. You had to have all kinds of skin grafts and plastic surgeries-"

"What's a skin graft?" she asked, interrupting.

"Oh. It's where they take skin from another part of your body like your butt and put it somewhere that has been badly damaged."

"Oh, gross. I had butt skin on my face?"

I shook my head. I could see why that might be a little disturbing to a twelve-year-old. "Yes, but they had to do something. Your face was damaged really badly. But, you had to have all those surgeries and the kids at school made fun of you a lot. A whole lot. The kids were really mean to you, Lanie. Your mom ended up moving you away when you were fifteen. I don't remember where, but she got you away from here."

I didn't know much about her after she moved away because we hadn't kept in touch. I raised my hand to my face, pressing it against my mouth as I thought. "I remember my mom telling me a few years back that you had a really active role in the ASPCA helping to rescue dogs."

"What's that?"

"What's what?"

"The ASP whatever you said."

"Oh, sorry. It's the American something something Cruelty to Animals. I can't remember exactly what it stands for. I would Google it, but I won't have an Internet connection for another twelve or fifteen years."

"A what in what?" she asked.

"Sorry, Lanie." My mind was going a million miles a minute and I kept forgetting that she and I were from different decades. "Never mind. You took a job rescuing animals."

"Why would I do that?"

"Well, the best I understand, that dog was mean because it had been mistreated. You wanted to help keep animals from being mistreated so that the same thing didn't happen to some other little kid."

"Oh."

"Oh my God, Lanie. I changed everything. In that one moment, in that one second, I changed so much. My dad, you, everything. I changed your whole life! I may have changed *my* whole life." The possibility that I might not meet Sarah and fall in love was starting to creep in.

"But that's good right? Your dad isn't going to die. I don't have a bunch of scars and I don't have to move away from my friends. What's wrong with that?"

"It doesn't sound like anything is." But I wondered how much impact there might be that I hadn't intended – or even thought of.

SEVEN

"My mom has to work this afternoon, so she's taking me to hang out at my dad's restaurant until he gets done. You want to come?" I asked.

"We get to eat?" Lanie asked.

"Yep. That's the plan, anyway."

"Yum." She rubbed her belly as she said it, signaling her assent.

"Hey, what's it called, anyway?"

"What's what called?"

"My dad's restaurant."

"You don't know what your own dad's restaurant is called?"

"Lanie, it's been twenty-five years. There's a lot I don't remember."

"Really? I remember lots of stuff from when I was little."

"Yeah, way back in the day. What? Four, five years ago?" I threw a dried-up piece of bark at her, hitting her in the chin.

"Okay, fine. Good point."

"So?"

"Oh yeah. You did ask me, didn't you? Eggin' It."

"That's right. Now that you say it, I can remember. Isn't it set up to look like a fifties diner?" I felt like I was an amnesia victim, constantly trying to remember things that were just out of reach.

We dropped from the log we had been sitting on and started the walk back to her house. There was so much I had figured out and our excursion to the creek helped out a lot, but there was still so much I didn't know. Every new development helped me fill in a piece or two, but I still didn't really know what it all meant. Grabbing Lanie's arm had set off a chain reaction that affected me and everyone around me.

That one, small action changed the course of all our lives. What was scary about that was that I didn't know what the new trajectory looked like. I didn't really know what all I had affected. And, if I did suddenly wake up to find myself in my old life, what would that life look like? I wondered if I really would be like an amnesia victim with no memory of what led me up to that point.

But even with those fears, I couldn't help but have a newfound spring in my step that I hadn't had since before I woke up to this insane replay of my childhood. The inevitability of my father's death had weighed on my shoulders like a stone hung around my neck. I didn't want to live through it again, but I had no idea how to stop it. Little did I know that I already had. And now, he could be there to teach me the things that had been imparted to him by his own father.

Then there were the changes to my mom. I didn't know if I could picture her as anything but the alcohol dependent person she had become. But the possibility was real that there was a new woman for me to get to know. I didn't know how long it might take to let go of the sins of the past, but I was actually looking forward to that new component of my future.

We reached the fence and Lanie placed her hand on top, getting ready to jump. "I still don't see how this could happen."

"So, that means you believe me?" I asked.

"I think so. I don't know. I mean, you don't sound like you. You don't sound like a kid. It is hard for me to get, you know? Grownup words coming out of a little twerp." She leaped up to the fence, swinging her legs over and landing on the other side.

"Ouch! That hurts." I followed after, climbing over only slightly less clumsily than I had before.

"Well, at least it makes more sense now why you suck at climbing fences. You climb like my grandpa."

"Bite me, Lanie," I said, smiling. "I'm not ancient. The fence is almost as tall as I am."

Walking in the through the back door, Lanie's mom was standing at the sink, washing dishes. "Hey, you two. Have fun down at the creek? You didn't get all wet did you?"

"It was good. And no, we didn't get wet. Hey, Andy's mom is taking him to eat and then to hang out until his dad gets off work. Can I go?"

Lisa finished with the glass she was washing, running it under the faucet to rinse it. She placed it in the drying rack and turned around. As she turned, there was a flash of what almost looked like disapproval. Her lips were slightly pursed; her brow forced downward, but she replaced it with a smile before she finished her rotation. "I guess so. Hey, Andy. Why don't you wait outside for a sec? Lanie will be right out."

"Sure. Okay." I said, walking through the kitchen and into the living room. Lanie's house was a split-level just like mine, only backwards. As I stepped out through the kitchen doorway, the stairs led up to my left and the front door was in front of me, tucked in a shallow alcove beside the stairs. As I reached the door, I placed my hand on the knob but paused, waiting to see if I could overhear a snippet. Lisa's reaction had seemed a bit odd. Listening, there was only silence from the kitchen. Evidently, she was waiting to for the door to close behind me.

I wasn't sure what made me so curious, but I briefly thought about opening and closing the door to create the appearance that I had gone outside. I thought better of it since I would still have to find a way out without making any noise. Instead, I opened the door and stepped through into the rising heat of the day. The eastern sun hadn't broken over the roofline, so its full force was coming down on that side of the house. It was only late April so it would be relatively cool by July standards, but it was still warm for spring.

I sat down in my customary spot on the steps and waited. It looked like Mr. Johnston had gotten the mower to start. His grass was freshly mowed and he was using a push broom to sweep the grass clippings from the driveway back into the yard. In the opposite direction, I saw the now familiar black car with the lightning bolt. It sat there almost as though it belonged. This time, both windows were open about a third of the way. I guessed that they hadn't wanted to run the air conditioner since I was nowhere to be seen when they arrived.

I strained to see into the darkness of the car, but it was no use. The windows were tinted limousine black and all I could see through the open section was the top of a man's head. He was facing my direction and I could see the front view of dark hair that was combed over to one side. We sat there looking at each other, but he had the advantage. I was certain that they knew who I was, but who they were was still a mystery to me. A part of me wanted to know who was behind the glass, but I would have rather had them drive away, never to be seen again.

Behind me, the front door unlatched. The smaller latch on the screen door clicked as Lanie pushed it open as well. "Sorry about that," she said, stepping through the door and letting it fall closed.

"What was that about?" I asked. "She didn't look very happy about letting you go."

"Oh, she was mad because my room was a mess"

"Just checking to make sure everything was okay."

"Thanks, Dad."

"Oh, great. Here we go with the old people jokes. So glad I told you."

"You know I couldn't let an opportunity like that go," she said, patting the top of my head as she came down the steps.

At home, the three of us piled into my mom's red Escort for the short trip to my dad's restaurant. It was just on the other side of town. As we pulled out, I tried to be subtle about watching behind us to see what the black car would do. It let us get a couple hundred feet up the street before it pulled out, keeping its place behind us. We pulled up to the stop sign and it visibly slowed, seemingly to avoid getting too close to us.

It followed us all the way to the restaurant, but it didn't pull into the lot. My mom made the left turn and the car kept on going, turning right at the next cross street. As we got out of the car, I looked up at the sign that read *Eggin' It* in red and black letters. I had a few vague memories about coming here as a kid, but I couldn't remember much else.

Walking in didn't help much with the memories either. I had hoped that being inside would bring back a flash of memories like what had happened at home and at school. Instead, the white and black walls with the bright red booths were just familiar. No epiphanies came as I saw them.

It was clear that my dad had done a good job at giving the place a fifties feel, though. It wasn't anything like the normal, poorly done, decade based montages that are designed to evoke as many memories as possible. Walking in made you feel like you were stepping backward into the past. I chuckled to myself as I noticed the irony that my dad's restaurant was set thirty years in the past, just a few years farther than I had travelled.

"Why don't you two find a place to sit? I'm going to go let your dad know we're here," my mom said. She turned and walked through the padded red door that likely led to the kitchen.

The lunch rush was well underway and the place was fairly busy. The counter was dotted with people, some of them sitting and having coffee, some making their way through an omelet, a plate of eggs benedict, or maybe a cheeseburger. Two older men were sitting at the end having a heated discussion about baseball, from the sound of it.

We found a booth at the back. We slid into the seats and I grabbed two menus from the chrome wire rack attached to the wall over the booth. I hadn't even handed Lanie hers when one of the waitresses came over to take our drink orders. I guess that's one of the fringe benefits of being the owner's son.

"How you doing, Andy?" the waitress asked. I looked up at her and I had no idea who she was. She was in her fifties, her black hair streaked with gray. She was a barrel of a woman and had bright red glasses that rested on the top of her head.

"I'm good. How are you?"

"Oh, good, I guess. Just the normal aches and pains from being on my feet all day. I'm guessing you want a Dr Pepper. How about you, young lady?"

"I'll have a Sprite."

That actually freaked me out. Having a person you've never met before know what your drink order was going to be was a little unsettling. I knew it was because she knew me and had likely taken my order several times, but it was still weird.

Looking at the menu, it was definitely fancier than the straight diner fare I expected from the décor. There were omelets with ham and gruyere cheese; there were stuffed pork chops, and there were cheeseburgers with a thin slice of portabella mushroom and Swiss cheese.

As I was poring through the selections, I glanced up and Lanie was looking over the table at me. "What?" I asked. "You're making me feel like a circus freak."

"That's because you are," she said, smiling now. "I think I'm just waiting for you to grow a beard or maybe a sixth finger. Or maybe some horns."

"A sixth finger? Horns?" my mom asked, now standing over the table. "What in the world are you guys talking about over here?"

"Holy cow, Mom. You're sneaky like a ninja. Remind me to never get on your bad side."

"A ninja, what do you mean?"

"I don't know. You keep sneaking up on me, scaring me half to death."

"That's me, the silent stalker." She raised both hands to mimic a fight stance before bringing a hand to my head like she was going to karate chop me. Instead, she ruffled my hair. "I've got to take off. You guys go ahead and order. Andy, only one pop, okay?"

"Okay, mom. Bye."

As she walked toward the doors, I looked back at Lanie. "That was a little weird." I almost felt like I should stop saying that. Just about everything was weird.

"What do you mean?"

"I'm thirty-five. I don't think my mom has ruffled my hair in twenty-five years."

"Twenty-five years? Man, you're old. If your body wasn't so small, I'd get you a walker."

"You just can't let that one go, can you?" I said with a smirk.

The waitress came back to take our order and to bring us our drinks. As she walked away, Lanie asked, "So, how did you get here, anyway? What happened?"

"I really don't know. I woke up Thursday morning in my bedroom. I saw my mom and she looked so young. It was crazy. It freaked me out so much I fell backward off the bed."

Lanie laughed, spraying Sprite out on the table from her nose and mouth, which made us both laugh. "Oops. Sorry," she said, reaching out with a napkin to wipe up the scattered spots. "No, I mean before that. What caused it?"

I have no idea. The last thing I remember was my wife and I going out for Italian food. Everything was great. We drove home, went to bed. Now I'm nine."

"What was she like?" she asked, running her finger around the rim of her glass.

"She was… is amazing. Sorry, sometimes this whole situation makes me forget that she is still back there, waiting for me." I took a drink of my soda, thinking for a moment. "She's beautiful. And she's very compassionate. She has a heart to help whoever she can. Sometimes even to the point that we would argue about it because she wanted to help more than I thought we should have. And she's funny, always laughing."

"She sounds great."

"She is." I smiled as I thought of a memory. "I remember one time, our cat got out and she made me drive all over the neighborhood at midnight looking for that thing. I think we were out there for like two hours. All I wanted to do was go back and go to bed, but she wasn't having it. She didn't want to leave him out there without looking first, at least. The next day, she printed up posters and put them all over the neighborhood. I remember that she went all around the neighborhood, talking to people."

"Did you find it?"

"Well, yes and no. He showed up on our doorstep about four days later with his fur all matted. So, I guess you could say he found us."

"That's a nice story," she said. She pinched her straw between her thumb and forefinger, pulling it into her mouth.

"That's just who she was. That time it was a cat, but she was always going out of her way to help people. I miss her."

"Do you have kids?"

"No. She has always wanted them, but I never did until recently. We were just starting to try before... this happened."

"You didn't want kids?"

"I don't know. I guess I just had such a crappy childhood that I didn't want to take the chance of doing the same thing to my kids."

"Crappy childhood? But your parents seem so cool." She looked at my nine year old form before looking around the restaurant. She was seeing my childhood as we spoke.

"Well, remember I told you my dad was supposed to die?"

"Oh, right. Duh. I wasn't thinking about your dad."

"He was supposed to die the day after tomorrow. What happened to you devastated my mom. She blamed herself. I think she blamed herself for my dad too. She became an alcoholic. So, I guess I grew up without a dad and with an absent mom."

The waitress I couldn't remember came back, balancing a tray with our plates on it. She slid a cheeseburger and fries in front of me. In front of Lanie, she set down an omelet with cheese and bits of bacon spread across the top. "That plate's hot, hon. Be careful not to burn yourself."

"Thanks," Lanie said as the waitress walked away.

Lanie placed both hands on the table on either side of her plate, locking her eyes with mine. "Okay, so you've got to tell me. Is the future like the Jetsons? Do you have flying cars and stuff?"

I raised my hand to my mouth to keep from spitting chewed burger as I laughed. She made me think of all the little pictures and stuff we did in grade school of what the year 2000 would look like. I remembered one year that we actually did a time capsule, putting in pictures and letters addressing the people of the future. We had pictures of flying cars and automatic food dispensers that would create full meals; there were pictures of people teleporting to work and all kinds of stuff that may not even exist in our lifetimes. But, to us, the year 2000 seemed like it was a lifetime away.

"No, Lanie. Sorry. There aren't any flying cars or teleportation machines. Although you can see people when you talk to them on the phone, though. But not very many people actually use it."

"Why not? That would be cool."

"I'm not sure. Maybe because people don't like to be all made up just to talk on the phone."

"Hmm. Well, what is like then?"

I thought for a moment as I dipped a fry in ketchup. "It really isn't all that different from now. Not really. We depend on computers a lot."

"You mean like the Macintoshes we have at school?"

"Kind of. They are just a lot more advanced and a lot smaller. We have phones that we carry around in our pockets or on our hips that are way more powerful than those computers."

"Phones you carry around with you? No cords?" she asked. I laughed as I thought about the phone we had at home with its thirty-foot long cord. Wireless house phones weren't common yet. Actually, many people still hadn't moved away from the old, rotary dial phones.

"Almost no phones have cords anymore." I wondered if I should say *had* or *will have*. What verb tense should you use to describe the future that is your past?

"Wow. That would be cool. But, why would you need a phone that is a computer? That seems silly."

"Well, you can play games or get on the Internet. You can listen to music-"

"What's the Internet?" she asked, showing me a puzzled look.

Wow. Maybe it was a lot more different than I thought. There are so many things that we take for granted as being a normal part of everyday life. All that stuff grows just a little at a time, each thing building on the thing that came before it. It made me think of how my mom didn't get a digital video recorder until just this year. She still had her stacks and stacks of video tapes that she used to record her daytime shows.

"Hmm," I said, trying to think of a way to explain the Internet to someone who had only seen computers that barely count as predecessors to modern technology. "Well, it connects millions of computers together and it allows you to have more knowledge at your fingertips than is in the world's biggest library. So, you don't even have to leave your house to look up stuff."

"Sounds lazy," she said, taking a bite of her omelet.

"I suppose it does. So many of the advancements over the next couple of decades are all about making things smaller, faster, and easier."

"So, no flying cars, huh? I was really looking forward to flying."

"Nope, sorry."

"How about robots?"

"Not really, no. I mean there are, but not like C-3PO or Roxy or whatever."

"Then what are they like?"

"Well, most robots are built for a purpose, like assembling cars or putting together tiny microchips for computers."

"You can't talk to them or get them to do stuff for you?"

"Nope."

"Well, do cars drive themselves at least?"

"No. I mean they do have a car out now that can parallel park itself."

"Wow," she said, rolling her eyes at me. "Can you teleport?"

"Nope."

"Are there laser guns?"

"Guns, no. They do have lasers that cut things, though."

"What a letdown. Who knew it would be so boring?"

We sat and talked for a while longer as we finished our meals. We talked about the world that was her future and my past. We talked about school and the neighborhood. There was so little in the way of details that I remembered. She helped me fill in some of the gaps, but there was nothing she could do to dispel the lost feeling that I felt almost constantly. Only time was likely to fix that. Hopefully I would be able to find my way out of the past before that happened.

When closing time came, the last of the customers filed out the door and the restaurant staff began rushing around, trying to get everything ready for the next day. The waitresses cleaned the tables and the floors and filled the salt and pepper and other condiment containers while the cooks cleaned the kitchen. They made quick work of it with the precision that comes from much practice.

The door to the kitchen made a swooshing sound as my dad pushed through. "Sorry it took so long, guys."

"No worries," I said. "We were just hanging out."

He walked over to our table and bent forward, placing a hand on either edge of the table. "What do you guys think about some ice cream? I thought maybe we could stop on the way home."

"Um," Lanie said, instantly smiling. "You felt like you had to ask?"

"I guess that would be a yes," my dad said as he straightened, returning the smile.

We drove the short distance to Dairy Freeze and pushed through the doors. I hadn't been there in years. It was our favorite place to go back before my dad died. My mom and I went there a couple of times afterward when she was trying especially hard to make life seem normal, but I think it brought up too many memories, and it ended up on the off-limits list.

The interior was all white except for the bright, red tables and the pictures of menu items spread across the walls. There were banana splits, and shakes, and, of course, the Peanut Blast. That was my favorite. It was vanilla ice cream with layers of peanuts and rich, dark chocolate syrup. They were huge. Looking up at the picture, I remembered that I almost always had a bellyache when I finished, but I tried to keep that a secret. I loved the flavor combination and I was afraid that they wouldn't let me have a whole one if I said something.

We each placed our order before stepping back to wait. "Are you cold?" my dad asked, looking over at Lanie. She had hunched her shoulders and was holding her arms in close to her body.

"It's freezing in here."

"Really? I don't think it's that bad. I do have a jacket in the backseat if you want to go grab it."

"That would be awesome," she said, turning toward the door. She pushed out into the bright sunshine and jogged across the parking lot to the car. Almost as though it were waiting, the black car pulled behind the Nova, blocking her from view. Ten seconds turned into twenty and Lanie still did not emerge from around the car. She should have been back by now.

"Dad, I think something is wrong," I said.

"What do you mean?"

"Look," I said, pointing toward the car. "As soon as Lanie opened the door of our car, that car pulled up. She still hasn't come back."

"I'm sure it's nothing." He turned and took a step toward the door anyway, trying to get a better look. As I watched, the side door of a nearby minivan opened and a group of kids started climbing out. Five or six kids shepherded by a man and a woman crossed in front of the car when the window rolled down quickly. Lanie was inside.

Her face was shaped by terror, her eyes wide. Lanie pushed her head out the window and yelled to the adults, "Help! Help me!" The man turned toward the car and Lanie jerked back inside. The car accelerated, pulling out of view. My dad and I both broke into a run, shoving through the double doors. We stepped into the parking lot just in time to see the car swing hard right onto the street. The engine screamed as the driver pushed the car to accelerate as quickly as it could.

We both ran across the lot and got into the car. My dad rammed the key into the ignition and, twisting it, the Nova roared to life. Moving forward, my dad bumped the car up onto the grass strip separating the lot from the street. We dropped back down on to asphalt and turned in an attempt to catch up to the black car with Lanie inside. It was about a hundred yards ahead of us and we were losing ground.

"Hold on," my dad said, pressing the gas pedal closer to the floorboard. We weaved in and out of traffic and the black car changed from a small dot to a slightly bigger one as we slowly began to catch up. Just when we got within fifty yards or so, the car swung hard left with a screeching of breaks all around as the car ran a red light to make the turn. The intersection was a jumble of cars pointed in various directions as they tried to avoid hitting the offending Camaro.

We took advantage of a green light at the intersection before that one and turned left onto a parallel street. It was fairly empty, so my dad floored it, bringing us up to an alarming speed. I looked away from the buildings as they whizzed by to see that the speedometer read seventy-five.

He pushed on the brakes, shoving me forward in the seat until the belt locked and jarred my forward motion to a halt. He spun the wheel quickly to the right, bringing the back end around in a slide. Without waiting for the car to come to a stop, he pressed lightly on the accelerator again, waiting for the tires to catch. The tires regained their traction, and we raced toward the next intersection.

It was his turn to run the red light to make the left turn. We threaded in between two cars, one leaving the intersection and one about to enter. The car that was behind braked and swerved, producing a cacophony of sound as its horn blared and rubber protested against the stop with a scream. We made the turn, but the black car had disappeared. The road ahead of us was dotted with several cars, but the one containing Lanie was not there. I spun around in my seat to look behind us. It was about fifty yards back.

"Dad, they're behind us!" He checked his rearview mirror and slammed on the brakes as he yanked the wheel, this time pulling us around one-hundred-eighty degrees. The car shuddered as it came to a stop. There were thick, black strips of rubber on the street marking where the wheels locked and lost traction.

Again, he pressed down on the accelerator, racing back toward the car, but it was turning right. When we made it to the place where they turned, we turned left to come in behind them, but they had disappeared yet again. There were several pickups and cars parked along the side of the road, but the street was empty of traffic.

"Watch the side streets," my dad yelled as we continued down the street. As we crossed each street, I watched my side and he watched his. We hoped for a glimpse of the car as it tried to make its escape. Each street was just as empty as the one before. Finally, after about six blocks, I saw it a couple hundred feet away.

"There it is!" My dad slammed on the brakes, causing me to lurch into my seatbelt again. My small form felt like a ragdoll as I tried to fight against the inertia of the car. We were too late to take that street, so he chose the next one instead. He turned right and sped up and the black car crossed several blocks in front of us. It had turned left as it worked to throw us off its trail. When we reached the street where it passed, it had disappeared again, probably turning onto another side street.

We canvassed the area for another several minutes, but the car and Lanie were gone. They had disappeared into the maze of buildings that surrounded us. We came to a stop, this time much more gently than before. He hit the wheel with his hands, wrapping his fingers around it into a tight grip. "How am I going to tell Lanie's dad?" he asked as he stared out the windshield.

EIGHT

The buildings on either side us had taken on a menacing feel, almost mocking us with the fact that Lanie was out there somewhere. The driver in the black Camaro was racing away as we drove, taking her to suffer whatever fate her captor had planned. I didn't know who he was, and I didn't know what he wanted. What I did know was that I couldn't shake the feeling that he had taken her because of me. In my heart, I knew it was somehow my fault.

"Where are we going?" I asked. Looking over at him, I was surprised to see that he suddenly looked much older than his thirty-five years. The events of the past several minutes had already taken a toll on him. His hair was mussed where he had been running his hands through it. The lines on his face seemed harsher, more defined. He looked tired and he looked like there was a heavy weight on his shoulders.

"We have to go to the police. We have to tell her parents and we have to call the police."

At his mention of the police, I couldn't help but feel like they wouldn't be able to help us. What were we going to tell them? The truth sounded ludicrous. I travelled back in time and someone who knew about it left me a note. When I refused to follow their instructions, they kidnapped her instead. It all seemed so impossible. But the events of the past few days had shattered my ideas about what was normal and about what could or couldn't happen. If there really was a supernatural element to all of this, how much could the police help us? They definitely wouldn't believe me if I told the whole truth.

"Dad, I'm not sure calling the police is a good idea. I think I know what happened." I sat for a moment, feeling as though that wasn't right. "I mean, I think I know why it happened." That wasn't right either. I didn't *know* anything outside of the obvious. Someone took Lanie.

Instead of trying again, I just said, "I think he took her because of me."

"You what?" he asked. "That's silly. Why would you even think that?"

I didn't know what to tell him. I thought it was my fault because I had gone against the note. The note told me to let things take their natural course and I hadn't. Now, whoever was in the car had taken her. The note and the car had to be connected. I wanted to tell him that, but I didn't know where to start. He didn't know that I was really an adult. He didn't even know that Lanie was supposed to get attacked. And until he did, I didn't think he could understand the truth of what happened. To him, I was just a boy without the benefit of an adult's perspective.

I knew I had important information that could mean the difference in finding her or not. But in order for that to help, I would have to tell him everything. I would have to make him understand that I wasn't just a nine-year-old boy. As I thought about the prospect of telling him, the same feelings I had with Lanie came back, only they were worse. Lanie had already suspected something was amiss. She had been asking questions. Then, there was the fact that she was a kid. I believed her youth helped her to accept the impossible a little more easily.

As the buildings raced by on either side, I couldn't make myself follow through. I couldn't deliver the truth. Not yet. So instead, I just said, "I've seen that car before. It's been hanging around the past few days."

"It has?" he asked. He veered to come alongside the curb, slowing the car to a stop. Without putting the transmission into park, he turned to face me. "What has it been doing? Have you seen anyone get out?"

"No. He was just watching us. Sometimes he would just sit there; sometimes he would pull up or drive past. He was even there when the dog almost attacked us."

"How long has it been hanging around?"

"Since Thursday after school," I said.

He reached forward and lifted the gear selector until the thin, green indicator sat in front of the large "P" on the column. Turning to face me again, he raised his elbow to rest on the back of the seat. "So it was there after school on Thursday and then what? Before and after school on Friday?"

"Yeah. And it followed us to the restaurant this morning, but it didn't turn in."

His eyes went out of focus as he stared through the window beside me. A mom and her son moved past us, the boy trying to stuff a hotdog into his mouth as he walked. There was an orange balloon floating above his head with *Bert's Brats* printed across it in large, black letters.

"He must have been waiting for an opportunity to grab her," he said, pulling his eyes back into focus. He faced forward again and dropped the car into gear, checking the mirror for traffic.

Of course, that was the most logical explanation, but it went against my screaming instincts. Everything in me said that I was at the center of it. It had to have something to do with me. The car didn't show up until I did. Coincidences happen every day, but this couldn't be simple chance.

I tugged at the seatbelt to keep it from digging into my neck as I tried to figure out what to do next. He couldn't see the connection because he didn't know what had happened. To him, it was a simple but horrible kidnapping.

My palms instantly started to sweat as I understood that I was going to have to face the inevitable. I was going to have to tell him if I wanted him to understand.

My dad glanced down at me as we pulled away from the curb. "Son, that didn't have anything to do with you. Don't even worry about it. It wasn't your fault."

I took a breath and braced myself for the conversation to come. Once I started, I knew there was no taking it back. "I'm older than you think I am, Dad. I don't know how it happened, but somehow I've come back in time. I'm not a nine-year-old boy."

He let out a heavy breath as he looked down into his lap for a moment. He tapped the side of his thumb against the steering wheel several times. In that moment, I would have given almost anything to be inside his head. I couldn't tell what he was thinking. I wasn't quite sure how I expected him to react, but I had thought it might be… different. I thought he might slam on the breaks, laugh, something. Instead, he stared down toward his lap as he drove, tapping his thumb against the wheel. Finally, he just said, "I don't think Lanie has anything to do with that."

It took a second for his words to register. I replayed his voice in my head a couple times to make sure I heard it correctly. He had said, "With that" as though he already knew about my coming back in time. But that couldn't be true. There was no way he could have figured it out.

"How…" I started, but I was so dumbfounded that I could hardly get the words out.

"I know you aren't a boy, but that doesn't change anything. It still isn't your fault," he said

"But how…" I tried again. How could he possibly know? Was I that inept at acting like a child? Surely not. People don't travel back in time. Except for when they do, of course. But still, there was no way he would have guessed that. There was no way to guess it. I placed my hands on my thighs, trying to control the shaking that had erupted. "You can't. You can't know. That's impossible."

"No, not impossible. I do know. I know you arrived Thursday morning. I know about the dog and Lanie. I know she was supposed to get attacked."

"I… I don't understand." As I listened to my own stilted words, I felt as though my faculties of speech had abandoned me. I felt as though I must seem even younger than my body's age. And I wanted to be angry with him, but I was so overwhelmed with confusion that any anger was diffused before it had a chance to erupt. "How could you know that, Dad?"

"You're not going to like this, but I can't tell you how I know. I didn't want to even tell you that I knew, but you didn't really give me a choice."

"I didn't give you a choice? You didn't want to tell me?" I asked. For some reason, that began to spark the anger that was unable to surpass the feeling of confusion moments ago. "You knew this whole time and you just let me stew in it?"

"Hold on a minute, Andy. You don't understand-"

"You're right, Dad. I don't understand. I wake up to find someone hit the rewind button on my life and now Lanie's missing and I don't know what's going on and you're telling me that you knew this whole time?"

"I didn't know Lanie was going to get taken. I only knew you were older. I can't tell you how much I hate this, Andy. I want to tell you everything. I want to put your mind at ease, but I can't."

"Why not?" I demanded.

"Because you won't forget if I do."

"What? What are you talking about?"

"In a few weeks, you should start forgetting how you were before. Eventually, the only Andy left will be the nine-year-old Andy. Talking about what happened can keep that from happening."

"Whoa, wait. What did you just say?"

"You have to let yourself forget. It's the only way for you to live a normal life."

I suddenly felt as though my lungs had lost the ability to expand. It was like my chest had just collapsed under the weight of his words. I had feared that I might be stuck here, but to hear him say it hit me in a way I could never have expected. It was like being told I was about to die.

"No, no, no. You're wrong. I've got to find my way back to normal, because this isn't it. This is not normal. You don't understand. I can't forget. If I forget, then I won't know there's anything to go back to."

The conflict in my dad was obvious. There was a sadness in his eyes that penetrated all the way to his soul. "I'm sorry, Son. I am so sorry.

You can't go back, at least in the way you're thinking. The only way to get back is to live it."

"Well then, I don't want to forget." The thought of losing my memories was even worse than the knowledge I couldn't go back. If I forgot, I wouldn't even know who Sarah was. If she was in the future and I was stuck here, my memories were all I had left. "I don't want to lose Sarah."

"Was she your wife?"

"Yes, she is. We've been married for ten years. I don't know what I would do without her."

"Then you have to trust me. You have to let yourself forget."

"Why, Dad? I don't understand."

"Forgetting is your best chance of ending up with her again."

"No, I can choose her. I can court her. I will do whatever I have to do to win her love."

"But it isn't that simple. Your life is the result of your choices. And your choices are based on what you know at the time you are making the choice. You can guess at the outcome and you can even be right a lot of the time, but the only way you can truly know is to experience it. And that experience is more of a threat than you realize. Your experiences will affect your choices."

"But not that choice. I know that's where I want to go."

"Have you done everything the same so far?"

"No." I thought of Lanie and the dog. I thought of my dad. And my mom.

"You did things differently because you knew the outcome. You have been here, and you have done it before. You made different choices because you had more information. The only way to make the same choices as before is to allow the new information to pass away."

"But I will make the choice to court Sarah."

"What makes you think this is just about you?"

"What do you mean?" I asked.

"Sarah has her own choices. She has her own decisions. She fell in love with the man that existed when you met her. If you don't forget, that man will never exist outside of your memories."

What he was saying was finally starting to break through. His words had brought the realization that Sarah wouldn't be meeting the same man she met the first time. She would be meeting a man who has gone through all the changes that years of experience bring. There were no guarantees that she would even like that man.

"How do I forget, then?" The idea of forgetting scared me to death, but I didn't want to lose her forever.

"You have to do things the same way you did before."

"I don't understand."

"When you do things differently, your new memories conflict with your old ones. When they conflict, they become linked. Once a memory is linked it can become imprinted on your brain, making it permanent."

"Imprinted? Linked? Permanent? Are you saying my memories aren't real or something?"

"No, they're real, but they came with you. I know it doesn't make sense; I'm not even sure I understand it, but they don't exist inside your brain. It's complicated."

Something told me that he was lying, or at least not telling the whole truth. He understood better than he was willing to admit, but I didn't think I was going to get him to budge. In light of what he had told me, I wasn't sure I wanted him to budge. "So, you're saying that I brought memories with me that aren't really inside my brain the way other memories are?

"That's exactly what I'm saying."

"And talking about all of this can turn them into normal memories?" I asked.

"Something like that. It makes the old memories act like new ones. But the real danger comes from doing things differently. Then you'll have two versions of the memory and the connection between them makes you remember both."

"How do you know all of this? You talk like you've seen it before."

"I've already told you too much. I know you don't like it, but you have to trust me. Forgetting really is for the best. It is vital that people forget. That is the only way they can live their lives ignorant of what lies before them."

I thought I understood what he was saying, but it was so much to take in. Every moment of the past couple days was a complete wreck and I couldn't understand what was happening. And now, Lanie had been kidnapped and I still couldn't shake the feeling that it was tied directly to me. I felt like I was trapped in the center of something I didn't understand and couldn't control. Every time I thought I might be starting to get comfortable with the rhythm of the whirlwind, it just got more intense. I didn't feel like I could take much more before it shook me apart.

As we turned into Lanie's driveway, the magnitude of how the situation had progressed weighed on me like a giant, concrete pylon. We were going to have to go in there and tell her parents that their daughter was missing. We were going to have to tell them that someone had taken her and that we didn't know what to do. Or at least I didn't. My dad knew much more than he was willing to admit, but I didn't know how far that knowledge went.

We walked up the steps to Lanie's door and rang the bell. After several seconds, the door opened and Lanie's mom, Lisa, stepped into view. "Hey, guys," she said. "Where's Lanie?"

"Hi, Lisa. Is Tony here?"

"Yeah. Where's Lanie? Wasn't she with you?"

"Can we come in?"

"Of course, but why won't you answer me? Where is my daughter?"

"That's what I've come to talk to you about, but I need to talk to you both." A mix of fear and concern showed in her face as she pushed open the screen door, allowing us to enter. As we stepped across the threshold, my dad turned to me. "Andy, why don't you have a seat on the couch?

We're just going to step outside to talk for a minute. We'll be back soon. Lisa, can you get Tony? I think Andy will be fine by himself."

Her face was slack and white as she turned to make her way up the stairs. After a few moments, she returned with Tony following behind her. As he reached the bottom step, he looked from me to my dad before turning to walk toward the back door. He didn't say a word, but he didn't have to. The look on his face said that he knew something terrible had happened. Something he didn't want to deal with, but had little choice. I could relate much more than he could possibly know.

My dad opened the back door and the three of them stepped through, closing it behind them. They walked out to the back fence that ran along the edge of their yard. I didn't really understand why they were going through the trouble of separating themselves. I was there when Lanie was taken, so they couldn't possibly talk about something I didn't already know. I couldn't understand how hearing a conversation I already knew about could keep me from forgetting. I knew my dad was worried about it, but I wondered if he was taking too much of a precaution.

I rose from the couch and crept toward one of the windows that overlooked the backyard. Kneeling down, I got as close as I could to the window and tried to peek out without disturbing the way the curtains hung. They were too far away for me to hear anything, though. My only cues as to what was happening came from their gestures and movements.

Even without the benefit of sound, it was clear that my dad had delivered the bad news. Now, Tony's face had lost its color just as Lisa's had. Her darker complexion was now a pasty white. Her eyes were wide and her lips pulled back into a dark perversion of a grin. After a moment, she turned her back on my dad and buried her face into her husband's chest. I was seeing the difference between knowing something was wrong and knowing what was wrong.

The discussion between Tony and my dad seemed to devolve into a disagreement. Their volume began to rise, almost to the point that I could hear them. Muffled, isolated syllables penetrated the panes of the window, but there wasn't enough there to be able to understand.

My dad began to pace and Tony held his wife. He started shifting his gaze toward the house, moving his attention between it and my dad. I wondered if he could see me, but he didn't seem to be looking at me, exactly. He was looking at the house as though it were my proxy.

Lisa finally pulled away from Tony, joining in the continual glances toward the house. Was my dad blaming it on me? Was he telling them it was my fault? No, surely not. But I did wonder if he had told them I had suggested that we not go to the police. To two people who had just had their daughter kidnapped, that had to seem ludicrous. The alternative was for us to go after the kidnappers ourselves, taking vigilante justice into our own hands.

After a few minutes, the volume of their conversation began to subside. Lisa appeared calmer, but none of the color had come back into her or Tony's faces. They looked as though their worst nightmares had just been unleashed upon them. In truth, that was probably because they had been.

The trio turned and started making their way back toward the house. I crept away from the window as quickly as I could, being sure to stay below the level of the window. My new height made that easier to do. I quickly dropped onto the couch and scooted backward, hoping that it looked like I had been there the whole time. I had no more than settled in when the door opened.

"It looks like you were right not to want to go to the police, Andy," my dad said as he walked into the living room. "They can't help us. Tony and I are going to go see someone who might be able to, though. We'll be back in a little while."

"Hey, wait a second," Lisa said, shooting a look of disapproval toward my dad. "You aren't expecting me to stay here with him, are you? That's my daughter out there. I'm not going to just sit here while you guys are looking for her. Besides, what if he's after Andy too? I don't know if I can protect him."

"Lisa, you know we can't take him with us," my dad said.

She does? Why would she know that? What in the world was going on? "How does she know that? Do they know too?"

"Yes, we know too," Tony said.

"How? How do you know?"

"You know we can't talk about that. We have to go, Andy. I don't know how much time we have. We don't understand why this happened."

I couldn't help but feel conflicted. One part of me was terrified of learning more because of what my dad had said. If there was no way back, I didn't want to risk losing Sarah. But I also felt like I was in the middle of something so much bigger than I could have ever imagined. I simultaneously wanted answers and was afraid to get them.

"Okay, fine." I forced the words out of my mouth even though I couldn't quite silence the part of me that wanted to know more. "But why can't you take me with you? Lanie is part of the present, whether it happened the first time or not. I can't live my life hiding from anything that seems different from the first time around. And besides, I might be able to help somehow."

"You're right, Andy, but this is different. We're going to get Lanie back and, when we do, things can get back to normal again. You shouldn't be mixed up in getting things back to normal."

"We've got to get moving, Joe," Tony said. His hands were stuffed in his pockets and he was staring at the floor. Somehow he knew what was happening just as my dad did. I could see the conflict in his face as he understood what I was going through, but needed to get things in motion so he could get his daughter back. I still couldn't see how my helping could keep me from forgetting, but I had to let them go.

"So what do I do, then?" I asked.

"I'm going to try to get your mom on the phone. You can stay with her, but you need to keep your eyes out. Lock up the house and don't let anyone in. Anyone. Pretend like you aren't home, no matter what happens. Oh, and your mom doesn't know any of this, so she has even fewer answers than you do. I'd appreciate it if you can keep it that way."

Before I could say anything, he turned and walked into the kitchen, lifting the receiver off the phone on the wall. I heard the minute clicks as he punched in the numbers. He stood quietly, waiting for an answer, but it didn't look like an answer was coming. He waited for several more rings before I heard him punching in another series of numbers. The second number had the same result as the first.

"She must be on her way home," he said as he replaced the cradle. "Tony, I know we need to hurry, but do you mind if we run down to the house for a few minutes? We'll give her just a bit and see if she shows up."

"Yeah, but let's be quick. Worst case, Andy can lock up and wait for her," Tony said as he looked down at his watch. I could only imagine how much he dreaded seeing each second click by. Every moment that passed was likely reducing his chances of seeing his daughter alive.

Tony, my dad, and I stepped out into the bright sunshine of the late afternoon. The roofline hid the sun from view, but it still felt unseasonably warm. I was glad I had chosen shorts that morning, although I was sure the temperature would dip down enough to make them uncomfortable later.

As we cleared the hedgerow that separated the Parkers' yard from their neighbor's, I could see the familiar red of my mom's Escort as it sat in the driveway. The front door of the house was standing open as well.

"Looks like you called just a bit too early, dad."

"Figures."

Inside, the television was on, but it was playing to an empty room. It was an old episode of Mork and Mindy. It looked like the one where Mork falls victim to advertising and starts filling the house with everything from baby formula to four-wheelers. "Hon?" my dad called out. He peeked into the kitchen and then sprinted up the stairs. There was no response to his calls.

From upstairs, he yelled down, "Check the garage. Maybe she's putting in some laundry." I pulled open the door, but she couldn't be in there. The darkness of the garage was a sharp contrast to the well-lit living room.

"Nope." I walked into the kitchen and around to the dining room. Her purse was sitting on the table, her keys lying on top. "Her purse is still here, though."

The three of us converged on the living room, but my mom was still missing. My dad turned and went out the front door and I went out the back. She wasn't there either.

Back in the living room, Tony asked, "Think she could have run over to one of the neighbor's?"

"Your guess is as good as mine. Maybe she did. Let's give her a few seconds. I'm sure she'll turn up." That didn't feel right and I could tell he felt it just as much as I did.

I turned to walk toward the couch, but I nearly fell over in horror as I noticed a spot of yellow on top of the television. It was the small, rectangular shape of a yellow sticky note. I was too far away to read the words written across the surface, but I knew they weren't good. "Uh, guys. Look," I said as I changed my course to head toward the television.

As I approached, I could see that the note contained the same words as before, written in the same block letters: LET IT HAPPEN. The crease where I had folded it in half ran down the middle of the paper just as it had when I threw it away.

"It's the same note," I said.

"The same as what?" Tony approached the TV and grasped the corner of the note, pulling to separate the sticky edge of the paper from the wood top. "What do you mean?"

"I found that on the bathroom mirror Thursday night."

"What does it say?"

"Let it happen," I said. "That's it. Just those three words."

"Let it happen? Let what happen?" my dad asked.

"I didn't know what it meant and I threw it away. But after Lanie... I thought whoever wrote that wanted me to let the dog attack her."

"That doesn't even make any sense," my dad said.

"Welcome to my world, Dad," I said, but there was no satisfaction in it.

NINE

The city's river district was about a half hour away. The area was a transportation hub for the region where rail lines, water routes, and trucking came together into an interchangeable network that allowed various goods to be transported around the country. Along with the transportation facilities, there were also various warehouses, grain silos, and small factories that dotted the area. The building we were interested in was a relatively small warehouse that was tucked in among several others.

Stepping into the building, the appearance of a warehouse gave way to that of an office as the doorway opened up into a large foyer. The harsh, fluorescent lights above our heads reflected in vague stripes across the black granite beneath our feet. To our right, there was a large, reception desk intended to greet visitors as they entered.

A smallish woman in her late fifties sat behind the desk, her skin the color of rich chocolate. Her face lit with recognition as we moved closer and she lifted herself out of her chair. "Well, look who we have here!" she said, smiling. "Joseph Myers, it has been forever since I have seen you. Get your butt over here and give me a hug."

"Hi, Kim," my dad said. He moved around the desk and pulled her into an embrace. "It's been a long time."

"Yes it has. What's it been? Twelve, fifteen years?"

"It hasn't been that long, has it? Ten years, tops."

"Ten, he says," she said, looking over the top of her glasses at Tony. "I'm sure it's closer to fifteen if it's been a day. You here to see your dad?"

"Yes ma'am."

"Must be a big deal if you're coming down here. He was expecting you."

"He was? He was expecting me to come here?"

"Yep. Who is this little man here?"

"Oh, sorry. This is my son, Andy."

"Well, hello, Andrew," she said, extending her hand.

"Hi. It's nice to meet you." I allowed her hand to swallow my own and give it a quick shake.

"Well, aren't you the most polite, cutest thing ever. Don't tell your dad, but I've got some chocolates hidden away if you can find your way back down here," she said, winking.

"I'm right here, Kim."

"I know that, you're supposed to pretend not to hear. Do I have to tell you everything?" she said, glancing up at him with a smile. Standing up straight, she walked back to the phone and lifted the receiver off its cradle. "Let me just tell him you're here."

She put the receiver up to her ear and mashed a couple buttons on the phone. After a moment, she said, "They're here... Yep ... I'll send them up." She hung up the phone and turned back to us.

"You guys can go on up. Tony, you know the way, right?"

"Yeah. Thanks, Kim."

A set of elevators sat behind the reception desk. I don't know why, but I kept expecting the office to be a façade like a movie prop – where the entrance looked like an office, but the rest was just a warehouse. If that was the case, the elevators were an excellent part of the illusion.

The elevator chimed softly and the doors slid open. The elevator was just as elegant as the foyer, with mahogany or maybe cherry wainscoting that covered the bottom half of each wall. Mirrors meant to decorate the top only served to remind us of the stress we were all feeling. Our reflections looked as though we hadn't slept in at least a couple days.

"We're here to see Grandpa?"

"Yeah."

"I don't remember him much," I said as the doors closed.

"You don't? I'm surprised. We don't spend a lot of time with him, but he's no stranger." Sometimes it was difficult to remember that none of the people around me shared my perspective. My past was still their future. Even still, I wondered why I didn't have many memories of my grandpa. I couldn't remember if something had happened to him or if he had just found his way onto my mom's list of stuff that reminded her of my dad.

"Why did the lady downstairs say it must be a big deal if you were here?" I asked. I wanted to ask why we were here, too. I would have if I had thought I would get an answer.

"Kim? I don't know. I guess I just don't have much reason to come down here." As the elevator doors opened, he continued, "I stopped working for your grandpa about the time I married your mom."

On the top floor, a woman sat behind another reception desk, her hair short and dark. She mustn't have been around as long as Kim had; there was no warm recognition as there had been downstairs. "Afternoon, Tony," she said. Her tone and her mannerisms were much more businesslike.

"Hi, Sonya."

"You guys can go on in."

"Is it okay if my son hangs out here for a minute?" my dad asked, resting his hand on the top of my head.

"Actually, Jonah specifically asked for both of you to go on in. And Tony is welcome too, of course."

"He did? Okay. Thank you."

As we swept open the office door, my grandpa leaned forward to push himself up from behind an enormous writing desk. He moved with a deliberate slowness that didn't quite seem to match his age. His lips pulled tight into a thin line as though the exertion of rising from the chair pained him.

As he rose, I searched my memory for any trace of him, but there was very little if there was anything at all. His thinning wisps of white hair were a stark contrast to his eyes, so dark they could almost be black. The look about him was very distinctive; it seemed as though he would be hard to forget. He carried an honesty in his face that said he should be listened to and that he meant what he said.

Still there was nothing solid for me to grab hold of. I had no memories of Sunday picnics, birthday cards, or anything else. There was a small spark of something, but I couldn't place it. Even with my mom's aversion to things that reminded her of my dad, it seemed odd that I had so little memory of him.

He still managed to smile as he rose, even with the apparent pain that had come from standing. But the smile only lasted for a moment before it faltered and then faded into a look of concern. "You guys look like death himself. Is something wrong?" he asked.

"Yeah," my dad answered. "It's Lanie and Donna. They're missing."

"Missing? What do you mean?" My grandpa asked, his look of concern giving way to alarm. His eyebrows shot up, causing the thin lines across his forehead to become broad canyons.

"The kids and I went for ice cream and Lanie went out to the car for a jacket. Someone took her when she did. And then Donna was gone when we got home. Her car and her purse were there, but she wasn't."

"Oh my! That is terrible. Do you know who did it?"

"We think it might have been Ray Thompson," Tony said. "From the way Joe described the car, it sure sounded like Ray's car."

"But he's a Timekeeper. Are you certain it was him?"

"Certain? Well, he's the only person I know who drives a black Camaro with lightning bolts on the sides."

"Yes, that does sound like his car." He lifted his eyes toward the crown molding above our heads as though in thought.

My grandpa lowered himself into the chair behind him, taking as much care as he did when he had stood up. Leaning back into the cushion of the chair, he asked, "Why would he have done this? Could he have a grievance against one of you?"

"I don't even know him," my dad said, sitting in one of the leather chairs that faced my grandpa's desk.

"And I don't know him that well," Tony said. "Not really. I mean, we don't hang out or anything. I just remember him having lightning everything: tattoos, necklaces. And I remember him showing off the custom paint job on the car."

"It is very confusing, I must say. It seems foolish for him to commit such an act in a car that would be so easily recognized. Raymond can be a bit reckless, but he is not a stupid man." My grandpa sat still for a moment, looking again at the decorative molding that ran along the joint between the wall and the ceiling. Dropping his gaze to meet my dad's, he said, "I suppose the most obvious solution is that he wanted you to identify him. The question I do not know the answer to is why."

My grandpa's fingernails clicked against the top of the desk as he drummed his fingers. "Surely your wife could not be a coincidence, but I do not understand the connection."

"The note," I said. "Dad, tell him about the note."

Tony stood from his chair and fished the yellow sticky note out of his pocket. He crossed the short distance to the desk and pressed the note onto its surface.

"What is this?"

"I found that stuck to the bathroom mirror Thursday night."

"The same day you arrived? That seems like another odd coincidence."

At his words, I flipped my head around to look at my dad. How did they all know? My dad, Tony and Lisa, and even my grandpa. And they talked about as though it wasn't anything out of the ordinary. What in the world was going on?

Reaching over to the phone on his desk, my grandpa removed the receiver from its cradle. He punched in a few numbers and pressed the handset to his ear, waiting for an answer. "Hello, Jacob," he said. "Can you come up to my office for a minute? Thank you."

Setting the receiver back in its place, he said, "Perhaps he can help fill in some of the missing pieces."

"What are you thinking?" my dad asked.

"Well, I am not sure. But I don't think the note could have been written without the assistance of The Sight, but I hesitate to say anything beyond that."

The Sight? What was he talking about? This was too weird. "What is going on here?" I asked.

"Andy, we-" my dad said, cutting himself off in mid-sentence. "Dad, maybe we should have Andy wait outside. I don't think he should be hearing all this."

"Oh, I think it is too late for that."

"Too late? Why is it too late?"

My grandpa looked across the desk at my dad and said, "Because the events with Lanie and the dog changed much more than you know."

"What do you mean?"

"I hate to tell you this at all, but especially on such a terrible day. And there is no easy way to say it, so I will be blunt. Son, you were supposed to die the day after tomorrow." My grandpa's face reminded me of the police officer who had come to tell us my father had died. He looked like he would rather be talking about anything but this.

"I was supposed to what?" My dad's mouth fell open as he tried to make sense of what my grandfather had just told him.

"It is true. The vision you saw was limited because the events affected your own future. You could only see up to the point where it began to impact you."

My grandpa sat in silence for a moment before he continued. "When the dog attacked the girl in the original past, she was hurt quite badly.

Donna spent a lot of time at the hospital watching over her. You tried to spend as much time with her as you could, but you were still trying to work. Monday morning, you brought her home to get some sleep, but you went back. You fell asleep at the wheel and you crashed."

"Oh my God," was all my dad said. He squeezed the arms of the chair, the upholstery bulging in small rises on either side of his grip.

"The fact that you are still alive created a new future in many ways. Andrew's life was permanently changed in that moment," my grandpa said.

My dad turned his attention to me, his eyes wide and his face taut. "That must have changed everything for you. Absolutely everything."

I wasn't sure what to say to him, so I didn't. I didn't want to increase the blow by telling him just how much it had affected me. How much it had affected Mom. That was a discussion we might need to have eventually, but this wasn't the time or the place.

The four of us fell to silence as we waited for my uncle Jacob. The news of my father's death in the original past seemed to have shaken him and he sat looking down at the floor. Tony sat quietly as well, his knee bouncing rapidly with apparent anticipation.

In the silence, my mind returned to the words my grandpa had spoken. He knew I wasn't a child. He talked about it as though it were completely normal. And he said something about visions. Something he had called The Sight. And Timekeepers. I knew I wasn't supposed to know, but I the question popped out before I could stop myself.

"Grandpa," I said. "What were you saying before? You said something about Ray being a Timekeeper. What does that mean?"

"Oh yes. I imagine you must have many questions. This is probably very confusing for you. What has your father told you?"

His response had caught me off guard. There was none of the hesitation or avoidance my dad had shown. Instead, he lifted a pen from his desk, turning it end over end in his hands. The light from his desk lamp reflected off the shiny surface in a fine point, moving with the angle of the pen as it turned.

"He told me that my memories came with me, but they weren't really in my brain. Not yet. He said I would start to forget my past and that I would become the nine-year-old me. But he also told me that I wouldn't be able to forget if I did things differently."

"Did he tell you why it was important for you to forget?"

"He said my experiences will change my choices."

"That is true, but there is more to the story."

"How do you know this?" I asked. "Why aren't any of you surprised? You act like this happens all the time."

"All the time?" Grandpa asked. "No, no. Not all the time, but it does happen." He laid the pen back down and leaned forward, resting his arms on the surface of the desk in front of him. "Andrew, the people you see in this building are called Timekeepers. We are here to guide people like you, although most of you never know it."

"Guide us? Guide us how?" I asked.

"It is so very important that people who come back forget about their old lives. We are here to make sure things don't get in the way of that. You could say that we are here to maintain balance. You see, the effects of a person knowing the future could be devastating. It could be disastrous. But it is also more than that."

"What do you mean?"

"There is a downside to forgetting. It is very likely that you could end up making all the same decisions you did the first time around. Let me ask you something. What do you think would happen if every decision you made was exactly the same as before?"

I could tell there was something deeper I supposed to be understanding, but I wasn't putting it together. He sat patiently as he waited for me to answer. "I don't know," I said. "My life would go on just like it did before?"

"Yes, but more so than you might like. Something brought you back here to this time, did it not? If you made every choice exactly the same way, wouldn't you end up back here again in... how old were you?"

"Thirty-five."

"And how old are you in this body?"

"Nine. Almost ten."

"Thank you. Wouldn't you end up back here in twenty-five more years?"

"I guess so."

"And what about twenty-five years after that? And after that and after that again?"

The implications of that were startling. "Are you saying that I would keep going around and around, living the same twenty-five years forever?"

"Well, probably not forever. There is always some chance involved, but yes, you would be stuck for quite some time. That is unless you make things just different enough."

"Just different enough?" I asked.

"Another part of our job as Timekeepers is to nudge you a tiny bit to change your course. Our goal is to keep you from doing the loop-the-loop over and over again, but without throwing you so far off course that you cannot forget. It is a very tricky thing to manage, to tell you the truth."

"So, you're saying that stopping Lanie from running was what I was supposed to do?"

"Oh no. Not exactly, anyway. It was unavoidable. You could no more have let that girl run into the jaws of that dog than you could have attacked her yourself. We couldn't have made you allow that to happen even if we had wanted to."

"But someone wanted me to," I said, thinking of the note.

"That appears to be the case, yes."

"But why? Why would someone do that?"

"I do not know, Andrew. I wish I did, but I do not. The important thing is that you followed your heart and not some terrible note. But that meant you received a bit more than the nudge we wanted. You could say it was more like a shove, or a kick, perhaps. That kick had a ripple effect that changed your entire future."

"What is it too late for, Grandpa? Are you saying I won't forget?"

"I'm afraid so."

"What does that mean?" I asked. "Does that mean I'll never meet my wife? That we'll never be married?" If what my dad said was right, everything I knew was gone forever. She may as well have died.

"No, Andrew. That is not what I'm saying. It doesn't mean anything except that your future is unwritten. You still have a life full of choices and you can do whatever you wish with them." My grandpa's voice softened as he spoke, but it didn't have the effect he was going for. He was trying to set me at ease, but I took it as an omen. To me, the change in his voice was like the darkening of the sky just before a storm.

"But even if I pursue her, she might not fall in love with me."

"Might is a big word that can apply to anything, Andrew. I believe in free will, which means that we each get to make our own choices. The tricky part is that those choices build on one another. You cannot choose to turn left at a certain point if you did not first choose to make the turn that led you to that choice. But that is not to say you cannot take a different route to the same destination."

I pushed myself out of my chair, turning to face a large bookcase that lined one wall. I scanned the array of books without actually seeing them as I tried to fit my brain around this new reality. Being overwhelmed was something I had thought I understood before these past few days. But as I stood under the onslaught of so much information, I thought I just might collapse under its weight.

He said the future was unwritten but, to me, it felt like it had been erased. Nothing was as it used to be. My life with Sarah, college, the military, even my years in high school were gone. The path of life that I looked back on was now nothing more than a story I might have read in a book. None of my memories had any substance and nothing I knew was real. Even if I was able to get Sarah to fall in love with me one day, none of what I carried in my memories had actually happened.

"Andrew," my grandpa said. "Try not to feel discouraged. I know it feels like everything you knew is at risk to be lost and, in some ways, it is. I do not want to lie to you. You deserve more than that. But I also want you to know that you haven't lost anything yet. Your future is full of possibilities. It truly is unwritten."

I knew what he was saying was true, but it didn't feel true. It felt like everything was gone. It felt like my life had not only been flipped upside down and dumped out, but like the wind had carried everything away.

"So, what is The Sight?" I asked, ready to move away from the conversation of what I had lost. I needed time to think, and certainly I wasn't ready to feel better. I didn't know how to feel hope for the future. I was still trying to understand it, and I had no idea how to accept it.

My grandpa let out a breath before he answered. I could tell he wasn't happy with where we had left the discussion, but he was gracious enough to let it be. "The Sight is what allows us to know about people like you. When it is fully developed, you can see a brief window into the lives of people who travel back to a point in their youth. You can see who they are and where they land. You can also see the surrounding events of the original path, but never the future or even the present."

"Does every Timekeeper have it?" I asked.

"No. Very few do, actually. The Sight is a genetic mutation that only affects men in the ruling line. And, even then, not every man. In fact, this is the first time every living male in our line has had The Sight in ten or more generations. I believe it is a way to keep too many people from having uncontrolled access to people who know the future. The consequences of such a thing are unimaginable."

"Every living male?"

"Yes, there are four of us. I have it, as does your father. Your uncle Jacob has it and so do you."

"Me? What do you mean? How can I have it? I've never even heard of such a thing."

"It is not developed. You do not know how to use it. But there are other ways it shows up. Do you ever find yourself knowing something that you should not be able to know?"

"I don't think so, at least not in ways that can't be explained in terms of simple luck or coincidence."

"Well, I do not know about luck, but I will grant you that there is coincidence, but think back. Think about your own past and I bet you will find things that cannot be explained away as simple happenstance."

"I… I don't know. I've never thought of myself as psychic." Even as I said the words, the event with Bobby Richardson on the playground came to mind. The way I seemed to know things I shouldn't have been able to know. But the notion that I might have some psychic gift seemed silly.

"Who said anything at all about being psychic? We are not fortunetellers. We do not do parlor tricks. We simply have the ability to see into a person's soul. Sometimes we know specifics, but sometimes it is more… rough. It can be an emotion or a sense about who someone is. It can tell you what drives a person. The trouble with it is that you cannot turn it on or off. Sometimes it is there and sometimes it is not."

Behind us, the doorknob clicked as it turned. The door swung open on its hinges and my uncle Jacob finally walked through the door. As I turned to face him, I couldn't help but be amazed at how much he looked like my dad. He was a good five years younger, but he could have almost been his twin. Aside from my uncle's neatly trimmed beard that was barely more than a heavy shadow, it looked like the only substantial difference between the two was age.

He surveyed the small group as he walked in, his eyebrows going up in surprise. "Hey guys, what's up? What are you doing here?" he asked, closing the door behind him.

My dad rose from his chair, turning to him. "Something's happened, Jacob. Donna and Lanie are missing. They were kidnapped."

"Kidnapped? Oh my God! What happened?"

"I took Andy and Lanie to get ice cream and a black Camaro showed up. It took Lanie and it raced off. Later, we found Donna's purse at the house, but she wasn't there. But we did find this."

My dad walked to the desk and pulled off the sticky note, handing it to Uncle Jacob. He looked down at the message scrawled across the front before flipping it over to examine the back.

"I... I don't understand," he said as he turned it around again to look at the words.

"Andy found it the night before last. Before Lanie was supposed to get attacked by the dog. And it showed up again after Donna came up missing."

"Before Lanie? Do you think this was telling Andy to let her get attacked?"

"Well, that's our theory," my dad said.

"But... that would mean they had to know it was going to happen. That would have to mean that a Timekeeper took her! Oh, God no. You said it was a black Camaro? What else? Was there anything else with the car?"

"There were lightning bolts on the sides. Tony thinks it was-"

"Ray," my uncle finished for him. "This is my fault. Oh my God, I'm so sorry." He covered his mouth with his hand and collapsed into the remaining chair.

"Your fault? What are you talking about?" my dad asked.

"I... I don't know. I mean, I had him watching Andy. You know, just to see whether he saved her. He was just watching and he called the other morning to say that Andy stopped her from running like we expected. I had no idea, Joe. I didn't know he would do something like this, that he *could* do something like this. I'm so sorry."

"That doesn't make it your fault," my dad said. "Besides, we can't worry about who let what happen. We have to focus on getting them back. Do you know how to find him?"

"You're right. Of course, you are. But I just feel so- No, you're right. I know where he lives. We could check there. And I can make some phone calls. I can talk to folks who know him. Maybe we can catch a lead or something."

"That's good, Jacob. I think that's a start. How about if you start making calls while we go check out his house. Maybe you'll find something by the time we're done."

"Yeah, okay."

"Why would he do this, though?" I asked. "I mean, there's the obvious reason. You know, that he wants to do something very bad to them. But why the note?"

"I don't know. The way he left the note when you first arrived. Taking Lanie after you didn't listen. Then he goes after Donna and leaves the note again. It's almost like he's trying to make it look like the Timekeeper's are punishing you." My uncle rubbed his fingers across the stubble on his chin as he spoke.

"I don't know," my dad said. "No one's going to buy that. We would never kidnap innocent people because a time traveler didn't do what they were told."

"Well, why else would he leave the note?"

"What if he just didn't think that far ahead?" Tony asked. "The guy doesn't have to be a mastermind, does he?"

"You mean that he didn't think we would dismiss the idea of the Timekeepers punishing Andy?"

"It's the only thing I can think of."

"Me too," my uncle said. "I can't think of anything else either. But something bothers me about it, you know? I've never even suspected that he was like this. That's got to mean that he's not stupid, right?"

"Not if this is his first time," Tony answered.

"That's true, I guess," Jacob said.

"Guys, what if he took her on impulse?" I asked. What if he took Lanie and realized that we would identify him? What if he took Mom just to make it look like he wasn't specifically targeting Lanie? Maybe he left the note the second time to make it look like someone else was calling the shots?"

"Okay, but that doesn't explain why he left it in the first place. It has to be that he was trying to divert our attention. What I don't understand is why," Tony said.

"Maybe the only reason why is so he could buy himself some time. Maybe he wanted to throw us off his trail for just long enough for him to…" I let my words trail off, not wanting to finish the sentence. I didn't even want to think about the rest of that sentence.

I couldn't be sure, but I thought a look of gratitude flashed across Tony's face before he spoke. He probably didn't want me to finish that sentence any more than I did. "You know guys, we could stand here all day and try to figure out what he was trying to do. The fact is that Donna and my baby girl are out there and we need to rescue them. I don't really care why he did it. I care about finding Ray and getting them back."

"You're right, Tony," my dad said. "Let's go. Jacob, if you can't reach us at my house, you should be able to get a hold of Lisa."

"I'll call as soon as I know something," Jacob said. "And, Joe, be careful."

"I don't think it's me you need to worry about. If Ray happens to be there, he's going to have a very, very bad day."

TEN

Ray's house was on the south side of Kansas City, maybe twenty minutes from the Timekeeper warehouse. The neighborhood's streets were dotted with older bungalow style houses with broad, gabled porches that faced the street. The area had definitely seen better days, most of the houses suffered from peeling paint, distressed yards, and general disrepair. We pulled to a stop in front of one that looked like it had sat abandoned for several years. The porch canted to one side with a gentle slope through the middle.

"Is this it?" I asked. I felt a twinge of nervousness as I thought about the prospect of entering. The porch looked as though it could collapse at any moment and the house itself didn't look much safer.

"No, it's up there," my dad said, pointing to a carbon copy of the one I had pointed to, except that it wasn't quite so dilapidated. While the porch may not have looked like it was about to collapse, the house still appeared to be in need of attention. The whole street seemed to be the model of poverty. Almost every house was badly neglected in some way. Across the street, an old, faded Buick looked like it might have once been purple. Rust had spread along the lower portion of its doors and quarter panels like a fungus that threatened to cover every surface.

As we got out of the car, each of us locked the doors nearly in unison. Speaking in a low tone, my dad asked, "Doesn't my dad have you guys on the payroll?"

"Yeah. We're not rich, but we certainly make enough to live better than this," Tony said.

"Maybe he wants to live in a neighborhood where he won't attract attention to himself," I said.

"Makes sense, but it's a little disturbing."

As we got closer to the house, we could see that the driveway was empty. The small carport alongside the house was empty as well. We hadn't expected him to be home, but we still parked several houses down just in case. There was no need to alert him if he did happen to be there.

We cut across the yard and walked up to the chain link fence that sectioned off the back yard. Vines had grown up through the lattice-like pattern of the links, twisting around the rusted latch for the gate. Tony rested his hand on the latch, but didn't raise it.

"What's wrong?" my dad asked. "Do you hear something?"

"No. I don't like this," he said, twisting his head around to look at my dad.

"This isn't safe. We should have taken Andy back to my house. I don't feel good about this."

"What is safe right now?" I asked. Besides, you act like I don't have a say in any of this.

"But you're a kid. I know you're thirty-five inside your head, but you're just a kid."

"Just a kid? You know what? I do have a kid's body. You've got me there. And I'm an adult on the inside. You're correct again. But what you seem to be forgetting is that I can make my own decisions. I have been living on my own for nearly twenty years. The fact that I'm trapped in this little body doesn't take away from that."

I didn't know why that had gotten under my skin like it did, but I was suddenly angry with him for treating me like a child. Maybe it was all the stress from the past few days, but all the pent up anger, frustration, and despair that I been trying my best to contain wanted to explode like a cork from a champagne bottle.

"Now I know how older people feel," I continued. You ever see someone treat their elderly parent like they are a kid? They talk to them like they no longer have the ability to make rational decisions. They can't decide what to eat, where to live, what to wear. The fact that they don't hear as well or move as well suddenly implies to the very people they raised from birth that they have also lost the ability to think."

"I..."

"Stop it, okay? Just stop it. I am a grown man, even if I don't look like it. Even if going inside that house is the worst idea of the century, I am perfectly capable of making the decision to put myself in that situation."

"Guys!" my dad whispered. "Andy, lower your voice. Do you want the whole neighborhood to know we're out here?"

"I'm sorry. It's just that you're so... small. No matter how many times I see this, it doesn't get any easier. It's like it violates all the natural laws or something. And Lanie is already missing. I just don't want to take the chance that something will happen to you too."

I knew I was overreacting, but the words had just popped out. I felt like I was on edge and things that should have been insignificant were setting me off.

"You know what? You're right." Tony said as he turned away from me, raising the latch and pushing open the gate. My dad and I followed him through as we made our way toward the back door. Before stepping around the corner, Tony pulled his pistol out of his holster and surveyed the yard.

"See any dogs?" he asked.

"Nope," my dad said. There were no doghouses, no tie-outs. There were none of the telltale signs of a dog in residence.

"Andy, you're not armed, so can you hang out on the porch at least until we clear the house?"

"Sure," I said. He did have a good point, as much as I hated to admit it.

Tony tried the knob, but it was locked. He twisted his upper body, doing his best to survey the inside of the house for any signs that someone might be home. The bottom floor of the house was dark and quiet. The only visible light came from the various windows and there didn't appear to be any sounds emanating from the inside.

Satisfied enough to take the next step, he turned around and backed up against the door. He did a quick scan of the surrounding backyards and then brought his elbow up, smashing it through one of the small panes of glass in the door's window. Even though we seemed to be alone, we all winced at the harsh crash of the glass breaking and then shattering against the vinyl floor below.

We froze and watched for any reactions – either from inside Ray's house or from the neighbors. No doors opened, no one came out. No curtains pulled back and there were no faces peeking out at us that we could see. Tony reached through the empty pane and unlocked the door. Turning the knob, he pushed the door open and he and my dad moved through the door being careful to avoid the bits of broken glass on the floor.

There were two interior entrances to the kitchen; one directly in front of us and one to the left. Tony took the one on the left and my dad went forward, their guns drawn and pointed at the ceiling as they went. It was almost uncanny how quiet they were as they stepped through the house. The only thing I could hear was the occasional whisper or shuffle. There wasn't much I could see from my vantage point at the door, but I could see my dad making his way up the staircase. He hugged the wall as he climbed, trying to keep his weight away from the center of the boards to avoid potential squeaks. From elsewhere in the house, I heard the telltale click of a door latch as Tony entered some closed off section.

It struck me as odd that they were trying so hard to be quiet. Tony had just broken a window. If Ray hadn't heard that, he probably wasn't going to hear them trying to creep through the house either. But, as I stepped through the doorway, I too tried to avoid the shards. I didn't want to invite trouble by making noise.

My small feet made it much easier to maneuver the bits of glass, but I didn't move with nearly the practiced ease as the two men. They definitely looked like they had done this before. I hunched my shoulders in frustration each time the glass crunched under my feet.

Finally through the gauntlet of glass, I was struck by how much different the inside of the house was from the outside. The exterior had looked severely neglected, but the inside looked as though Ray had taken great care to make it seem almost brand new. The paint was fresh and rich and the dark finish on the oak cabinets reflected the few remaining remnants of sunlight that came through the kitchen windows.

I stepped through the doorway in front of me and entered a small sitting room. The layout was much different from newer houses that were designed to allow televisions to be the centerpiece. In the days this house was built, activities such as conversation and reading were probably the most common sources of entertainment.

Behind me, I heard the same door latch sound that I had heard before. I spun around on my heels, ready to run, but it was just Tony. "I thought you were going to wait outside until we cleared the house," he whispered.

"I saw my dad going upstairs. I thought that meant this floor was good."

"Yeah, okay. You're right, but we have to be careful. This guy isn't playing around."

"Upstairs is clear," my dad called from upstairs. He had stepped around the corner at the top and was looking down at us. "You girls still arguing down there? I thought you kissed and made up."

"Eat it, Myers," Tony said.

"Nice," my dad said. "You guys see anything interesting down there?"

"Not really, but I was more interested in making sure I didn't get shot. There was a locked door downstairs, though. I didn't hear any movement, so I don't think anyone is in there."

"Maybe we should check that first," my dad said as he came down the stairs much less cautiously than he went up. "Let's be careful. It's the only room we haven't checked and it's the only room that's locked."

Tony crossed the doorway that led to the basement as my dad came in behind him. My dad brought his finger to his lips in a silent shush gesture and then pointed from me to the doorway. Evidently, he wanted me in between the two of them. That was probably smart, since I was the only one without a gun. If someone came at us while we were on the stairs, I would just be in the way of a clear shot.

The three of us kept to the sides of the stairs as my dad had done when he had climbed to the second floor. At the bottom, a single bulb hung from a chain, casting sharp shadows that stretched out in every direction. In my mind's eye, I could see the bulb swinging back and forth creating a kaleidoscope of disorienting shadows in horror movie fashion. Of course, the bulb wasn't moving and the shadows stayed put, but it would certainly have matched the tension in the air. We were approaching a locked door in the basement of a kidnapper. The fact that it was cliché did nothing to alleviate the sense of dread that grew with every step.

The door sat in the center of a wall at the back of the basement. Tony came up alongside the door on the hinge side and brought his gun up so that it was ready to aim at a moment's notice. My dad looked at me and pointed toward the bottom of the stairs. In a low whisper, he said, "Anything happens, you run."

I nodded and crept back to the bottom of the stairs, placing a foot on the bottom step. As I looked back toward the door, my dad stepped in front of it and took a deep breath. He leaned backward on one leg and kicked at the door with a solid bang. The wood splintered with a crash as the door flew inward, slamming against the wall.

Almost immediately, Tony rushed into the room and spun to his right, clearing the corner. He turned just as quickly to his left and took a step back, disappearing from view. My dad regained his footing after the kick and followed in after, holding his gun parallel to the ground. There was only silence for a moment, before I heard Tony shout, "Clear! My God, it stinks in here!"

As he spoke, my breath hitched in my throat as the acrid combination of ammonia and soured urine wafted out through the doorway. Tears came to my eyes within moments as the smell assaulted my senses. My dad exited the room, wiping tears from his own eyes as he came. He coughed and then tried to take a deep breath, but the air outside the room had become almost as bad as the air inside.

He turned to face the wall and snaked his arm around the inside of the doorway for a few seconds before he said, "No switch."

"Is this it?" I asked, flipping a switch on the opposite side of the wall on the other side of the door. The bulb came to life, bringing only a dull glow to the room. It was a low wattage bulb and it didn't do much to dispel the darkness around it.

I stepped into the room, holding my shirt against my face as a makeshift filter. It didn't seem to help. The room was nearly naked. There were no windows and the only door was the one I had just passed through. The only thing inside was a steel, gray chair that had been welded to a black metal plate. The plate looked as though it had been bolted to the floor. Around it, the concrete was stained a dark brownish red, much like old blood that had dried. Exactly like old blood that had dried, in fact.

"That's messed up," I said, pointing at the chair.

"Yeah. You could say that. I've got to get out of here. I can't-" Tony pushed past me and went back up the stairs two at a time. It didn't take much in the way of detective work to figure out that he was picturing Lanie trapped in here. I think we all were.

My dad and I followed him out and made our way up the stairs as well. The basement was almost completely devoid of anything, save the chair. Upstairs, Tony had gone outside and was trying his best to empty the contents of his stomach onto the lawn. The only problem was that we had not yet eaten dinner, so there probably wasn't much for him to purge.

"Sorry, guys," Tony said as he came back inside. "I just saw that room and that chair and smelled that awful smell and I had to get out of there. I just keep seeing Lanie and I... I'm sorry."

"Hey, no worries. I'd be lying if I said I wasn't thinking the same thing about Donna. But I don't think they've been in that room or even in this house. We'll find them. Don't worry, we'll find them."

"Well, let's get to looking so we can get out of here. I don't want to be here anymore."

"What are we looking for anyways?" I asked. "I mean, the room didn't tell us anything good."

"No, it didn't," my dad said. "In a perfect world, the girls would have been here and we would be on our way home, but nothing is so easy. Just look for anything that will tell us the girls were here or maybe where they went."

"Maybe he'll have an address book with an entry under 'S' for secret hideout," I said without any real humor. Standing in Ray's living room was a sharp reminder of just how little we knew. We had a culprit and the room downstairs told us it was all too real, but we still didn't have much to go on. We didn't know where he might have taken them. We shared a sick feeling that we knew what he wanted, but we had no idea where to go next. There were no clues that led anywhere. Our only hope was to find something that might give us a next step.

"Everything looks so normal," I said as I looked around the room. There was a gray, suede couch and a matching chair. A large console style television sat against one wall. Everything was neat and tidy; there was no clutter, the carpets were clean, and the walls looked just as new and fresh as those in the kitchen. If not for the downstairs, I might have thought a completely normal person lived here.

"What were you expecting?" Tony asked. He opened the closet door and pushed the coats around so that he could see the bottom and back of the closet.

"I don't know what I was expecting. Maybe an Anarchist's Cookbook or something on the coffee table. But there isn't even a coffee table."

"It does look pretty normal. I'll give you that. But there has to be something. There has to be."

The main floor was just as fruitless as it looked. We found telephone books, magazines, and a couple of old TV Guides. It almost seemed impersonal, like it was set up for show without giving away anything. There didn't seem to be anything that showed Ray's personality, particularly its darker side.

The top of the stairway opened up into a long hallway with bedrooms on one side and at the end. As with the downstairs, the bedrooms looked very normal, except that they were almost sterile. There was no personality to them. They reminded me of the model homes you find in new subdivisions where the builders show you what you could build. There was no wax fruit and there were no fake books and TVs, but it all felt staged just the same. It was as if he knew we were coming and had set it up for us.

At my first glance, the bedroom at the end seemed just as artificially normal as the other bedrooms. It had all the normal accommodations. A queen bed sat in the center of one wall with dark, cherry nightstands on either side. The opposite wall contained a matching dresser.

"What is that?" I asked as I saw the picture frame on the wall above the dresser. The background inside the frame was black and several women's pictures were spread across it. Under each picture, a small personal item was affixed with a bit of black thread. There were rings, necklaces, and other jewelry. Other pictures sat above small locks of hair or ribbons.

"Oh, dear Jesus," Tony said. "I think they are trophies."

As I stepped closer to the frame, I could see that all of the women looked miserable. Many of them had streaks of mascara running the lengths of their cheeks where they had been crying. Most of them had a wild, disheveled look to them. It was easy to imagine that they had gone through horrors that would break most of us.

"Do you think he killed them?" I asked, remembering the brownish stains surrounding the chair in the basement.

"I don't know. I hope not," Tony said.

"It looks like they're alive in the pictures, at least. And none of the trophies look like they would have had to come from a dead body. Maybe he let them go."

We didn't really believe that he had. Not really. It was one of those things that you say to make yourself feel better, even if you didn't really believe it is true. The man in the car was real and the threat was real. My mom and Tony's daughter were somewhere with the man who had taken these pictures. I didn't want to imagine the terror that they might be facing at that very moment. I didn't want to think about the room or the chair. I prayed that we would find them before there was cause for them to end up in this display.

"It kind of makes me feel dirty just looking at it," I said, even though it was hard to force myself to turn away. The wide eyes stared at me, pleading for help. "But at least we know for certain that Ray is behind this."

"Yeah. Let's see what else we can find," Tony said as he willed himself to turn away from the pictures. "The only thing I really know is that this guy's hours are numbered. I don't know how many hours, but there aren't a lot of them. I can guarantee you that."

The room and the trophy display managed to drain a lot of the enthusiasm for the search that had been there when we arrived. We came hopeful that we might find something, anything that would give us a next step. Instead, we found both more and less than we had hoped. We found evidence of the macabre, of the sick and twisted, but we found nothing helpful. We found nothing that made us feel any better.

We searched the entire upstairs, but it was just as generic as the downstairs. It seemed like we were only going to find what he wanted us to find. Back in the living room, I asked, "Now what do we do?"

"I don't know, Andy. I don't know." Tony sat down on the couch and massaged his temples.

"I know it was my idea to not get the police involved, but that was when I thought there might be some big supernatural element to all of this. I mean, not that there isn't, but this is different. We're dealing with a total sicko who is one hundred percent flesh and blood. And I get the sense we're in over our heads."

Tony leaned forward, resting his arms across his knees. "Oh, I want to, you better believe it. I want to bring in the cavalry. I want to bring every resource there is to bear so that we can find this guy. And when we do... But we can't."

"What do you mean we can't? The police are here to serve and protect right? We have a psycho rapist slash killer slash whatever on our hands and he has Lanie and my mom."

"Yes, that's true. But Ray is a Timekeeper. We can't draw attention to ourselves."

"Even at the expense of innocent lives? I think I get this whole 'keep everything on track' bit you guys have, but there has to be limits."

"You don't understand," Tony said. "If we start a formal investigation, the police are going to start to dig. They are going to look at employment records. They might start talking to co-workers. If that happens, how long will it take before they see through the business façade? When they do, they might find that we don't really earn revenue like normal businesses."

"What, do you steal it?"

"No, nothing like that. Nothing illegal, but we don't want to end up looking like some weird cult. You know how much media attention things like that get. We'd be instantly infamous."

"I don't get it. You are so afraid of being exposed that you would risk losing your own daughter to protect it. If it were that important, wouldn't you have a better front? One that isn't maybe so easy to see through?"

Tony stood up from the couch and pointed his finger at me. "You think I would risk my own daughter? That this is easy for me? This is killing me, Andy. It is taking everything I have to keep it together because I know that I'll never see her again if I don't."

"That isn't what I meant. I just meant that I figured the Timekeeper's secret wouldn't be so fragile."

He dropped his arm and looked down at me, studying me. I could see in his eyes that he knew what I meant, but there's something about a bad situation that can make a man look for a fight, even if it isn't the right fight. But instead of countering, he said, "It isn't that it's that fragile, it really isn't. Maybe you could say that we have a pretty strong aversion to testing it out, okay? It's kind of like how protective cases for stuff say that they can withstand a fall on concrete. That doesn't mean you want to go dropping it on purpose to test it out, does it?"

"No, I guess not. But I don't like it. It seems like there should be certain cases where you bring them in. Cases like this one. What about the Timekeepers? Aren't there more of them we can bring in on the search? Maybe someone knows something."

"That is the angle Jacob is working," my dad said. "Look guys, whatever we do, we need to do something. If there's one thing that is clear from this visit, Ray really isn't messing around."

"Then what do we do next?" I asked.

"Well, that's the million dollar question isn't it? We've been through every inch of this house and all we've found is bad news," my dad said. "I say we go back home and see if we can find out what Jacob has turned up. We can hope he's had better luck than we have."

"Okay, let me give Lisa a call and let her know to expect us." Tony lifted the handset off the phone by the couch and punched in the numbers for his house. He held the phone against his ear for what seemed like an eternity. Every passing ring seemed to exaggerate the stress that was visible on his face. Thirty seconds turned into a minute before he finally hung up the phone.

"We have to go," was all he said, but it was all he needed to say.

ELEVEN

We rejected any sense of caution as we raced down 71 Highway, making our way back to Tony and Lisa's house. If the car had wings, it wouldn't have surprised me a bit to see the ground moving away from us as we lifted off the pavement. We shifted from lane to lane, weaving our way through traffic with expert precision.

My dad's driving skill was hard to comprehend. The way he had whipped the car around when we were pursuing Lanie's abductor had been more than impressive. He had subjected the car to his bidding almost as though it were an extension of him. On this particular trek, he showed an equal confidence and sureness in his control of the car. We leapfrogged traffic as we moved in and out of lanes and drew several alarmed horns as it seemed that we missed clipping the surrounding cars by mere inches.

The sun had finally dropped below the horizon for the night, so there were a lot fewer cars than there might have been earlier in the day. Even still, the roadwork that brought this stretch of road from two to three lanes wouldn't happen for another five or six years. The current width of the road didn't really allow for the volume of traffic that travelled south.

Watching him navigate through this labyrinth of cars reminded me just how little I knew about him. There were the obvious aspects of him that I couldn't know because his life was cut short when I was just a boy, but this was like a whole other dimension that I probably wouldn't have known about even if he had lived. I still didn't know what it really meant to be a Timekeeper, but it was obvious that it brought a number of skills with it that were not generally a normal part of life.

As we raced forward, I gripped the sides of Tony's seat hard enough to turn my knuckles white. There was something about racing down a crowded highway at ninety miles-per-hour that caused your adrenaline to spike. Off to the right, I saw the familiar black and white of a police car just a few cars ahead.

"Dad! Police car!" I shouted, releasing the seat in front of me and pointing toward it.

Without a word, he pressed the brake pedal nearly to the floor, making me thankful that I had worn my seatbelt as I felt the ribbon of fabric press across my waist. The backseat only had a lap belt, so my upper body still lunged forward. My face would have mashed into Tony's seat if I had only been a few inches taller. Instead, I found myself staring down at my feet as the shift in inertia carried me forward.

The police cruiser was riding in the right hand lane, probably on patrol. "Come on, come on, come on," my dad said as he tapped his hand against the steering wheel. Every few seconds, he looked from the watch on his wrist to the police cruiser. The seconds seemed like hours. The chances that we would arrive in time to save Lisa from the same fate as Lanie and my mom were probably nonexistent, but we couldn't dismiss the urgency of the situation. None of us were willing to accept the day's events as passive bystanders.

After what seemed like forever, the patrol car finally took an exit ramp on the right, freeing us to continue our pursuit. My dad tromped on the gas as soon as the car was off the highway, pressing me back into my seat as the Nova shot forward.

Back on our street, the tires squealed as my dad whipped the wheel around to bring us into the driveway. Tony's door popped open before my dad could even get the car into park, let alone kill the engine. He launched himself out of the car and sprinted toward the front door of the house, vaulting the stairs in a single leap. He flung the screen door open and gripped the handle, but it was locked. He shoved his hands into his pockets and ripped the keys out, fumbling for a moment to find the correct one.

My dad and I joined Tony on the porch just as he managed to jam the key into the lock. He twisted the key and then the knob, giving the door a shove. It swung inward with a solid thump as it collided with the doorstop attached to the wall. From inside, we heard the sound of Nancy Sinatra singing about how her boots were made for walking and that was just what they were going to do.

As we pushed through the doorway, Lisa was standing at the dining room table with a laundry basket in front of her. She had turned at the sound of the door smashing into the doorstop and stood looking, eyes wide with alarm.

"Tony! You almost gave me a heart attack," she said.

"Gave you a heart attack? Why didn't you answer the phone?" Tony asked through heavy breaths.

"You called? Oh, I'm sorry, I didn't hear you. I must have been downstairs switching out the laundry."

"The laundry? You're doing laundry?" he asked incredulously. Looking around, the house was immaculate. Every bit of clutter had disappeared and every surface practically shined. The only thing out of place was the occasional bottle of cleaner. A roll of paper towels sat on an end table and a broom leaned against one wall. "You okay?"

"Yeah... No." She threw the socks she was folding back into the laundry basket. "I can't sit still. When I sit still, I think. When I think, I can't get Lanie out of my head and then I just cry. And then I start thinking about Donna and I get even worse."

Lisa pulled out a chair and lowered herself into it. She laid her arms across the table, placing each of her hands on the opposite elbow. "I keep thinking I don't have any more tears to cry, but then there they are. It's like I have an unlimited supply. I'm so tired of crying, but I can't help it."

"We're going to get them back. I swear it."

"Be careful what you swear," she said. Lisa's face was drawn and tired. Several strands of hair had come loose from her ponytail, adding to the effect. "Oh yeah, Jacob called while you were gone. He wants you to call him."

"Thanks," my dad said, turning toward the kitchen to find the phone.

"Tell me something good. Tell me you found something out."

My dad stopped where he was and turned; he and Tony locked eyes and the thought between them was almost audible. We had learned much over the past few hours, but we still knew nothing. At least nothing useful or encouraging. I could see the battle going on inside Tony at that moment. Should he tell her about the trophies? Should he tell her about the room, the chair, and the smell of urine and ammonia?

"What? What did you find?" Lisa asked as my dad resumed his trip to the kitchen. Tony walked over to the dining room table and pulled out his own chair to sit in.

Looking at him, I was struck by just how much he and Lanie looked alike. The stress of the day had distorted his features a little, but it was still clear that she favored his side of the gene pool. They shared the same fair hair and skin and they even had the same curl to their hair, even though his was cut short to his head. He even had the same light freckles that dusted his cheeks.

"I don't know," he said. "Everything. Nothing."

"What do you mean? Can you try again without the riddle?"

"Well," he said and then stopped for a moment, tracing his finger in a small circle on the tabletop. "We found out that Andy probably isn't going to forget." He didn't want to tell her and he was stalling.

"Why not?" she asked, turning her gaze to me.

"Well, it looks like he changed a lot more things than he intended to when he saved Lanie. So much so that Jonah doesn't think there is any chance of him forgetting."

"That sucks. How can he be sure, though? There has to be a way."

"Well, it looks like Joe was supposed to die in a car wreck on Monday."

"Whoa." Lisa blinked her eyes at her husband, unsure what to say.

"Yeah. When the dog attacked Lanie in the original past, Donna spent a lot of time at the hospital. Joe was going back to sit with her and he fell asleep at the wheel."

"How did he take it?"

"As well as he could, I guess."

"What about you, Andy? How are you doing with this?"

"I don't even know how to answer that. Today has been…" I trailed off looking for the right word. "Impossible. Today has been impossible. I started out knowing nothing and now I have more information than I know what to do with. I don't even know if I can take anything else in, you know? And it seems like everything that can go wrong is going wrong. But other than that, I'm great."

"I can't say I ever expected to be in a situation where no one in the room envies anyone else's situation. It sounds like we've got more than enough crap to go around." Looking back at Tony, she said, "Okay, so about Lanie. What did you find?"

Tony pursed his lips instead of responding right way. "Well, Jonah and Jacob confirmed that the car was probably Ray's, so we went to check out his house."

"And?"

"Nothing really. The house was so clean it seemed staged. It was like he set up everything perfectly so we would find just what he wanted us to."

"So, you did find something then?" she asked, noticing his word selection.

"Yeah." With my dad in the kitchen, it was my turn to exchange glances with Tony. I looked down at my shoes almost immediately, suddenly entranced by the stitching that ran along the sides. I didn't want to play a part in deciding how much he told his wife. There are some decisions in this world that you have to make all on your own. "It doesn't look like this is the first time he has done this."

"You mean he has taken other girls? What did you find?"

Tony let out a long, slow breath and began tracing circles on the tabletop again. "We found a picture frame filled with pictures of several girls. But they were all older than Lanie. They were all in their twenties and thirties."

"Pictures. You mean?" She sucked in air in a quick blast. "Were they-"

"No. They were all alive. They didn't look happy, but they were all alive."

Lisa let out the breath she had been holding. "Thank God for at least that. Did it look like Lanie and Donna had been there?"

"No, it didn't, but they were just taken today."

"Well, what do we do now, then?"

"Pray that Jacob finds something. He's doing some digging to see what he can find."

Almost as if on cue, I could hear my dad finishing up on the phone in the kitchen. There was a soft click as he set the receiver back into its cradle. He entered the dining room and pulled out his own chair at the table, sitting down to join Tony and Lisa.

"So?" Tony asked.

"Well, Jacob called a few folks and is starting to piece together a picture. All he really knows at this point is that Ray has a place down in Warsaw. I don't know how solid a lead I think it is, but it's more than we have now."

"Warsaw? That's more than two hours away. If he's wrong, we're could waste five or six hours."

"I know. What's worse is that he doesn't have the address yet. He's still working on that."

"Still working on it? When does he think we're going to be able to leave?" Tony asked.

"Not until morning. He wants us to meet him at the Timekeeper building at 7:00."

"Man, you've got to be kidding me! The best lead we've got is over two hours away and we can't leave for what?" Tony craned his head around to look at the clock in the living room. "Nine hours? Anything could happen in that amount of time. Call him back. Tell him we need to figure this out. Tell him we need to go now."

"Go where, Tony? Look I agree with you. I want to go now, too. But we can't just go looking randomly. You know we can't."

"I know. I just think… Okay, I don't know what I think. But I know I can't sit here on my hands while she's out there. There's got to be something we can do."

"We can get ready. We can make sure we're prepared for whatever we find down there. Jacob doesn't the have address yet, but he does seem confident that he's onto something. I'll give him that."

"Well, if you can't leave until morning, you may as well try to get some sleep," Lisa said.

"Sleep. That's a joke," my dad said. "That's something I can't see happening. We have to get ready. If the girls are there… we can't screw this up." He lowered his head into his hands, fixing his gaze on the dark grain of the tabletop beneath his head.

Lisa reached across and rested her hand across his arm. "You're not going to screw this up. I know you won't – unless you don't get some sleep, that is. We've all been through so much today. You've got to be just as exhausted as I am and you're going to be prone to making mistakes if you don't rest." She patted his arm and gave it a squeeze before pulling her hand back and placing it in the crook of her elbow.

"You're right. I know you're right, but I'm just… I'm worried and I'm stressed and I'm tired and I need to get myself together."

"No, you need to chill out and stop putting so much pressure on yourself. No one expects you have it all together. You're not alone in this. You don't even have to worry about being the leader. We can share the load."

As she said that, my dad lifted his head from his hands and turned to face her. "Thank you, Lisa."

"Leader?" I asked. I knew my timing was bad, but I was having a really hard time getting my head around the whole picture. "Are you a leader in the Timekeepers? Is your restaurant just a cover or something?"

"No, Son. No cover. The Timekeepers aren't part of who I am anymore. I used to be the heir, but I walked away. I left that life behind when I married your mom. I realized that wasn't the life I wanted for your mom and you, so I stepped down. Being a Timekeeper brings too much stuff with it that I didn't want for you – and that's especially true for the guy in line to lead them. You're always rushing off to some crisis, either trying to keep someone going in the right direction or intervening when they jump off the path."

"So, you're not even a Timekeeper, then? Man, I feel so lost." I leaned back against the wall behind me. "What about you guys?" I asked, looking at Lisa. "You're Timekeepers though, right?"

"Oh, not me," Lisa said. "Tony's the only one. Our situation isn't too different from yours, actually. At least in this regard. Tony kept the job and I know about it, but Lanie doesn't. To her, he just travels a lot."

That was one of the few things I did remember from this far back in the past. I didn't remember Tony very much at all. I think I spent more time with him today than I had before in total.

My dad pushed himself up from his place at the table. "As much as I don't feel like sleeping, Lisa's right. Tony and I aren't going to be of much use in the morning if we don't at least try."

"Tony and you? You don't mean to leave me here do you? Didn't we have this conversation already?"

My dad fixed his eyes on me in a piercing stare. "Yes, we did. But Tony is right. Your body is nine years old. I am not going to bring you into a fight with a grown man who is probably armed. If Jacob is right and Ray is there, it is going to get ugly."

"Look, Dad. I do understand that you are my father. And I understand that I should give you respect, but the gray matter between my ears is the same age as you. That means I've been walking on this earth just as long as you have. That means that I am just as capable of making decisions as you are. I am going."

"Come on, Andy. Why are you being so difficult? Do you know what a grown man could do to you? Have you looked at yourself in a mirror lately? You're like four feet tall and you weigh maybe a third of what I do. I'm not letting you commit suicide."

"Dad," I said, returning his stare. "A bullet would stop you just as easily as it would me. We're going in armed, right? I know how to handle a gun. I know how to hide and I know how to move. I can use my size and my agility to my advantage."

"Fine. You want a gun? You want to kill yourself? Tony," he said, "Get him a gun."

Tony got up from the table and ran up to the second floor, taking the stairs two at a time. After a few moments, he came back downstairs and dropped a behemoth of a pistol on the table with a solid thud. "Here you go," he said.

Before I even picked up the weapon, I knew what they were trying to do. There was little chance I'd even be able to fit my hands around it, let alone be able to shoot it with any accuracy at all. They were trying to prove their point and they did, but it hit a nerve. In fact, it made my blood boil.

"Really?" I asked, looking up at Tony. "Hardy har, freaking har. Joke's on me. I get it. I'm puny. I'm short and I'm weak. You don't have to go get the biggest gun you've got in your collection to make me see that. My size and my physical age have been on the forefront of my mind since I woke up in this crazy mess. Get me a .22. A well placed shot will drop a man just as easily as this will, just with less kick and less mess."

"Oh, come on, Andy. Don't get so worked up. You know we had to try. We're just worried about you. Your brain says you're big and capable, but your body doesn't agree."

"I know that. Believe me I do. But I'm going."

"I know, Andy," my dad said. "But I had to try to talk you out of it, even if I knew it probably wouldn't work. I hope you can understand that. Let's go home and try to get some sleep."

"Home?" Tony asked. "No way. Every time someone is alone, something bad happens. I'm done freaking out because someone didn't answer the phone. Andy can sleep in Lanie's room and the couch is actually pretty comfortable."

"Yeah, you're probably right. Sounds like you have some experience with sleeping on the couch though," my dad said.

Tony just shook his head as he got up from the table. "Yeah, whatever. I plead the fifth."

TWELVE

I headed to bed after grabbing a bite to eat and settled in for what looked like it was going to be another long night. I lay in Lanie's bed looking up at nothing. I barely noticed the long shadows cast along the rough texture of the ceiling like bony fingers reaching for some hidden secret tucked away in the closet.

I had only been in this rehash of my past for a few days, but it seemed the new normal was that nighttime was to be dreaded. At night, I was alone and everything was quiet. There was nothing to keep the memories away. There was nothing to keep my mind from brooding over all that had happened in the past few days.

My eyes focused on the room around me and I knew that this night wasn't going to be any different. I turned over and adjusted my body to get more comfortable, but it was no use. It wasn't long before the weight of everything settled along my body like a lead blanket. As hard as it was to come to terms with the present situation, I still couldn't escape the sense that everything was my fault.

My logical mind said that was a lie and that I couldn't possibly have known what would happen. It said that there was no way I could have let that dog attack Lanie. In fact, just the thought of making the conscious choice to allow my memory of the past to play out in this time brought on a feeling like dread and revulsion mixed together. It was not possible for me to have made a different choice.

In my mind, I saw that original memory in startling detail. I saw the way she lay on the ground in a futile attempt to protect herself. I saw the savagery of the dog and the way it attacked without mercy, without remorse. I could remember the aftermath and how she looked as she lay there in the hospital. She was like a mummy wrapped in clean, white gauze. The embalmed remains of a corpse wasn't what was hidden beneath, but rather the mauled and torn remnants of a little girl.

As I lay there thinking of the torment she had to endure, both in the physical from her attack and subsequent medical treatment and in the mental from her classmates, I knew there was no other choice to make. But, even with that knowledge, I couldn't reconcile the things I had lost because of that choice. That old story called *The Monkey's Paw* kept invading my consciousness like an insidious virus chomping away at my peace of mind.

I envisioned the houseguest from the story who gives the family a monkey's paw, insisting that some magic man had cursed it to show that we should not attempt to change fate. Fate was a fixed and steadfast beast that would only change with an unacceptably high price.

There was no walking corpse at my door showing the telltale signs of decay. I had not made an intentional wish to save Lanie or my dad. I had been presented with a choice that I did not ask for, but I made my selection just the same. In doing so, I created a ripple effect that altered the course of everything I knew. It stopped my history from becoming my future and it changed the course of all of our lives. In the story, the husband knows that that their only hope is for things to go back to the way they were. Trying to change fate only brought disastrous consequences. For me, there was no third wish coming. There was no way to put things back the way they were.

I flipped over in Lanie's bed, tossing the blankets away from me. The small, bedside clock read 11:32. Its electronic numbers cast a soft, red glow across the top of the nightstand. Outside, a lone cricket played its evening tune in a droning rhythm that was both soothing and obnoxious.

My first price was Sarah. I had lost my wife. She had no knowledge of me. She did not share the love I had for her. I thought back to the night I proposed. We had taken a trip to Los Angeles and we had spent the evening on a pier out in Long Beach. I remembered that there was a hole-in-the-wall Mexican restaurant at the end that overlooked the water. The dining area was outside and there were seagulls everywhere. They rested on the posts and beams and they scurried around the floor. They waited at our feet for scraps of food to hit the floor.

She said I had made her the happiest woman in the world that night. I know that I felt like the happiest man in the world when she said yes. But that memory was just a vapor with no substance. I could see it as it surrounded me. I could feel my love for her and the love she had for me, but if I reached out and tried to take hold of it, my grasp would only come back with empty air.

That memory and memories like it only served as a reminder of what I had lost. They were like knives that sliced my heart in two. No, they were more like a plastic butter knife that could only cause a raw and irritated abrasion that might never heal. They took minute fragments of my heart a bit at a time and kept me from fully embracing my new present. Silent tears dripped from my face onto the sheets beneath me as I grieved the future that could never be.

My dad had been right when he said it was better if I forgot. But it had nothing to do with money, power, or anything else. It had everything to do with being the only cure for my situation. The only way I would stop missing Sarah was if I forgot her. As much as that thought scared me to death, I felt like it was the only way. How else would I keep from constantly mourning my loss?

I found no solace in my grandpa's belief that nothing had been lost. He said that my future was unwritten and that I had choices to make. He believed that it was not too late to find a life with the woman I love, but I could not help but feel like that future was beyond my grasp. I felt like it was far away and that I could only look on it as a distant oasis in the desert of the present. The chances that I might reach it before I die of thirst seemed remote.

My thoughts kept returning to the monkey's paw and how it represented the persistence of fate. I wondered if these events said that my fate included life lost. I wondered if that was an aspect that I couldn't choose. What I could choose was who I lost, but not the loss itself.

There was a convenience store in my youth that displayed a banner over the soda machines that read: "Freedom of Choice." It was supposed to represent the customers' freedom to choose the soda they wanted. What always struck me about that was that the owners of the store picked the sodas you could choose from. They never had Dr Pepper, which was the soda I would have chosen. So, it was freedom of choice, but I didn't really get what I wanted. I had to choose from the options they had picked for me.

In this moment, in this redo of what had come before, loss was the predefined parameter. It was a foregone conclusion. If I left Lanie to her fate, I would lose her and my father and I would lose my mom to her own choice to numb her pain and to hide from her reality. If I saved Lanie, I would also save my dad, but it seemed that saving Lanie was really just an illusion. She was lost as was my mom. Both of them were lost in different ways, but they were lost just the same. Fate, destiny, or whatever demanded its due. If we did not find a way to save them again, I would have only succeeded in prolonging the inevitable.

Where the guilt came in was the fact that I did not know what choice I would make if I were allowed yet another redo. Seeing my father again brought back so many memories. I could only hope to count all of the times I had wished for my father to be back in my life. When Sarah and I had just been married, I had come home one night to find her standing in the kitchen stuffing towels, buckets, and bowls under the sink to catch the water spewing from a pipe that had sprung a leak.

We were both just starting out in our careers and money was something of a rare commodity. A plumber just wasn't in our budget. So, I went out and got some solder and a torch. I bought a pipe cutter and some copper pipe. I cleared everything out from under the sink and set about trying to fix the leak myself.

The only problem was that I had never done it before. I had seen someone do it once, but I had watched in that barely interested way that you do when you don't have to do it yourself. I could remember the stuff he needed and basically how to do it, but that was about it. I was willing to give it the old college try, though. Or at least my bank account said I was.

As it turned out, there was one critical piece of information I was lacking. I didn't remember that I needed to clean the copper with a wire brush before soldering. Cleaning the copper makes it easier for the solder to adhere to the pipes and to create a good seal. As I sat under that sink running that torch forever, I think I raised the temperature of the copper to a near nuclear level. I cussed and I groaned while I tried my best, but every time I thought I was done and turned the water back on, a thin stream of water would shoot out, spraying the wall or the cabinet or my eyes.

I remember sitting there looking at that pipe and watching the water drip down the inside of the cabinet. I remember wishing that my dad were there to show me how to do it. I was angry at him in that moment. I was mad that he left me even though he had no choice in it. It made no sense, but I was angry just the same. I was angry about every lesson I had to learn on my own. I was angry that he had left me alone.

That anger made it even more difficult to leave Lanie to her fate. Granted, I had not known that my saving her would save my dad as well. But, now that it had, I didn't know if I could take it back if I had to make the choice again. I felt like I would have to choose between my father and my wife, Lanie, and my mom and it tore me up to not know the answer.

How do you choose between people you love? How do you choose life and death for people period? I knew that the choice didn't involve Sarah's death like it did my dad's, but it wasn't about them. I hated that my turmoil was all about me and what I wanted. Lanie and my mom, Lisa and Tony, my dad, and even Sarah were all secondary characters in my plight even though I was afraid to admit it. In that moment, I was ashamed of my selfishness and that fact intensified my anguish.

I twisted and turned in the bed that belonged to the girl I had saved and then consigned back into torture. Even in my exhaustion, the waves of sleep took a long time to wash away the sands of grief and guilt that littered my conscience. I did finally fall asleep, but I dreamt of three black caskets in a black room. My mom, Lanie, and Sarah were in them, dressed all in white. Their arms were folded across their chests as they slept a forever sleep. My dad stood with me as I looked on. We were both crying in our grief as we said our goodbyes.

As I watched, the two women and the girl started to cry as well. Tears ran from their closed eyes and slid down the sides of their faces. Small, dark spots grew slowly on the pillows beneath their heads with each falling tear. I looked on in hope as I watched the tears flow. Corpses don't cry;

the dead don't weep. Maybe they were safe. Maybe they were just sleeping.

Any hope in their safety turned quickly to horror as I watched circles of red spread from the centers of their chests. The white of their dresses that covered their breasts turned into a crimson circle that grew until there was no white left. I was rooted in place as I watched, unable to turn away even as I felt my shoulder being shaken. I could only watch in revulsion as the shaking became more insistent. It was my own version of the foreboding door knock in *The Monkey's Paw* and I did not want to turn to see who was behind me. But my feet betrayed me as they turned my body to face my fear.

My father had moved behind me and was clutching my shoulder. It was he who had been shaking me. He was now dressed in a suit that was all black. His jacket was completely black as was his tie and his shirt. His eyes had gone black as onyx as well and he held a shimmering knife in his hand. He did not wield it as a weapon, but rather as an item on display. He raised his hand, offering the knife to me.

"No," I said in my dream as I took a step backward. As I moved, my father moved with me without even taking a step. It was as though he was tethered to me and he floated along as I moved.

"You must take it. It is yours," he said. His voice was far away and had a strange echo to it. It was as though he were speaking to me from the bottom of a well.

"No. I don't want it. It wasn't my fault."

"But it was your choice."

"I didn't know. I didn't know!"

THIRTEEN

The dream was cut by another version of my father's voice. It was a version from the here and now that didn't have that eerie, distant quality from the dream. My eyes fluttered open to see him standing above me, his arm extended with his hand on my shoulder. The shaking sensation from the dream really had been him as he tried to rouse me from sleep.

"It's time to go," he said.

"Okay. I'm ready." I blinked my eyes several times trying to flush away the last vestiges of sleep. My eyes felt like they had been coated with tiny grains of sand.

As I walked downstairs, the rich smells of bacon and coffee filled my nostrils. Lisa was standing at the stove pulling slender strips of bacon from a pan, laying them across a plate covered with a paper towel to soak up the extra grease. Tony was at the dining room table, sitting with both hands wrapped around a mug of steaming coffee as though it might try to run away.

"Mmmm, that smells awesome," I said. "Where do you keep the coffee cups?"

"Cabinet to the right of the sink. Sugar's in the bowl by the machine. Milk's in the fridge," Lisa said as she placed the last strip of bacon onto the plate.

I pulled a cup from the cabinet and poured some coffee. Caffeine was a welcome addiction, particularly on the mornings that come after a night of not enough sleep. "You guys sleep okay?" I asked.

"Well, that would require me to sleep first, wouldn't it?" my dad said as he waited in line to pour his own cup.

"Touché."

I dropped in a spoonful of sugar and gave it a quick stir before making my way to the table. Lisa had been busy this morning. The table was loaded down with pancakes, eggs, sausage, and even some sliced up apples and pears. "Um. Wow," I said as I slid into one of the chairs.

"Well, I wanted to make sure you guys had plenty of fuel for the day ahead. Maybe it's wishful thinking, but I just know that the girls are going to be there. I don't want empty bellies to be the reason for anything to go wrong. Plus, I found myself with plenty of time on my hands this morning."

"So it sounds like it was a pretty sleepless night all around then."

Tony still hadn't said anything. He just kept sitting there gripping his coffee cup and looking down into the ebony surface of the brew. He occasionally lifted the mug to his lips for a small sip.

"You okay, Tony?" I asked as I started loading down my plate with some of the early morning goodness on the table in front of me.

"Yeah. Just tired," he said. He kept his hands on the coffee, not yet moving to get a plate.

"Anthony Parker, don't make me hold you down and force feed you," Lisa said, pointing a serving spoon at him before burying it in the platter of eggs.

"You know I'm not a big breakfast guy," he said as he reluctantly pulled a plate from the stack.

We ate mostly in silence. I thought everyone was too tired from the night before, but it also seemed like more than that. It felt like shock had set in to sap the normal banter that might occur even in times of high stress. Breaking the quiet, I finally asked, "So, what's the game plan?"

"I'm having Jacob meet us at the Timekeeper building at 7:00. He's going to ride down to the cabin with us and we'll see what we see." After a short pause, he looked up at me from his eggs, adding, "and shoot who we shoot."

I stretched my body to see the clock mounted on a living room wall. The little hand was on the three and the big hand was almost to the six. "It's only 3:30," I said.

My dad said, "Yeah, well, we figured we'd get there early. I have a feeling that firing a weapon at your towering height of four foot nothing will be a completely different experience than doing it as an adult. I thought it might be a good idea to test that theory before you're under fire."

"Yeah, smart plan," I agreed.

After breakfast, we cleaned up the mess as quickly as we could and the four of us walked out to the car, locking the door behind us. "Lisa, you're coming with us?" I asked.

"No more alone. Alone is bad," Tony said. "Bad things happen whenever someone is alone, even if it is just me crapping my pants because they didn't answer the phone. I've got a couple folks meeting us there that Lisa can hang out with. She'll be safe."

Like breakfast, the ride out to the Timekeeper building was quiet. Each of us was staring out the windows, watching the traffic and the trees and other scenery pass by. As much as you could in the dark, anyway. I was thankful that the drive was quite a bit more docile than the ride back from Ray's had been. There was no weaving in and out of traffic. No one honked at us even once.

When we arrived at the Timekeeper building, my dad guided the car around the opposite side of the building from the main doors we had entered before. The back of the building overlooked the Missouri River as it snaked off to the east and to the west. Off to the west, I could see the large grain elevators in the early morning light. They stood like individual columns that pointed up into the sky. The edges of each one were joined together to form a single building with a series of cylindrical humps like corrugated metal.

My dad guided the car alongside a large dock that ran down the length of the building. We parked at the end alongside an older Ford LTD. It was a tank of a car, painted a light blue with strips of faux wood running down the sides. Spots of rust decorated the metal body like small, brownish polka dots.

As we got out, I noticed two men standing on the edge of the dock near a door that sat off to the side of an array of larger doors designed for moving boxes and equipment in and out. The men were dressed in black and each had an AR-15 rifle slung over their shoulder. The AR-15 was the civilian version of the M16, although I think the Air Force used it at one time. We approached the steps and the taller of the two men dropped a cigarette to the pavement of the dock and crushed it under his shoe. He blew out his last drag in a plume that spread slowly across the parking lot as it was picked up by the light, morning breeze.

"Not taking any chances, huh?" I asked, pointing to their weapons.

"Nope."

Tony, Lisa, and I climbed the stairs while my dad pulled a large, black duffle from the trunk of the car. Tony stepped forward, taking the taller man's hand into his own. "Thank you for coming, you guys. Nothing feels safe anymore."

"Don't mention it. I'm glad we could help."

Tony turned to Lisa and pulled her close to him, wrapping his arms around her middle. Lisa looked up into his eyes, trying to hold back tears. "Don't worry, babe. We're going to be just fine. You, Lanie, and I will be sitting and talking and laughing before you know it. Same for them," he said, nodding toward me.

"I'm glad you're so confident. I hope you're right."

Tony leaned in, lowering his forehead to rest on the top of her head. "I am." Pulling back, he brought his hand up to her chin and tilted her face so that she was looking into his eyes. Leaning forward, he brought his lips against hers in a soft kiss. The tears she had been fighting to hold back spilled over and ran down her cheeks. Tony broke the kiss and ran his fingers down her cheek. "I love you."

"I love you too. Be careful."

The two men had moved to the top of the steps and were waiting quietly for Tony and Lisa to say their goodbyes. Lisa pulled away and, turning to look at me, said, "You guys better not get killed. I'll have to find a way to resurrect you so I can kill you myself. I've had enough emotional torture the past couple days." With that, she and the two men descended the steps and got in the LTD, driving back around to the other side of the warehouse.

After watching the car drive away, Tony punched a code into the door that elicited a soft click from the tumbler in the door's lock. He pulled open the door and we stepped through into a large bay that took up maybe a third of the building. From the way it looked, it seemed that I wasn't too far off in my assumption when we had been here before. I had kept expecting the office to be a façade with the remainder of the building being empty warehouse.

The area we were in had indeed been a warehouse, but it wasn't empty. To our right was a single doorway interrupting a wall that ran the length of the building. The wall on the far side held a row of doors spaced several feet apart. Some were standard doors, but a couple of them looked like large, metal, fire doors. My guess was that the Timekeeper's armory sat behind those doors. They looked very reminiscent of the armories present in many Army battalion buildings.

Tony opened the door to our right and stepped inside. He flipped on a bank of light switches that vanquished the complete darkness within. The room was a long shooting range with a row of stalls that ran perpendicular to the room's opening. My dad set the large duffle on the floor pulled on the zipper, revealing the arsenal that was tucked away inside.

He started pulling out a wide array of weapons. There were shotguns, AR-14s, and even an old M16A2. This version of the M16 was in the process of being introduced on a broad scale during my stint in the Army. Now, of course, the weapon was brand new and was likely only in use in the most elite groups within the Marine Corps and Army. I still couldn't quite wrap my head around the nature of the Timekeepers. I wondered just how deep their resources went if they had weapons that weren't only illegal in the civilian sector, but in limited supply even within the U.S. military.

With all the rifles out, my dad started pulling out several pistols as well. Tony bent over and scooped up three different ones, carrying them over to the counter and setting them out in a line.

"Okay, Andy. Check it out. I've got three choices for you here."

"One of them isn't a 357 Magnum is it?" I joked, referring to their attempt to dissuade me from coming.

"No. The goal is to keep everyone alive." He didn't appear to be in much of a joking mood. "Your first choice is a snub nose revolver. This particular one is designed for a woman's hand, so it will likely be the most comfortable for you, but it comes with a downside. It is a revolver so you don't use a clip. We do have speed loaders, but they are going to take up more room than regular rounds."

"Okay. And the second looks to be maybe a .22 pistol and the third a nine mil?"

"Very nice. So, maybe you really do know how to handle a pistol."

"I'm a lot more comfortable with the M16, but I do okay with pistols."

"All right then, do your worst," Tony said, laying out a variety of ammunition. He pressed a switch on the side of the shooting lane that brought the target to within about ten feet. "None of these have a really strong kick, but I think they are going to be a lot worse than your brain thinks they are going to be."

I stepped up to the counter and lifted the nine millimeter. It felt huge. Without trying to shoot it yet, it felt like it would require two hands. I would need one hand to hold the grip and one to sit higher to squeeze the trigger. I selected a magazine off the counter and slid it into the pistol. Switching the safety off, I took aim and squeezed the trigger.

The shot went high and to the right, nearly missing the target sheet entirely as the kick lifted my arms. The guys did manage a bit of a snicker as they watched my arms jerk.

"Want to try another?" my dad asked. "It's okay if you do. We won't judge."

"Just give me a second," I said as I lined the sights up with the target for another attempt. This time, I aimed about six inches lower than I wanted to hit and a bit to the left. Bull's eye. Okay, almost a bull's eye. I hit center mass of the target and would have certainly dropped a man with the shot.

Next, I tried the revolver. It fit better in my hand, but it was still quite heavy, so I would have to use two hands again just to maintain control. The bad thing about using two hands is that only one of them could stabilize the shot. That meant that I wasn't going to be shooting in a hurry. I needed to actually stop, brace myself, and take the shot with care.

It looked like my initial guess about the .22 was right on. It had less of a kick, so it didn't take as much effort to keep my shot stable. It was just as big as the nine, but lighter, so I was able to be more accurate without having to focus so much.

"Looks like we have a winner," my dad said after I put ten rounds in a row into the bull's eye on the target. "My turn. It's been a while since I've shot a pistol."

My dad stepped up to the counter and lifted the nine millimeter off the counter. He slapped a fresh magazine into the weapon and raised it to the target. He fired off ten rounds in quick succession, dotting the inside of the bull's eye with maybe three distinct holes visible through the paper.

"Show off," I said jokingly. "What do the Timekeepers do, anyway?"

"What do you mean?"

"I don't know. It's like you're soldiers or something. Yesterday in the car when we were chasing Ray, you drove like a stunt driver. It was the same thing last night when we thought Lisa had been taken. And you and Tony knew exactly how to clear Ray's house. Now, you pop ten rounds into the bull's eye in like four seconds. Tony has an arsenal in his house."

"Yeah," my dad said. "A lot of different skills are useful in that line of work."

"But Grandpa said the Timekeepers were all about nudging people just enough to keep them from doing the loop-the-loop. Car chases, guns, and knowing how to clear houses don't sound like nudges to me. They sound quite a bit more violent than that."

"Well, sometimes nudges don't work. Sometimes, people find themselves in situations where they don't forget and then they start using the future to their advantage. Sometimes, they start investing in things and sticking their noses into future events. Sometimes, they use their acquired money and power to gain even more money and power. When they do that, they start upsetting the apple cart."

"So, when that happens…" I started, letting my words trail off.

"When that happens, we have to make things right. We nudge people to make sure they don't go off the rails. But, even with the best effort, things don't always go right. And we have to fix it."

"Is force the only way you fix it?"

"No. It is actually the last resort. We keep tabs on people who… who come back to make sure they really do forget. We watch to make sure they don't start showing signs of using the future to their advantage. If they do, we start with more subtle ways. We have conversations. We try to convince them."

"I'd rather have one person coming along willingly than five who are just cooperating because they're intimidated," Tony added.

"Exactly. But sometimes that doesn't work. And, when it doesn't, we have to use force."

"But you're so good at it," I said.

"We have to be. First of all, we don't want our folks to die. Second, we don't have many options after we apply force. We need to make sure it works."

"I see," I said. Automatically, my mind started chasing that idea to its natural conclusion. "That means you probably do assassinations, too."

"If we have to. Andy, I don't know if you understand just how much damage a person with knowledge of the future could do. If the right person with the right knowledge used their information to their advantage, they could rule the world. What if someone went back to 1939 with knowledge that would have allowed the Nazis to win World War II?"

"Whoa." The implications of that were staggering. I could see how one person's knowledge could change everything. It made the ripples in time I created seem miniscule by comparison.

We exited the range and turned toward the metal doors on the adjacent wall. It was an armory and a large one at that. All three doors opened into a large room that was lined with just about every kind of small arms imaginable. There were M203 grenade launchers, M16s, AK-47s, and scores of pistols. Tony walked into a large wall unit and came out with three black vests with built in body armor.

He handed one of the vests to my dad and one to me. Both of them burst out laughing when my vest hit the floor. Tony put it into my hands and the weight ripped it straight out of my hands, sending it to the ground at my feet. It wasn't so much that it was that heavy, it was just much heavier than my brain said it was supposed to be.

"That was awesome!" Tony said.

"Yeah, a real laugh riot."

"Here," Tony said, picking up the vest from the ground. He undid the clasps and held it open, motioning for me to step into it. Instantly, I knew what David felt like in the story of David and Goliath. When he volunteered to fight the giant, they put armor on him that was way too big, weighing him to the ground.

Also like David, I opted to go without. "Sorry, guys, this isn't going to work. I'll get killed just trying to maneuver. I will take this, though." I lifted a large knife off the shelf. It was tucked away in a sheath that was meant to be fastened around a forearm.

"I was afraid you might say that," my dad said. "Why don't we take it with us in case you change your mind? Maybe it will still come in handy."

"We can take it, but I can tell you right now that I'm not wearing it." I shrugged off the armor and handed it back to Tony, glad to be free of its weight.

Holding the knife up against my forearm, there was no way it was going to fit. The straps were much too big and it was just too long for my short, skinny arms. Instead, I pulled up my pant leg and fastened the knife around my calf. It was uncomfortable, but it worked.

We packed the weapons into the duffle and my dad closed the zipper, hiding them from view. He hefted the bag off the floor, using the large shoulder strap to help absorb some of the burden. I had no idea how much that thing weighed, but I was sure it wasn't light.

Back outside, Jacob had already arrived and was leaning against his car, smoking a cigarette. It was odd seeing so many people smoke. They were everywhere. Of course, people still smoked in the future, but they have almost become an endangered breed. Back in this time, people could still smoke in stores and airplanes, even hospitals. It was still an ingrained part of the culture.

"Hey guys," Jacob said as we came down the stairs. "You ready to go check this place out?"

"Yep," my dad said, pulling his brother into a hug. "I figured you would bring the cavalry with you."

"There're a few folks that are going to meet us near there. I didn't figure we needed to mess with a two hour convoy." Looking down at me, he said, "How you doing, sport? I bet talking to me is just like meeting me for the first time." He clinched the cigarette between his thumb and middle finger and flicked it in a high arc to land several feet away.

"Yeah, something like that."

He smiled, extending his hand and saying, "Well then it is nice to meet you. Or for you to meet me since I've already met you."

"Likewise." As he took my hand in his, I felt as though a jolt of electricity overtook my body. The sensation reminded me of one time that I grabbed ahold of an electric fence when I was a kid. It felt as though I had been kicked in the chest and a weird tingly feeling raced down my arm to my heart.

For a moment, I thought I was fainting because the area around me grew dark. Only the area directly in front of me was still visible, only it was different. Jacob wasn't shaking my hand. He was standing about six feet in front of me and he was holding a pistol. I could see my dad sitting on a gray, concrete floor and it looked like his hands were tied behind his back. Lanie sat on the floor beside him and Tony sat next to her. Beyond that, everything faded to black. Everything outside of that center of focus became nothing. It was only darkness.

I was hallucinating. I had to be. Jacob was speaking, but I couldn't tell what he was saying. It was like his voice was out of a dream. The words were distant, and they were garble. To my ears, they sounded like tinny gibberish. Jacob was moving back and forth, swinging the weapon in his hand as he yelled. He brought the gun back toward my dad and squeezed the trigger. The sound of the shot was deafening. It didn't have the same quality as his speech. Instead of sounding far away, it sounded like the shot had gone off in my head.

The shot hit its mark and I watched as the insides of my dad's head were suddenly on the outside. They spread across the concrete wall behind him in a gory explosion. I tried to scream at the sight, but I was frozen where I stood. I couldn't move and I couldn't speak. I could only look on in horror as my dad fell over on his side, his head landing in Lanie's lap. She screamed as his blood ran down her legs and pooled between her feet.

As quickly as the darkness came it was gone. The morning sun shone in my eyes and my uncle Jacob was still holding my hand in a friendly handshake. "You okay, bud? You look like a goose just walked over your grave."

"Yeah. I'm good. I just… I just got a little dizzy there for a second."

"You'd better watch that. You don't want to fall over and knock your brains out." The similarity of his comment to whatever I had just seen made me want to bend at the waist and spill my breakfast onto the ground. I tightened my throat and willed the sensation away. With brute force and maybe some luck, I managed to keep my breakfast where it belonged, but I couldn't do much about my head spinning.

FOURTEEN

My pulse raced as I looked up at my uncle Jacob. What I had just seen was unlike anything I had ever experienced before. Was it a vision? A hallucination? Was it the future or was it make-believe? I didn't know. But the image of my uncle putting a bullet into my father's head was burned into my brain for eternity.

"Ready to go?" Tony asked as he opened the passenger side door of my dad's Nova. "It's a long drive and it will be past nine o'clock when we get there."

"Yep," Jacob answered. He turned toward the car and said, "You guys couldn't have brought a four door? At least the back seat is better than mine." He pointed toward his own car sitting in the next space, a red Dodge Daytona.

"I didn't know you were riding with us. I hope you have a ride back, otherwise it's going to be a tight squeeze to get everyone in the car."

No one had seen what I had. But the weird electrical feeling I had felt, did Jacob feel it too? Was there some connection between us? They had said something about the thing they called The Sight, but it didn't sound anything like this. This was *crazy*. They had said The Sight could give you feelings about a person. This was no feeling: it was way more than that. It was an immersion. It had been nearly as clear as if I were really there. I saw him raise the gun. I heard the shot. I saw the life go out of my dad as he fell into Lanie's lap. It was all so real and it was right in front of me.

As Jacob opened the driver's side door and climbed into the back seat, the pounding in my chest became even more severe. I wasn't sure what to do. My instincts told me that we shouldn't get into the car, but I didn't quite trust what I had seen either. As real as it had been, people don't have full on psychic visions of the future. At least I don't. But, then again, people don't travel back in time and land in their nine year old bodies either.

I don't remember telling my legs to move, but they did anyway. I found myself walking toward Tony's open door in a near hypnotic state as I tried to process what was happening. My indecision and lack of clarity about the situation was allowing me to go against my gut and climb into the car. I felt the weight of the pistol I had tucked into my waistband and at least had the knowledge that we wouldn't be defenseless victims as we rode together. I needed more information before I did anything crazy.

With the four of us in the car, we backed out of the parking space and my dad drove us out of the lot and toward Interstate 435. I-435 was an offshoot of I-35 that ran all the way around the city in a continuous loop. From there, we would head south for a couple of hours to some house or something near the town of Warsaw. Warsaw was a small lake town that sat alongside one of the branches of the Lake of the Ozarks in southern Missouri.

"So, you're expecting the girls to be there?" Tony asked, looking back at Jacob.

"There's no way to be sure, but I think it's a fairly safe bet. A couple of the guys I talked to said Ray sometimes talks about some pretty creepy stuff when he gets a few beers in him. He said something about his lake house and how quiet it was. He said he has a great big barn or something and how the neighbors were too far away to hear anything that went on in there."

"Wow. I can't believe he would indict himself like that. I didn't think he was that stupid," Tony said.

"Well, he didn't say all of it. I don't think he actually came out and said he is kidnapping and raping women. I just kind of put the pieces together, you know? I mean, we already know that he has Donna and your daughter, right?"

As my uncle Jacob spoke, I had the weirdest sensation. It wasn't the tingly, grab-hold-of-an-electric-fence feeling from before, but it still got my attention. The hairs on the back of my neck stood up kind of like they do when lightning is about to strike nearby. I wasn't sure why whatever was happening seemed to have a tie in with electricity, but the feeling was unmistakable.

I didn't see a vision like before either. Not really. As I looked over at him, it was like he had an aura except it wasn't made of light or anything like that. It was pure black and it came off him in waves that seemed to emanate from his hair, his clothes, even his skin. I sat transfixed. I couldn't believe what I was seeing. Then, as quickly as it came, it was gone. I was just looking at my uncle Jacob again and it was as though the aura had never been.

The vision, the aura, I didn't know what they meant. It did seem obvious that he was tied in with Ray somehow, but it was hard to put my faith in something that seemed like the effects of a hallucinogenic drug. Nothing like this had ever happened before. And, besides, he was my dad's brother. My dad grew up with him and knew him better than he knew just about anyone. Wouldn't he know it if Uncle Jacob were the type of man to partner up with rapists?

"Hey, you ok?" Jacob asked me, tilting his head in concern. "You still got that dizzy thing going on? You're not getting carsick, are you?"

A bead of sweat rolled down the side of my face. I reached up and wiped it away, saying, "Maybe a little. I'm fine."

"Well, say something if it gets worse. I don't really want to get puked on today."

"Don't worry, I won't puke on you."

"So, what kind of place are we talking about, here?" Tony asked.

"The lake house?" Jacob asked.

"No, the Ferris wheel next to the lake house. Of course the lake house," Tony said. He lifted his hand to his forehead and shook his head. "Sorry, sometimes when I'm stressed my mouth engages before my brain. Let me try again. Yeah, the lake house."

Even though Tony had pulled his words back and apologized, the flash of anger in Jacob was sudden and fierce. The aura came back, only this time it was a crimson red. As I watched, the aura filled in to the middle and out to my periphery in a smooth, sweeping motion. For a moment, my vision was filled with a crimson haze.

The red turned to black and then I could see again, but it was like the vision before. I could see Jacob and I could see my dad's lifeless body slumped over on the floor. Lanie's legs and feet were streaked with blood and her face was streaked with tears. She had thin, flesh colored lines running down her face where her tears had washed away the dirt. Jacob took a couple of steps until he was standing in front of Tony. Tony's eyes were like those of a trapped animal.

Jacob raised the pistol slightly and fired it, driving a round into Tony's foot. Tony howled, jerking his foot toward him in reflex as the hole appeared in the top of his foot and exploded out the bottom. Lanie screamed and recoiled away. From somewhere outside of my vision, I heard another woman scream. It must have been my mom.

Jacob moved his aim to the left and fired again, this time at Tony's other foot. He pulled his other leg up, throwing himself off balance and tipping over onto the floor. He lay there moaning an unintelligible string of syllables as he tried to express the pain.

"He's gonna retch!" broke through the vision as I watched Tony writhe on the floor. The scene before me faded back into red before my sight returned to the natural world.

"Okay, I'm stopping. I'm stopping," my dad said as the car started to decelerate.

Droplets of sweat covered my face and my hair had grown damp. I looked down at my hand and watched it shake uncontrollably. It was almost as though my arms and legs were not attached to me, but rather like I was looking at someone else's appendages.

I looked back at Jacob and everything was back to normal, at least as far as my eyesight was concerned. There were no auras, no visions, there was only Jacob. He had pulled away from me and moved as far as he could toward the far side of the car. His knees barely fit behind the seat in front of him, but he had managed to shrink himself down to put several inches between the two of us.

I looked from Jacob to my dad and then to Tony. As the car came to a stop, I knew that I had to act on what I was seeing. It felt like I had to choose between that and going mad from the visions that kept invading my consciousness. But, at the same time, I worried. I worried that what I was seeing was our fate and that I would not be able to do anything to stop it.

As soon as the idea of inevitability fully played out in my mind, it was followed with a much simpler thought: dead men don't shoot people in the feet. The car came to a stop and both doors opened. The four of us piled out of the car and onto the shoulder of the exit ramp.

Once I gained my feet, I looked again at each of the three men. What I was doing felt crazy, but, then again, crazy was the new normal. I reached behind me and felt the grip of the .22 caliber pistol against my back. I pulled it from my waistband and brought it around, pointing it at my uncle.

"Whoa, what are you doing? Put that thing away!" he shouted. The sound of a semi passing on the highway above us reduced his shout to nearly a whisper.

I glanced away from him, noticing the cars as they streaked by and I realized that a young boy pointing a gun at a man on the exit ramp might draw some attention. I lowered the gun so that it was less visible, but it was still pointed squarely at him. I hoped he didn't know I would have to use two hands to shoot.

"Andy, have you lost your mind?" my dad asked.

"Where are they Jacob? Are they at the lake house?" As I interrogated him, a gray Nissan truck exited the highway and pulled onto the shoulder a hundred feet or so behind us.

"I don't know. I think so. I hope so. Put that thing away." He took a step toward me and I brought the weapon out a couple of inches for emphasis. I decided not to count on my ability to bluff, bringing my free hand up to the grip in case he made a move.

"Andy what in the world has gotten in to you? What are you doing?" my dad asked.

"I…" I stammered. "I saw something. A vision. Three of them, actually. Well, two and a weird aura halo thing. He shot you. Both of you."

"He what? What are you talking about?"

"Right before we left, I saw uncle Jacob shoot you, Dad. Lanie, you, and Tony were there. That was all I could see. He was ranting like a lunatic and he shot you in the head. And then in another he shot Tony in both feet."

Tony and my dad exchanged confused glances. They looked like I had told them I saw a vampire or a werewolf or something. "I know what I saw, you guys. I'm not crazy."

"The Sight doesn't work that way. The only visions that happen are when someone rips, Andy. We don't see premonitions. We never see the future. I don't know what you saw, but it wasn't The Sight."

"Yeah, it doesn't work that way kid," Jacob said. Now it was his turn to sweat. Little dots of perspiration appeared across his forehead and threatened to run into his eyes. "Now, put the gun away and let's go get your friend and your mom, okay? Come on, Andy, you're freaking me out."

"I know what I saw!" I yelled. "The first time was when he shook my hand. The second time was when Tony made the wisecrack about the Ferris wheel. I saw him shoot Tony in each foot. You were dead, Dad. Dead."

I didn't know what to do. I knew what I saw. If it had only been the one vision, I might have been able to dismiss it. The aura and the second vision convinced me that I was seeing what was supposed to happen. I didn't know anything about The Sight, but every fiber of my being was telling me that Jacob was a very bad man. That he was every bit as bad as Ray, even if not in the same way.

But, I also knew that shooting him would push us even farther away from rescuing my mom and Lanie. He knew where this house was. He had connections that we didn't have. In that moment, I realized he didn't even tell us who told him about the house at the lake. If he died, our connection to finding my mom and Lanie were severed.

"Who told you about Ray saying stuff about women, Uncle Jacob? Who told you about the place at the lake?"

He hesitated and then stammered; trying to give an answer, but it was too late. "Bill Hammersmith. Ryan Jennings. I... I don't know. There were a few guys I got to talk."

"What's the address?" Again he stammered, but this time he had more difficulty coming up with an answer.

My dad fixed his gaze on his brother for several seconds, deep in thought. Finally, he met Tony's eyes for a moment again before repeating my question. "Where is the lake house, Jacob?"

Suddenly, the nervousness went out of my uncle. It was as though his countenance changed right in front of me. He no longer seemed worried about the gun that was pointed at him. He no longer looked as though he was worried we might not believe him. He looked back at the truck that had pulled to a stop at the top of the ramp and raised his hand in a wave. Instantly, the truck began to move.

It pulled away from the shoulder and accelerated quickly, the engine vacillating between quiet and loud as the driver worked through the gears. Jacob took a quick step toward the shoulder just as I realized that the truck had angled so that it was coming straight for us.

The three of us ran for the shoulder, trying to clear ourselves from the road. I felt a sudden push at my back that sent my head out in front of my body in a short arc. Jacob must have kicked or shoved me. My feet left the pavement and I watched in horror as the ground raced up to meet me. I thrust my hands out in front of me, mostly to make sure the pistol in my hand would be clear of my body. If the impact made it go off, I didn't want it pointing at any part of my body.

I hit the ground and rolled sideways, pulling myself up into a sitting position. I sat up just in time to see the truck pull away, the passenger door closing as they went. Tony and my dad ran back toward the road pulling out their weapons and aiming them at the escaping truck, but it had already gone too far to take the risk of firing shots in public. Our only connection to the girls had gotten away.

FIFTEEN

My dad looked as though he was shell-shocked. The three of us stood on the shoulder of the exit ramp, watching as the gray Nissan shot across the intersection and moved to merge back into traffic on I-435. No one said it, but the way the truck shrank as the distance between us increased seemed to symbolize what had just happened to our chances of finding my mom and Lanie alive.

"Now do you believe me?" I asked.

For a second, neither of the men said anything. They just watched the freeway above us even though Jacob had already disappeared. My dad turned to face me, that same shocked look still apparent on his face. "You were definitely right about Jacob. I don't know how I couldn't see it coming. I should have listened. Maybe we could have held him here. Made him take us to the girls."

"You can't blame yourself, Dad. It's not your fault. I could just as easily say that I should have acted sooner. I could have shot *him* in the foot."

Tony finally turned away from where the truck had disappeared. I expected to see the eyes of a man without hope. I had expected to see a defeated look, but there was a fire in his eyes. There was a deep anger that said he wasn't ready to give up. "It's no one's fault, guys. And, even if it were, we don't have time to get all twisted up about it. We need to figure out how to keep him from getting too far ahead of us."

"You're right," my dad said. He shook his head back and forth as though he was literally trying to shake off the setback. "Either of you have any ideas?"

"Well, Warsaw is pretty small, right?" Tony asked. Isn't it one of those small towns where everybody knows everybody? If the girls are there, maybe we can start asking around. Maybe someone's seen Ray's car. Maybe someone has seen that lightning bolt."

"But it's two hours away," I said. What do we have up here? Are there any leads we can follow in town before we make a drive down there? If we go down and get nothing, we've lost several hours."

"There's always Jacob's house," my dad said. "We weren't supposed to know he was involved, so maybe we'll find something. Maybe he made a mistake."

"That's good," Tony said. "Let's do that. I like that better."

We piled into the car and continued south. Jacob's house was in Leawood, a small suburb on the Kansas side of the city. At least it used to be a suburb. In the future, it would become one of the posh areas of Kansas City. It wasn't uncommon at all to find houses in the half million or three-quarter million dollar range. Even the least expensive houses were a quarter million. In some parts of the country, those might be cheap or even average houses, but they were near the upper end in Kansas City.

As we drove through the town, none of that existed in this time. The highway was a simple two lanes of blacktop with barely a stoplight to mark the town. Rolling hills surrounded the road on either side and were speckled with Herford and Black Angus cows grazing in the fields.

"Wow, this is crazy," I said as I stared out the window.

"What?" Tony asked.

"This area. There's nothing here."

"Nope. Just farmland. A couple subdivisions here and there. Why is that crazy?"

"It's just weird to see. There is supposed to be a movie theater right there with twenty screens. And over there was a frozen yogurt place where you fix your own dessert and then pay by the ounce. Seeing it all gone is strange."

We turned left on Barlin, making our way into a small subdivision that was pretty representative of what Leawood would become. The houses weren't gigantic by any stretch, but they were very different from the small split-levels and cracker boxes that filled our own subdivision.

We pulled into the driveway of a large ranch style house with a neatly manicured lawn. Decorative stones covered the front of the house, surrounding a large bay window that looked out onto the street. The three of us stepped up onto the porch and Tony pulled open the storm door. He reached out and tried the knob and it turned freely in his hand. We shared a perplexed look as the door swung silently on its hinges, almost seeming to invite us in.

"That's weird," my dad said.

"Maybe he just isn't that worried about locking his doors. I hardly ever lock mine," he said. "Until this weekend, that is."

"No. Not Jacob. He has always been worried about protecting his stuff. My dad even used to tease him about being a little OCD. It could be that he was in a hurry, but even then..." Dad allowed the words to trail off as he pulled his pistol from its holster.

Tony and I did the same as we all three stepped through the door. The house was dead quiet. The only sound was the soft hum of the refrigerator in the kitchen. There was no sign of life from anywhere within. Still, the two men moved with silent precision as they checked the house for occupants.

The living room was sparse, but nicely furnished. It carried on the impression that the outside of the house had started. My uncle Jacob did not appear to be hurting for money. The far wall contained a large front projection television that I could only remember seeing in very rare occasions because they were so pricey.

Behind the couch, a narrow table supported a speakerphone. Next to the phone, one of the now infamous sticky notes was stuck flat against the table. The words were written in a quick scrawl and contained message just as simple as the first one I had found, but this one sent a chill down my back. It said: Answer the phone, Joe.

"Hey guys, I don't think anyone's in here," I called out. "There's another note."

They came back into the room, guns lowered, but not yet put away. "Well, that's unsettling," my dad said as he read the note.

"Why do you think he's doing this, Dad?" I asked.

"I don't know. I've been asking myself that over and over again since it happened. I just can't get my head around it, you know?"

"Yeah." I didn't have any brothers or sisters, so I could only imagine how it would feel to have someone I've trusted my whole life betray me. Except that this was a completely new level of betrayal. To kidnap your brother's wife and a co-worker's daughter. Any kind of kidnapping was hard to comprehend, but this was downright impossible.

"I just never suspected anything. I don't think your grandpa did either. Or at least he hasn't said anything." He had started rifling through one of the end tables next to the couch. He threw each thing he pulled out onto the floor, no longer worried about leaving evidence that we had been here.

"Hey, Dad, is that...?" I asked, looking over at one of the dining room chairs. There was a black, knit jacket slung over the back of one of them. I walked over and lifted it off the chair, holding it up. "Isn't this your jacket? Could it be the one that Lanie went to get out of your car?"

He turned and looked, seeing his restaurant's logo on the right breast of the jacket. "I bet it is. I don't remember ever giving one of those to Jacob."

Tony crossed the room, pulling the jacket from my hands. He stood in silence as he looked down at it. The determination in his eyes softened for a moment as he held the last connection to his daughter. As I watched him turn the jacket over in his hands, I couldn't think of a single thing to say. His daughter had been taken and none of us wanted to think about what she might be going through at that very moment.

It wasn't quite the same as my mom. We all feared for her and we were just as terrified by the possibilities, but Lanie was just a little girl. I was a little boy, but I had the mind of a man. She had the innocence of youth and was just starting to go through the physical and mental changes that would carry her into womanhood. The possibility that these men might pervert that and crush her spirit in their hands was unthinkable.

He grasped the jacket by the collar, allowing the body of the garment to fall away so that it was hanging from his hand. He folded it over the back of the chair, seeming to take great care as he did so. To him, it almost seemed to be sacred. It was the jacket his daughter had been wearing at the moment she was jerked out of her innocence.

As he turned, it was easy to see that he had been fighting back the tears that wanted to come. The tendons and muscles in the side of his face bulged and twisted as his jaw clenched and relaxed. Slowly, the teary look of his eyes gave way to the steely anger that had emerged back on the exit ramp.

Without a word, he went to the closet and began digging through it. He was pulling out the jackets and coats, sticking his hand into each of the pockets before dropping the clothing to the floor in a haphazard pile. Each in turn, my father and I went back to our search as well, looking for anything that might help us.

Suddenly, the telephone broke the silence in the room as it let out a shrill ring. All three of us jumped, turning quickly toward the sound. We had known it was going to ring and that had almost made the contrast worse. It startled us, but it also scared us.

My dad looked down at the phone and let it ring. Once, twice, it called out. The note on the table implored us to answer it, but it was almost as though the phone was a live snake that threatened to bite if touched. For me, it was one of those moments of intense conflict where you wanted to answer it because you wanted another piece in the puzzle to save the girls. But, at the same time, I was afraid of what we might find out.

"Aren't you going to answer it?" Tony asked.

Reaching out, my dad's finger hovered over the button that would accept the call. Finally, he took a breath and pressed it. "Hello."

"How you doing, Joe?" said the voice on the other end.

"Oh, I'm just spectacular. Want to tell me what is going on?"

"And spoil all the fun? Why would I want to do that?"

"Why are you doing this?"

My uncle chuckled on the other end. Or maybe it was more like a snicker. "Joseph, Joseph. You were always so much slower than everyone gave you credit for. I'm so disappointed in you."

"That's okay; you'll only have to be disappointed for a little while. Where are you?"

"Oh, you'll find that out soon enough. I want you to listen to me, Joe. Can you do that?"

"I'm all ears." No one moved. My dad was staring intently at the phone, his hands balled into fists at his sides. Tony stood on the other side with one knee resting on the couch. He was flexing and relaxing his jaws again.

"I imagine you are," my uncle said as he laughed. He seemed to be genuinely enjoying himself. There was no sign of anger or malice anywhere in his voice. I think that was more disconcerting than anything. "In a couple of moments, some men are going to come to the door. I want you to take your weapons and lay them down on the floor by the door. Take off any watches and then I want you to go sit down at the dining room table with your hands on top."

"You're making a mistake, Jacob. Don't do this."

"I think that's enough commentary. You just be quiet and listen. Now then, if you try anything crazy, anything at all, you'll never see the girls again. Alive, anyways. And I want to make sure you understand something. Remember the display you found at Ray's house? It was real. You don't want to know the things those girls had to endure at his hands. And, if you resist in any way, Ray gets a free pass with your lovely wife and the girl. Do you understand me?"

"I'm going to kill you, Jacob," Tony said.

"Tony, so nice to hear from you, but no one invited you to the conversation. Joe, I asked you a question."

"Okay, fine. *I'm* going to kill you." This time, it was my dad saying it.

"You guys are just nasty. So mean. Maybe you just need a bit of encouragement. Hold on a sec, would you?"

The phone went quiet for a moment with just a couple of muffled words and movements. The three of us stood in anticipation as we watched the phone. We were afraid to move, afraid to speak.

"Baby, I'm okay. I'm okay," came through the phone. My mom's voice sounded strained and terrified, but healthy.

"Donna!" my dad yelled. "I'm coming for you. Where are you?"

"Tsk, tsk, Joe," Jacob cut in. "You know better than that. Here, there's someone else dying to talk."

"Daddy!"

"Hey sweetheart," Tony said. He was trying his best to sound calm and cool, but his face was anything but. He had pulled a tissue from the box on the couch table and was wadding it and ringing it in his fingers.

"Daddy, I'm scared. I don't know what they want. What do they want?"

"I don't know baby, but I'm coming. I promise that I will come for you."

"Aw, that's so cute. You're so hopeful. Take a listen to this, though," Jacob said. The line went quiet for another moment before a scream broke through the phone, distorting the small speakers in a harsh static sound. "Such a beautiful sound. It's the sound of your hope being dashed against the rocks."

"Don't do this, Jacob! Why are you doing this?"

"I want you to know who's in charge here, Joe. I want you to know that no matter who thinks you are the golden child, you are just a weak little boy. You could never lead. You're pathetic. And I want you to know it, but that's just the beginning. We have lots of fun planned."

"I don't understand." He paused, trying to push the uncertainty out of his voice. "This isn't over, Jacob. This isn't over."

"Wow, you really are slow. Didn't I just say it was only the beginning? Knock, knock guys. Remember, guns on the floor. Watches off. Sit at the table with your hands on top." The line went quiet as Jacob disconnected.

Almost immediately, my dad ripped the phone from the table and hurled it toward the TV. It flew outward, but the cord pulled taut, swinging the phone down in a tight arc. It shattered against the hardwood floor, sending bits of plastic shrapnel up and away from it.

Still not having satisfied his frustration, he grasped the couch table by its edge and pulled so that it tipped forward. It dug a small divot into the hardwood as one corner of the glass top collided with it and then broke into three large pieces. He bent down and closed his hand around the lamp that had been on the table and took a couple of quick steps in the direction of the television.

The cord on the lamp pulled tight just as the one for the phone had, but he yanked until the cord pulled free. My dad gripped the lamp near the top as though it were a crude baseball bat before aligning himself with the TV screen. He swung the lamp, seeming to relish the crash that occurred with each impact.

Having finally spent his anger, he dropped the lamp to the floor and stared at it for a moment. After several seconds, he looked up at Tony and said, "Give me your guns."

"What?" I asked. "You're not actually thinking about doing what he says are you?"

When he looked toward the sound of my voice, I expected to see the look of a defeated man, just as I had expected with Tony. I thought I would see an expression that said he had given up, but I was wrong. I can't say that there was a fire there, but it wasn't a man without hope. It was more like a quiet determination. He was still looking to find a way to get the upper hand. "Andy, what other choice do we have? Even if we killed whoever is coming, we wouldn't know what to do next. We don't know where they are."

"But my vision. He shot you, Dad. He shot you both."

"Andy, you were right about Jacob, but I don't know if I can accept that your vision was real. The Sight doesn't work that way. But even if it was, I can't believe that it is the only possibility. We can change what happens. I know we can."

"He's not going to let us out of there alive. If we go in there willingly, he will kill the girls and then us."

"We don't have any other choice, Andy. Your dad's right. Going with them is our only chance." Tony pulled his gun from his holster and handed it to my father.

"But... It's suicide." It was all I could think of to say. The thought of going in there without a gun terrified me, but it was hard to deny the fact that he was right.

"Gun," my dad said, holding out his hand. I started to pull it from its place in my waistband, but I had an idea. It was a gamble, but the reward could be great if it worked.

"Why don't I keep my gun?" I asked.

"Andy, you heard him," Tony said.

"Yeah, but I'm a kid remember? What if they underestimate me and don't check?"

My dad turned the idea over for a moment, a slight frown creasing his mouth. "I don't like it. We don't know what they'll do if they do search you."

"What else do we have, Dad? What else can we do?" I did still have the knife under my pant leg and I wasn't planning to say anything about that. But, still, a gun would be better. You don't have to get as close with a gun.

He walked to the front door and lay both pistols down so that whoever came through the door would be able to see them first thing. "I said I don't like it and I still don't, but you're right about one thing: I have no idea what we are going to do once we get there."

"Worst case, they rough me up. It won't be the first time I've been beat up."

"Tony? What do you think?"

"I don't like it much more than you do, but it could sure be helpful if it worked. I'm not sure whether I would search him or not if I were in their shoes. It could be a really good idea. Or a really bad one." He looked at the floor for a moment as he thought. Looking up, he said, "I say it's Andy's call. He's the one taking the risk."

"Then it's settled," I said.

The two men took off their watches and we sat down at the table to wait. In reality, it was probably only a couple minutes or so, but it seemed like much longer. It's funny how anticipation can draw time out.

Two loud knocks sounded at the door and someone on the porch called out, "We're coming in. You'd do good to listen to your brother, Joe. No funny business."

"We're at the table guys. Come on in," my dad shouted.

From outside, we heard the storm door open and then the front door unlatch. It opened just a couple of inches. Through the crack in the door, there was a single eyeball looking back at us. It opened a little more and a face appeared, looking down to find the pistols on the floor.

I was suddenly amazed at myself as I had to stifle a laugh. Watching the door open, I had the sudden image of attaching one of those noisemakers to the door – the kind with two strings attached to a small cylinder filled with a bit of gunpowder. You pull the strings apart and get a pop as the gunpowder explodes. In my mind, I saw them relaxing as they saw the pistols and swinging the door farther open only to get a pop from the noisemaker. It was one of those totally inappropriate ideas that get stuck in your head at the absolute wrong time, but it didn't keep me from finding it funny.

The door pushed all the way open – sans the explosive pop – and two men walked through the door, one of them in his thirties and the other probably wasn't even twenty yet. As worried as I was, I couldn't help but be amused. The two men were about as different from one another as you could get. One of them was dressed in khaki shorts and a collared shirt, his hair parted to the side and obviously stiff from some sort of gel. The other had hair half way down his back and was wearing jeans and an Ozzy Osbourne t-shirt that looked like it had been worn several times without washing. His hair stuck to his head in greasy clumps. I could only imagine the awkward conversations they had on the way out here. They were an odd couple if I've ever seen one.

"They only sent two of you?" my dad asked.

"Two is all we needed," the guy in the Ozzy shirt said. "You just try something if you don't think so." It did seem strange that they only sent two, I thought to myself. It was almost as if Jacob was inviting us to resist.

The straight-laced guy walked over to the table and dropped three short ropes on the table. He pointed at my dad and said, "You. Over here."

"Ooh, look, you brought gifts. I like gifts," my dad said, a smile spreading across his face.

"You're a funny one. See how I'm laughing? Now get over here."

My dad pushed up from the chair and walked over, putting his hands above his head and turning so his back faced the man.

"Oh good, you know the drill." The greasy guy ran his hands down my dad's form as he looked for weapons. Not finding any, he secured my dad's hands with the rope.

"Now you, Blondie," the other guy said with a smirk. I guess I hadn't paid any attention before, but Tony looked like he was exerting all of his willpower keeping himself from coming across the table after the guy. His eyes were wide and he was taking in breaths in short bursts through his nose. He had curved his fingers into claws, pressing them against the top of the table.

"Smirk while you can, Ray," Tony said as he got up from his chair. "I don't enjoy killing people, but I think your case will be an exception."

I sucked in my breath as the name clicked in my head. My uncle Jacob had sent the man who had taken Tony's daughter. We thought he was likely the person who had taken my mom as well, but we *knew* he was the one who took Lanie. And we had an idea of what he was capable of. I didn't even have a daughter, but I could only imagine the emotions that would play through my head if I came face to face with her abductor.

"Tough words from someone in your position," was Ray's response. The smirk was still there, but not without a twinge of nervousness. Sending two men had planted the thought that Jacob wanted us to resist. This almost guaranteed it. I wondered if Ray was smart enough to realize that.

Tony walked around the table and stepped in close to Ray. Their noses were only inches apart. "Sometimes, positions change, Ray. Sometimes, things don't go the way you expect." Tony lurched, bringing his head forward to head butt the man, but stopping short of hitting him. Ray jerked back, nearly falling over his own feet.

Tony turned around, putting his hands up as my dad had done. Instead of searching him immediately, Ray delivered a quick punch to Tony's side. The hit caused his knees to buckle slightly, but he didn't fall.

"Boss said not to do that," the greasy guy said.

"Shut up. What he doesn't know won't hurt anybody." He tapped Tony on the back with the muzzle of his pistol. "Except maybe for you."

"No wonder you go after girls. You're a coward, hitting a man with his back turned."

"Quiet. Hands behind your back."

Complying with Ray's demand must have torn Tony up, but he did it. Ray looped the rope around his wrists several times, securing them in place. What Ray didn't do was search him. Too bad Tony hadn't stashed another gun or something. But the good news was that Ray might be even more shaken up than he let on. I hoped that would work to our advantage.

"Your turn, short stuff."

I stepped up to him and started to turn around, but he stopped me by placing his hand on my shoulder. "You can leave your hands in front if you want." He applied a gentle squeeze to my shoulder as he said it. I wanted nothing more than to recoil as I realized the implications of what he was doing. To him, I was a young boy. He, on the other hand, was a demented creep who liked to take advantage of people who were smaller and weaker. I was simultaneously repulsed and terrified.

I was surprised that I was able to keep my composure, on the outside anyway. I lifted my arms for him to tie them and I hoped he wouldn't search me either. He didn't. Instead, he only tied the rope around my wrists in a secure knot. Maybe there really was a chance that my gamble would pay off.

SIXTEEN

Our destination wasn't in Warsaw and it certainly wasn't a lake house. I had no idea where my uncle Jacob had planned to take us, but the clean and greasy duo took us to a warehouse that was probably only a half-mile or so from the Timekeeper building. Like the other warehouse, it sat on the riverfront overlooking the Missouri River. It wasn't a huge building, but it was much bigger than the one where my grandfather had set up shop. It looked like it would be big enough for a great game of hide and seek if we could manage a way to get loose.

We pulled into the lot and parked on the front side of the building. The greasy guy swung his door open and stepped out. He raised his elbows into a stretch, putting his hands behind his neck. Turning back to the car, he pulled his pistol out of his holster and opened the door.

"All right, guys. Up and at 'em," he said, waving the gun as he spoke.

The three of us exited the car as the greasy guy watched over us. Everything that had happened over the past twenty-four hours or so was going to come to a head inside this building. I had no idea of the outcome, but it was clear that there was no escaping the inertia. Jacob had some kind of a grudge against my dad that seemed to extend well beyond him. It reminded me of a stereotypical mobster vendetta where they not only go after you, but your family and friends, too. But it was hard to believe that it could be something as simple and petty as sibling rivalry. It had to be bigger than that.

The inside of the building was very dark compared to the bright morning sunshine we left behind. My eyes had a hard time adjusting, making the cavernous room even darker than it really was. Toward the structure's center, there was a brighter area that stood out in sharp contrast to the surrounding darkness.

"That way," Ray said as he pointed his gun toward the light.

As we got closer, I could see that the bright area was an office that acted as an observation and control area for the warehouse. I could picture forklifts driving about with men and women manning the central office to guide operations via walkie-talkie. I wondered if the building had been some sort of distribution center for sending goods around the nation.

Beside the office, a small, lit up area was cordoned off by various shelves, barrels, and other implements that made the area its own room of sorts. Four men were waiting inside. A couple of the guys were sitting on barrels and one leaned casually against one of the shelving units. My uncle stood near the center of the area, his arms folded patiently behind his back. If they were in the makeshift room, my guess was that the girls were inside the office. He wouldn't want them wandering off.

We approached the lit area and Jacob smiled when he saw us. It was an odd thing, that smile. It was as though we were arriving for some casual, backyard barbecue and he was coming out to meet his guests. The smile truly seemed like he was happy to see us, which was probably the scariest thing of all. I had the feeling I was witnessing an actual, real-live sociopath: a brilliant actor with a heart of ice.

"You made it!" he said as he walked to the edge of the light. "I'm so glad to see you."

As he said the words, he wrapped his arms around my dad, pulling him into an embrace. I've never seen a person hugged by a snake before, but I would guess that this is what it would look like. My dad went stiff as my uncle stepped in, trying to pull away without actually moving his feet. His instincts probably told him that physically stepping away might be a bad idea. So, instead, he pulled away the only way he dared.

"Hey, why so stiff? We're not so big that we can't still give each other hugs are we?" he asked, doing his best to maintain the illusion that we were willing guests.

Without waiting for an answer, he released my dad and stepped over to me. He reached out and cupped the side of my face, almost as if in a loving embrace. Except that I knew there was no love in it. It was like being touched by the flat side of a knife. It was smooth and cool, but it could quickly turn and cut you.

"And Tony, we mustn't forget Tony. I'd shake your hand, but I can see that you're a little tied up at the moment." He grinned as if he had said something brilliant and funny. None of us laughed.

"Screw you, Jake," Tony said.

"Oh, come now, no reason to be crass. And, please, it's Jacob. I prefer Jacob." Turning to our chauffeurs, he asked, "You have their weapons?"

"Trip's got them," he said. Evidently, the greasy guy's name was Trip. I wondered if maybe he might be clumsy because I couldn't see how a name like Trip could be cool in any decade, even the eighties. But then, as soon as I had the thought, it came to me. Acid was a common drug in the eighties. Acid trip.

"May I see them?"

Trip stepped forward, lifting a weapon in each hand. Jacob looked down at them, a small frown crossing his lips for the first time. "Only two? I'm almost certain that all three of them had weapons."

This wasn't going to be good, I thought to myself. Apparently, the two men that brought us here had the same thought. They exchanged nervous glances as if to acknowledge their error. Ray had been sloppy and they both new it.

My uncle didn't wait for them to respond. Instead, he gripped my shoulder and spun me around. He pulled up my jacket, revealing the pistol grip sticking out of my waistband. He reached down and wrapped his fingers around the weapon, his fingernails digging across my back.

"You didn't even check him, did you? You treated him like a boy." The last trace of joviality had completely vanished. The coldness of a killer overtook his face as he shifted the weapon to his left hand. He turned, bringing his right hand up in a quick jab that collided with the side of Ray's face.

His head rocked as though it was on a hinge and he stepped back, trying to keep his balance. He made no move to retaliate; he only pressed his hand to his cheek while finding something interesting on the floor to look at.

Trip took a step back, putting his hands in front of him in surrender. "I'm sorry, Jacob. It won't happen again."

"I hope not," Jacob said. "Or, maybe you should hope not. Next time, I just might kill you with whatever weapon I find." Then, very suddenly, the happy-go-lucky uncle was back. The well-crafted smile played across his lips and he even had a little sparkle in his eye. I could see why no one really picked up on the evil that lay within. His act was well rehearsed and expertly performed.

"Let's let you guys find your accommodations and get settled. The festivities will begin soon enough, no need to be worried about that. You'll want to go through that door right over there." He pointed to the door that led into the adjacent office. My earlier assumption had been right; he wanted actual walls around his captives.

As we stepped through the door, I saw Lanie and my mom sitting on the floor in the back of the room. Lanie sprang to her feet and ran to her father. Restraints bound her wrists, so the best she could do was lean her body into Tony's in an attempt to hug him.

Tony bent at the waist and pressed his cheek into Lanie's before pulling back and kissing her forehead. "Are you okay? Have they hurt you?"

"I'm fine. They haven't hurt us, except, you know..." she said, referring to the phone call earlier. Her face was dirty and there were flesh-colored stripes on her face where her tears had washed the dirt away. She looked exactly as she had in my vision. The wall behind her was recognizable as well. The realness of it all brought a heavy weight to my stomach.

My dad had crossed the room while my mom pushed up onto her knees and then to her feet. They made the same crude attempt at a hug as they tried to compensate for being unable to use their hands. Pulling back, my mom looked at me and instantly lost any battle she might have been having with her emotions. Tears streamed down her face as she moved toward me. I could imagine the conflict in her heart at that moment: simultaneously happy to see that I was safe and horribly distraught that I was there. Our very presence meant that we were in danger.

As she bent in to kiss me, I found myself fighting the sudden, inexplicable urge to pull away. It defied all logic, but it was there just the same. I wondered if I would ever truly be able to move past the history that no longer existed.

Instead of pulling away, I allowed her to cover my forehead and cheeks with kisses. Finally pulling back, she asked, "How about you sweetheart? Are you okay?"

"I'm fine, mom. Really," I said, still fighting the urge to pull away.

In addition to the awkward feelings of resentment, I had spent the past two days being acknowledged as an adult again and I had to force myself to remember that my mom still believed I was a nine-year-old boy. I wondered if my dad had figured out what to do about that. I knew I hadn't.

"Hey, Runt, about time you showed up," Lanie said. Her forced smile was a thin veneer that did little to mask the fear underneath.

"Yeah, well, someone forgot to give us directions to the place. We had to wait for a ride."

Having said our hellos, everyone settled down onto the floor. The room itself was barren. There were windows on every side, but there were no desks, no chairs, and no decorations. Tony and Lanie sat along the back wall and my dad lowered himself next to Lanie. Finally, my mom joined them as she sat next to my dad.

As I looked at them, a memory of the vision filled my mind. I grabbed the window ledge in an attempt to steady myself because my legs suddenly became jelly beneath me. I saw my dad, then Lanie, and then Tony all in a row. In my mind's eye, I saw Jacob standing in front of them, waving the pistol erratically as he yelled. I saw my dad slump to the floor; I saw Lanie scream. I remembered Jacob shooting Tony in each of his feet. The idea of fate and inevitability crowded my sensibilities as I thought again of the story about the monkey's paw.

"You okay?" my mom asked, starting to push up to her feet.

"Yeah, I'm okay. Just got a little unsteady for a second, but I'm good." I had thought of the monkey's paw, but I also remembered what my grandpa had said. He said that the future was unwritten. What hasn't happened hasn't happened and nothing is fixed.

"Mom and dad, change places please. Tony and Lanie, you too."

"What? Why?" Lanie asked.

"I don't know, "I lied, remembering that my mom was still ignorant. "Something doesn't feel right."

Thankfully, they moved without questioning it further. I knew it probably wouldn't change anything. If Jacob was going to shoot my dad, a simple position change wasn't going to foil his plans. Still, it helped alleviate the feeling of dread. It reminded me that we had the power to change things. We weren't locked into a predefined path like rats in a maze.

I sat down between my mom and Tony, leaning back to rest against the wall behind me. The windows above me had once been used by the office workers to look out into the warehouse. Today, they served a different purpose. Our assailants could see in from just about anywhere in the building. Even from my viewpoint, I could see three of them just outside the window to my left.

"Have you guys been tied up this whole time?" my dad asked.

"No. They've just kept the door locked. They didn't tie us up until about twenty minutes before you got here," my mom said.

"That's weird that they would tie you up because we were coming. But I'm glad you weren't tied up the whole time. I can't imagine how sore you'd be having your arms in one position for so long."

"I bet I know why," I said.

"Oh?"

"Well." I stopped myself short, looking over at my mom. Trying to work through our situation without giving away my age was going to be next to impossible. "Maybe it was so we couldn't hug." I hoped they might take the thought the rest of the way. Thankfully, Tony caught it.

"You might have something there, bud. When we were on the phone with Jacob and your dad asked him why he was doing this. He said something about making sure we knew he was in charge."

"Oh, that's right," my dad said. "But why?"

"Napoleon syndrome?" Tony asked.

His thought was as good as any, but it still didn't feel like it was enough for all of this. We fell silent, unsure what to say next.

"Well, I have a question," my mom said. She leaned sideways and forward, using gravity to help pull her to her knees. She stood up and leaned against the windowsill behind her. "Jacob kept saying something about people called Timekeepers. He said that you used to be one, Joe. He said that Andy wasn't really a kid. He said that Andy was really our age. Why would he say those things? What was he talking about?"

As soon as she asked it, one piece of the puzzle clicked into place. He was trying to take away our sense of control. He had made us remove our watches to take away our sense of time. He forced us to make the choice to come willingly. He even tied our hands to limit our range of motion. Now, he was forcing my dad to reveal his secret and me to reveal mine. Taking a breath, I figured we might as well get the issue out of the way. At least we could talk more freely.

"What he said is true, Mom. I know it's impossible and I don't even understand it. Thursday morning, somehow, I traveled back in time."

"That's impossible. Look at you. You're the same Andy I've always known."

I stood and walked over so that I was standing in front of her. "My body is nine years old, mom. My brain is thirty-five."

"This isn't funny. I don't know how you could think this is funny at a time like this, but-"

"Mom, you have to listen to me," I said, cutting her off. "I am a thirty-five year old man and I'm married to a wonderful woman named Sarah. Thursday morning, I woke up here. Remember the spider I said I saw? Remember how I fell off the bed? It's because I totally freaked out when I woke up. I was in this body and you were young and we were in our old house and nothing was right."

"No, it can't be. Things like that don't happen. They just don't."

"If you said that to me on Wednesday, I would have agreed with you wholeheartedly. Things like this don't happen. Except for when they do. Listen to me, Mom. Do I sound like a nine-year-old to you?"

"I..." The color had gone out of her face and a ghostly countenance looked back at me. I could relate.

"It's true. Everything he's saying is true," my dad said.

My mom allowed herself to sink to the floor, her back sliding along the rough texture of the wall behind her until she came to rest on the concrete at her feet. She sat for a moment as she tried to sort between logic and trust. "But, how do you know, Joe?" she finally asked. "How do you know it's true? Why did he tell you and not me? Andy, did you think I couldn't take it? Is that why?"

"No, that's not why," my dad said. "I knew when it happened. He didn't have to tell me."

My dad and Tony spent the next several minutes walking her through the same story I had heard over the past day or so. She took it as well as I might have expected. It isn't every day you find out that there is this whole other element to our existence and that a band of folks are tasked with protecting it, not to mention the fact that your child is really a grown man.

Once they finished, my mom asked, "Why did you keep this from me all these years?"

"Because, Donna, I didn't want that life anymore. I wanted to leave it behind me. I wanted a family. I wanted you, and I wanted Andy."

"But you couldn't even tell me? How much of what you told me was a lie?"

My dad shifted uncomfortably where he sat. "Well, I guess that depends. If you're talking about lies of omission, then a lot, I guess. But I didn't lie about who I was. I didn't lie about my family or my friends or my childhood or any of it. I just kind of left the Timekeepers out."

My mom sat looking up at the ceiling, trying to control her emotions. "I don't want to talk about this anymore." More quietly, she said, "Not right now, anyway. We have to figure out what we're going to do. I don't want to die here."

She was right, of course. Eventually, Jacob was going to come through that door. He was having this party for a reason and I wasn't foolish enough to believe that he expected any of us to leave this place alive. We had to start putting together a plan and we needed to do it soon.

Looking down at my ropes, I started to wonder if I could cut them. If I held the knife toward me, I just might be able to work the blade into the ropes without cutting myself. The only problem was the windows above me. At any point, someone could pop over to the window and there I'd be, working at the rope with a knife I wasn't supposed to have.

My best chance was the window closest to them. If I sat directly under it, they would have to walk right up to the window and look almost straight down. Of course, if they took a trip around the outside of the room, my actions would be completely visible. There was a lot of risk, but I knew I had to take it. Jacob didn't seem to be in a hurry now, but we had no way of knowing how long that might last.

Almost as if in response to my thoughts, there was the clicking sound of the doorknob turning and the latch disengaging. The door let out a harsh squeal as it swung open. My uncle Jacob walked in and softly closed the door behind him. He had a joyful gleam in his eye, except in a different way than before. His look reminded me of a boy who was about to fry ants with a magnifying glass.

SEVENTEEN

"How are you guys doing? Are you comfortable?" Jacob asked. "Oh my, how rude of me. We should have put chairs in here for you. I'm so sorry about that. I'll tell you what; I'll get some in here straight away. I can't have you guys sitting on the cold, hard concrete."

He turned back to grasp the knob, but then stopped. He snapped his fingers and then pointed up toward the ceiling. "There is just one thing I need you to do for me first." He turned back to look at my dad before continuing. "Joe, I need you to ask for it. And say please. Pretty please. With sugar on top." He separated each phrase of his speech with apparent relish.

"You want me to what?" my dad asked.

"Was I not clear? I want you to ask me like you mean it." Jacob leaned back against the wall and crossed his arms, showing that he was prepared to wait him out.

"I think we're fine. Floor's not so hard, really."

"Suit yourself. Just ask if you change your mind."

"I'll let you know."

Jacob pushed away from the wall before walking in a slow circle around the perimeter of the room. He held the pistol out in front of him, pointing it at each one of us in turn. "Do you guys know why you're here?" Without waiting for an answer, he continued. "Of course you don't. Would you like to?"

The five of us responded only with silence. We all knew we were operating under his agenda. "Oh, come on," he said. "You've got to be at least a little curious."

He turned on his heels and moved so that he stood in front of me. He dropped down into a squat and said, "How about you? You've got to be just dying to know." He raised his pistol up, waving it around in small circles by his head. "Oh, not this. That's not what you're interested in. You want to know why you're *here*." He waved the barrel up and down the length of my body.

"Did they tell you? Did dear, old Dad let you in on it? How about Grandpa?"

When I didn't say anything, Jacob returned to a standing position, slapping his hand across his leg as he rose. "This is beautiful. B-E-A-utiful. Stand up, Andy. Do I have something to tell you. You're going to love this!"

I wasn't sure I wanted to hear what he had to say and I was certain that I wouldn't love it. There was no way he would be deriving that much joy from it if it were good.

"I said stand up," he said, this time with much more force. He reached down and grabbed my arm, jerking me into a standing position with such speed that it felt like I left my stomach on the floor.

"There, that's better," he said in a much softer tone. "Okay, now, you ready?" He looked at me with a smile that was almost inviting. It almost looked like he was going to share a wonderful secret. Almost. "Andy, I don't know quite know how to tell you this, but you died. That's why you're here."

"Say what?" I asked. My mind rejected his words as soon as they came out of his mouth, but the shock of what he said forced a reaction before I could control it. But he couldn't be telling the truth. He couldn't be. And, even if I were dead, he couldn't know that. My grandpa said we couldn't see where people came from. He said we couldn't see the future. But even as I rejected it, the vision played at the edges of my mind, rebutting the idea. Grandpa said we couldn't see the future, but I did.

"Oh, come on; don't act like you don't understand." He paused for a moment, the devilish smile frozen on his lips as he waited for me to react. "You bit the dust; you bought the farm. You're pushing up daisies, Andy. You're worm food!" He rose as he said the last sentence, his voice rising into a gleeful shout. He stretched his arms out as he twirled.

"Jacob!" my dad shouted.

"You shut up!" Jacob left me where I stood, rushing over to my dad. He thrust the pistol out in front of him, digging it into my dad's cheek. This guy was like nitroglycerin. Bump him wrong and he goes boom.

My head swirled as I watched these events play out in front of me. I watched as the skin on my dad's cheek bunched up from the pressure of the gun against his face.

"You know what? No. Tell him, Dad. Tell him what has to happen for people to rip."

Rip. There was that word again. My dad used it when we were back on the exit ramp. He looked up at his brother with a pleading look. "Jacob, don't. He's had to endure so much this week. He isn't ready-"

"I told you to tell him!" Jacob pulled the hammer back. "Tell him or I'm going to get your blood all over your pretty wife."

"The only way to come back is by dying, Andy. I'm so sorry you had to find-" My dad's words cut short as Jacob pressed the gun harder into his cheek, smacking the back of his head into the wall behind him.

"Shut up. You're done talking." Jacob pulled himself upright and turned away from my dad. "Isn't this exciting? I mean, how often does something like this happen? You were dead, man. Like a doornail!"

My uncle flipped over to smiling with a wicked glee as he delivered the news. For me, the room tilted on its axis and spun crazily. If I really was dead, everything I knew really was gone. They had already told me I couldn't go back and that had some finality to it, but this was... I didn't know what this was.

I knew it hadn't been rational, but there had been a faint hope that I might find my way back. I had held onto the dream that I might somehow go back the way I had come, finding myself back in my old life. If there were cosmic burps in the universe that could bring me backward, why couldn't there be one that would send me forward?

That glimmer of hope winked out like a flame deprived of oxygen. There was nothing to go back to. There was no life; there was no future. I had left Sarah behind to grieve my loss. I hadn't even been able to give her children so that she might keep some part of me.

"Yes, you're getting it. I can see it in your eyes." I heard the words, but they were far away. They were without substance.

As I thought about that version of the future, I remembered how much I had changed things. My actions might have completely destroyed the future I had left behind and the new version of me might not be dead. Still, I was plunged into a grief that burned me to my core. The memories of my past were real to me. None of this could change that.

Jacob stood and waited. His elation infused him with an uncanny patience. He waited for my eyes to come back to him. He waited for me to focus. He couldn't make it worse if I wasn't focusing.

Slowly, the world around me came back. Jacob was standing in front of me. His arms were crossed and he was all teeth. His grin stretched wide across his face and his eyes were lit up. He looked like a young boy on Christmas morning.

"You see, Andy, the universe is a crazy, complex place. You can't have a system with this much complexity without having a few bugs in the system. No. A bug isn't the right word. Bugs are bad. This is more like an anomaly. Yeah, that's better. You see, they don't just happen, they have to happen. Think about black holes. There has to be crazy, weird crap that doesn't make any sense. Without it, the whole universe would fold in on itself."

"I don't understand." My mouth betrayed me with that statement. I wasn't sure I wanted to understand. I felt like I had gotten enough answers for one day, but my mouth operated anyway. It was like looking at a car accident that you don't want to see. I couldn't help myself.

"That's okay. We're not here to talk about the why. The what will work just fine. Andy, your soul is kind of like energy. You know how electricity is attracted to certain objects, the way lightning jumps from one object to another?"

"Yeah."

"Well, your soul is like that. Normally when you die, you have somewhere you're supposed to go. It attracts your soul in the same way the ground attracts electricity. Sometimes, things don't work quite the way they're supposed to, though. You ever hear ghost stories, Andy? You ever hear about haunted houses?"

"Yeah," I said, finding myself confused by his new direction.

"Well, sometimes objects – houses, furniture, jewelry, whatever – can become spiritually charged. When that happens, that thing can catch your soul on the way by. Sometimes souls get attached to those objects and can't get away."

"Are you saying I'm a ghost?"

"No, no. Just trying to get the idea into that melon of yours," he said, tapping his finger against my forehead. "Sometimes your soul doesn't go where it's supposed to. For example, sometimes there are tiny rips in the fabric of time. They are very rare, but they do happen. Trauma causes them."

"Trauma?"

"Yep, trauma. When that dog attacked Lanie? Bingo. That's why you popped out right where you did. Lanie getting mauled and your dad getting dead created a little tear right here in time. Your very own Andy shaped rip in the fabric of time. But it gets better."

He looked at me and waited for me to ask the question, but I couldn't. I just looked back at him as I tried to wrap my head around what he was saying. Evidently, the joy of telling me outweighed his desire for me to ask, so he continued.

"You see, there has to be two rips. If you only have one, it's kind of like a hole in the ground. You can jump in it, but then you're just in the hole until you climb back out. That's no good. Your soul will just pass right on by. In order for you to pass all the way through, there has to be two holes and one of them has to be close to your death. You know what I think, Andy?"

"No," I answered. That devilish gleam was in his eye again.

"Well, I'm in a giving mood today, so I'll tell you. I think your wife is dead too, Andy. I think she bit it just before you did. And I'll bet it was a doozy. These rips don't just happen with any old trauma. No, they have to be big. They have to be earth-shattering, life changing, turn your world upside down traumas. Traumas with a capital T!"

"I bet you killed her, Andy. And I bet you held her in your arms as she died. I'll bet you kneeled there in a pool of her blood as she bled out."

What he was saying couldn't be true. I loved my wife. No, I love my wife. I could never do anything to hurt her.

Jacob fell silent as he pondered something. "Ooh, I've got something even better!" He practically skipped across the room and grabbed my mom by the arm, pulling her to feet. "What about Mom? I bet you couldn't stand to watch her take another drink. I'll bet you finally got sick of watching her waste away and I'll bet you put a bullet in her." He paused again, relishing the horror on my face. He hit a nerve with that one.

Of course, I couldn't have killed her, but I was so overwhelmed. I was so stressed out that I didn't know what to think anymore. I didn't know what to do. I tried as hard as I could to block him out, but I couldn't. I didn't want to hear anymore. I didn't want to know this. There was nothing in the world I wanted more than to just get as far away from him as I could so that his voice would stop.

"Shut up, Jacob! Shut up. You're lying. Why are you doing this to me?"

"But you're such a nice guy, Andy." He continued from where he left off, refusing to acknowledge the fact that I even spoke. "I'll bet the guilt swallowed you whole. You probably took your gun and put it in your mouth and whammo! No more Andy!" He repeated his little dance from before, spinning in a circle with his arms extended. This time, he nearly knocked my mom to the ground. Slowing to a stop, he said, "Except that there is an Andy and he's nine years old!"

"Dear God, stop it Jacob. Please, just stop." My dad had risen to his feet and was clearly battling between hatred and revulsion. Tony and Lanie sat at his feet, their mouths hanging open in shock. My mom's face was full of confusion, as though she couldn't comprehend what had just happened.

"Ding, ding, ding! We have a winner!" Jacob spun around again with that same horrifying glee. "It took you long enough, big brother, but I knew I could count on you."

"You did this to get me to ask you to stop?" my dad asked. The anger in his eyes burned white hot. I think I understood now why they had bound our hands. My dad would have literally ripped Jacob apart. Gun or no gun.

"Hey, don't look at me. I tried to let you take the easy path. You could have just asked for a chair." Jacob turned and walked out the door, closing it behind him.

EIGHTEEN

Once Jacob left, I pushed myself to my feet and staggered around the room in an awkward circle. My head was still spinning from the nightmare he had set before me. I stumbled to the corner of the room and dropped to my knees. My stomach twisted and pulled as it tried to force the remnants of my breakfast back up the way it had come. Instead, I heaved dryly with no reward except for the sickeningly profuse saliva flow that comes just before vomiting.

From behind me, I heard my mom ask, "Why would he say that? Why would he say that Andy shot me? I don't understand."

For some reason I couldn't comprehend, Jacob had fixated on this idea of control. He wanted to control my dad and he wanted to control me. This whole scene played out because my dad wouldn't ask for a stupid chair, or at least that was the start. Hearing my mom ask her questions told me that there was more to it. He wanted me to explain to my mom what happened after Lanie got hurt.

I couldn't do it. Short of Jacob coming in and holding me at gunpoint, he couldn't make me do that right now. I may have to do it in time, but not now. There were so many emotions, thoughts, and whatever else flying around in my head. I just couldn't deal with that right now.

"I didn't kill you, Mom. You can't listen to him. He's just trying to get in our heads." I believed what I was saying was true. But I also knew it wasn't the whole truth. Like my dad, I was committing a lie of omission.

Finally satisfied that I wasn't actually going to vomit, I stood up. I wiped the saliva from my chin and turned to face the others in the room.

They looked at me with so much pity. I hated that feeling. It made me feel helpless and weak.

"Is it true?" I asked. My dad dropped his eyes to the ground, not wanting to answer the question. "Dad, please."

"Yes. I'm sorry, Son."

"Wait, what's true?" my mom asked, probably still thinking about the possibility of me shooting her.

"Andy must have died. It's the only way to come back. Your soul..." He hesitated, hating that we had to have this conversation now. "Your soul has to separate from your body. That only happens in death."

"So, that's why I ended up here, in this time?"

"Yeah. Jacob is right about the childhood trauma." He stepped close and locked eyes with me. "Don't you listen to the rest. He was trying to terrorize you. Nothing more."

"But how did he know about Sarah? How could he know I am married?"

"I told him. When we talked last night, he asked how you were doing. I said the hardest part for you was probably missing your wife. I'm sorry, Andy. I didn't know."

"I know you didn't, Dad. There's no way you could've. Why can't I remember what happened?" I knew I couldn't have killed anyone, but he had planted a seed of doubt. If only I had some memory of what happened, I would be able to refute it in my own mind.

"No one can, Andy. Tony, do you ever remember encountering someone who actually knew they had died?"

"Nope. Closest I've ever seen was a guy that killed himself. He knew that he had planned on it, but couldn't actually remember doing it."

"You see, Andy. No one remembers. That's just how it works. I don't know why and don't let him tell you he does."

I took in a deep breath and let it out. I was going to have to work through all of this, but I was going to have to let it wait. Jacob's game would end eventually. We needed to get a plan in motion before that happened.

Through the window, I could see all six of them. Three of them were sitting on barrels talking. Trip was scribbling away on a small notebook while Ray and Jacob were off to the side discussing something. I was sure they weren't talking about anything good.

"Hey, Tony, do me a favor. Lean against the window there, but not like you're trying to purposely block it." I raised my hands to point to the edge of the window nearest the back corner.

Tony did as I asked and I retreated to the corner, dropping back into a sitting position. "Tell me if anyone comes close."

I lifted my pant leg and unsnapped the small strip of leather that held the knife in its sheath. I almost hoped Jacob would come back in while I had it out. Maybe I could catch him off guard. Even as I thought it, I knew it was a bad idea. The others would see and would rush us. We had no other weapons and didn't even have the use of our arms. It would be a bloodbath. Stupid didn't necessarily negate wishes, though.

"Nice job," Tony said as he saw the knife.

I held it so that the blade faced me, and I tried to work it under the ropes. I could get it in, but I just couldn't get at the rope well enough to cut it. My hands were too small, the knife was too big, and it took a little more hand strength than I had. Frustrated, I slipped the knife back into its sheath and dropped my pant leg to conceal it.

"What if one of us sat down and held it?" Tony asked. "Then you might be able to get at it better. Or what if you cut mine?"

"You're probably right, but I'm afraid that will draw a lot more attention from the goons at the window."

"Well," my mom said, "You're only nine. Your joints are a lot more flexible than ours are. Have you tried working your way out of them?"

I felt a little stupid that I hadn't thought of that before. "Duh. Well, there's that."

"What then?" my dad asked. "Say we get you out of the ropes and maybe you even get us out. What then?"

"I have no idea." Looking up at the windows, I asked, "Do those things open?"

Tony walked across and looked. "Looks like they do, but I'm clearly visible to our audience outside."

I looked up at the window above my head. It was on the back wall of the room and probably represented our best chance of escape because it was the hardest to see from their vantage point. I got to my feet and stood in front of it for just a moment. Reaching out, I gripped the window at the bottom and opened it about half way. I turned around and leaned up against the sill as nonchalantly as I could manage.

All three of them looked at me with wide eyes, unable to believe what I had just done. "Shhh," I said as quietly as I could. I had taken a big risk, but I was counting on their confidence. They locked us in a room that was in the middle of a warehouse. The room had windows on all sides, so we couldn't do anything without them seeing. If we did manage to get out of the room, the building was dark and any outside door would let in a flood of light that would alert them to our escape. We were tied up and unarmed. They had everything in complete control, or so I hoped they thought.

I stayed at the window, afraid to move. A couple of the guards outside glanced at me, but no one seemed concerned. They went back to their conversations as though nothing had happened. The risk paid off. I wasn't quite sure what I was going to do next, but it felt like progress.

"Andrew Meyer, you are not going out there. They will kill you," my mom whispered.

"Mom, they are going to kill us all if we stay in here. It may be our best chance."

"You're probably right about that," my dad said, "But that doesn't mean you're the one to go. Your mom's right."

"Dad-"

"Look, I'm trying really hard to respect the fact that you are a man. I really am. But they will kill you, Andy. There's no way you can win a fight with even one of them. It's suicide."

"Then I have to be smarter than they are. If you or Tony goes out, they're going to notice. If they look through that window and they don't immediately see one of you, they are going to come investigate. And it's going to be game over if they do."

"He does have a point," Tony said. "His size can help us. They are more likely to think he is just sitting where they can't see him and not get freaked out by it."

"I don't like this. I really don't. But I'm not too proud to admit you're right."

"What?" My mom said. "You're not actually considering this are you?" Looking back at me, she asked, "Just what do you think you're going to do when you get out there?"

"I don't know yet, Mom. But whatever we do, we can't do it in here. We're dead in here. Uncle Jacob hasn't signed the death certificate yet, but he's got the pen in his hand."

"Quiet. I think someone's coming," Tony said.

Sure enough, the door swung open with an obnoxious creak and Jacob walked through, this time carrying a single chair tucked under one arm. "Hey guys. What's up?"

His question just drew stares from around the room. Stockholm syndrome certainly wasn't something that Jacob needed to entertain fantasies about. We wouldn't be sympathizing with him anytime soon. I think any one of us, Lanie included, would gladly end him if given half the chance.

"You didn't really ask for it, but I thought I'd at least bring you one chair. Call it my good deed for the day." He spun the chair around so it was facing him and then set it down. He lowered himself into it, his legs straddling the back of the chair and his arms folded across the top.

"I see you opened the window. I don't remember anyone asking."

The power game continues, I thought to myself. I would happily play the game if it would keep the window open. "May we please have the window open, Uncle Jacob?"

He smiled at the question, but he turned his eyes to my dad. "Oh, not you, Andy. I would like your dad to ask."

"Can we have the window open, Jacob?" my dad asked.

Jacob raised a finger into the air with an expectant look on his face. "Aren't you forgetting something?"

My dad clenched the muscles in his jaw, but he continued, "Pretty please, can we have the window open?"

"With?"

"With sugar on top." My dad looked like he wanted to rip out Jacob's spleen, but he made the words come out.

"Very nice. It wasn't the most sincere request, but it will do. Yes, you may have the window open."

"Why are you doing this?"

"You mean to tell me you really haven't figured it out? You never cease to dissapoint." Jacob ran his finger back and forth across the back of the chair before continuing. He seemed to be savoring the suspense. "Joe, have you ever felt like the Timekeepers weren't fulfilling their calling?"

"No. I can't say that I have."

"Ha, I knew you would say that. You're such a good follower, never a leader. But everyone thought you were. You sure had them fooled, huh?" He extended his legs so that they stuck straight out, their weight causing the chair to top forward until his feet touched the ground again.

"I left, remember?"

"True. Anyway, think about it for a minute. We have a direct connection to the future. Don't you understand what that means? Can't you see the possibilities?" He pulled his feet off the floor, allowing gravity to pull the chair backward, clanking as the rear legs hit the floor. "All those memories rattling around in peoples' heads. They know which companies to invest in, who's who in politics, all of it. Imagine what could happen if you tapped into that knowledge!"

"That's a dangerous road." It was a road my dad had warned me about.

"Pfft. You sound just like Dad. It's shortsighted, Joe. It lacks vision. It lacks…" he tilted his head up to the ceiling as he looked for the right word. "Boldness. Yeah, that's it. It lacks boldness. You have to reach out and grab life, Joe. The Sight is a gift we shouldn't waste. We can't waste it."

"We have the gift so that we can maintain balance."

"Yes, exactly! Now you're getting it." He stood up and stepped away from the chair. "We have to maintain balance. What better balance than to keep the powers who have twisted everything up in check? I mean, think of all the wars and poverty and crime and drugs. What if we could end it? What if we could make it all better?"

"You can't make it better, Jacob. You could never have enough control."

"Man, you're such a puppet. You're like a dog lapping up whatever Dad throws out there."

"So, that's it then? Kill me so you can take control of the Timekeepers? It's almost funny, you know."

"What did you say?" Jacob asked.

"I walked away, Jacob. All you had to do was wait and it would have been yours."

"Yeah, you left, but I know you. I know you." He shook his finger at my dad, that happy, evil glint starting to come back into his eyes. "You loved all the attention you got from being the first born. Being the future leader."

"I hated it. That's why I left."

"No, you left because you were afraid. You knew that you weren't equipped for this kind of leadership. You ran away with your tail between your legs. But, you see, Joe, I know you secretly loved the power even if you didn't think you were man enough to handle it. I think you're going to try to take it back when the time comes."

"You're wrong, Jacob."

Jacob continued as though my dad hadn't even spoken. "Everything was supposed to work out, though. I didn't know it, but it was. Baby girl over there was supposed to be Puppy Chow and you were supposed to get your ticket punched. Everything would have been neat and tidy and that would have been A-OK with me. No muss, no fuss."

Jacob left his spot at the chair and walked up next to me. He lifted his arm and whacked the back of my head almost hard enough to knock me off my feet. "Hey!" my mom yelled.

"Shut it!" My mom looked as if he had slapped her instead. "Anyway, Andy here jacked it all up. I tried to tell him. I tried to tell him to let it go. Let the girl be lunch. All he had to do was nothing, but he couldn't even do that right. He had to be a good boy, just like his daddy. So now, I have to clean it up. I'm stuck making things right."

"Making things right? Is that what you call this? Why Jacob? Why? They don't have anything to do with this? If you want me dead, then just kill me. Let them go."

"Let them go? Where is the fun in that? Where's the imagination? You really do amaze me. No, Joe. Before I kill you, I want you to lose everything you care about. I want you to see how inept you are at leading. At protecting those you were supposed to protect."

"Why, Jacob? Why? I don't understand. Your hunger for power is so strong that you would kill me to get it? You hate me so much that you want to make me suffer with their deaths? You know, it isn't even your depravity that's the worst of it. You're like a little kid throwing a temper tantrum. Look at you. You're not just evil. You're pathetic!"

Jacob practically flew from where he had been standing and brought the gun up, cracking it against the side of my dad's head. "I'm pathetic? Me? You don't know me, Joe! You don't know anything about me!" It was no use. My dad couldn't hear him. He was unconscious before he even hit the floor.

"Enjoy the chair," Jacob said as he walked out, slamming the door behind him.

NINETEEN

We were never under the illusion that Jacob was planning to let us leave this place alive. It didn't take a genius to reach that conclusion. But, now, there wasn't even room for doubt. The only question was when. It could be five minutes or five hours. As much as he was enjoying himself, it could even be five days.

Of course, we still needed to find our way out of here. There was no other way to survive. If we didn't escape, it would only be a question of how he planned to kill us. A part of me hoped that he would opt for quick and painless deaths for us all, but my realizations about my uncle's character made that seem like a faraway dream.

Watching as Tony and my mom tried to maneuver my dad onto his back and to straighten his legs would have been comical if it weren't so sad. They had to sit on the concrete and back up to him, trying to get enough leverage and range of motion to turn him. Their shoulders weren't quite flexible enough for them to be able to flip him, so they had to scoot right up to him and let him lean into them as they backed toward him. After a couple minutes, gravity eventually helped rather than fighting against them, pulling my dad over with a painful looking drop.

As I watched, I scooted into the corner by the back window and started trying to wriggle my way out of the ropes. They were tight, but not nearly as tight as they could have been. Sicko Ray had been trying to be nice to me and the reasons for it made me want to take a shower, but I was also glad. Every situation presents advantages if you can find the right perspective. Ray's threat was his sexual deviance, but it was also his biggest weakness. And it was a weakness that just might have given us our ticket out.

"He's okay," Tony said as he and my mom straightened out my dad's legs. "He's out cold, but he's okay. He might wake up with a headache, though."

"Good. Jacob really whacked him. We've got to get out of here before this gets any worse."

"Yeah, I think our time is getting short. Is that working?" he asked, looking down at my wrists as I tried to work them free from the ropes.

"It's harder than I thought it would be. Or maybe hoped is a better word." I was flexing my arms back and forth, trying to work some slack into the knots, but the rope didn't seem to be getting any looser.

"Try forcing it over your thumb."

I hooked one thumb under one of the ropes and pulled. The loop started to ride up the first knuckle of my thumb, but there wasn't quite enough slack to let it pop over. I tried again, this time grabbing the rope with my teeth and pulling. It was almost there, but I couldn't quite get it over the joint.

"Anyone coming?" I asked, letting the rope fall from my mouth.

"No, but be quick."

I grabbed the outermost loop with my teeth again and pulled. Each time I pulled, it applied equal pressure on the opposite side of my hand and the back of my hand was beginning to throb from the abuse. I had to fight the urge to wince and let go each time I tried to force my hand through. Instead of giving up, I gripped my hand and folded it long ways, trying to take advantage of my youthful flexibility. It worked. I pulled on the rope and the top loop finally broke free, doubling the amount of slack. Now, it could actually come off if I unwound each loop in the rope.

"Don't take it all the way off," Tony whispered. He glanced behind him to see if there was any movement before continuing. "Leave it on until we're ready in case Jacob comes back in."

"But that's the question, isn't it? How are we going to know we're ready?" There were six men right outside the window. Getting it open was one thing. Going through it was another. Figuring out what to do after that felt almost out of reach.

"Maybe we need a distraction," I said.

"Like what?" my mom asked. "Got an idea?"

"Not really," I said, feeling a little despondent.

We sat for a moment in silence, each of us turning the different scenarios over in our mind. Lanie eventually broke the silence, saying, "I could throw a fit. Start freaking out." That didn't seem like a good plan. I could see them coming into the room to shut her up. In the best case, we're still stuck in here. In the worst, they would hurt her.

"That's a good thought, but I don't know. What if they hurt you to get you to shut up?" I pointed to my dad as he lay unconscious on the floor.

"Hmmm. What if I ask to go to the bathroom? Two of them take us when we go."

"I like that better, but it still leaves four of them."

My dad moaned and turned over on his side. He was starting to wake up. My mom rushed over and kneeled beside him. "Stupid ropes," she said. She could only look down at him, unable to help him sit up or even touch him.

"He left us the chair," my dad said as he struggled to pull himself up into a sitting position.

"Yeah, nice guy, your brother," Tony said. "You want to sit in it? It's got to be better than this floor."

My dad looked up at the chair for a second before responding. "Nah. Maybe in a bit, though. It looks like too much work. My head is pounding. Did he hit me with his gun?"

"Yep. You were out before you even hit the floor. You fell like a brick."

My dad scooted back toward the wall and leaned against it. "We've got to get out of here."

"Yeah. Welcome to the party. We were just talking about it. Our audience outside is posing a bit of a problem, though."

"Well, what time is it? They've got to go to sleep sometime, don't they?"

"That's true." As with the ropes, I felt a little foolish not having considered that. I was focused on the moment and not really looking ahead.

From outside, one of Jacob's crew looked in through the window and announced that my dad had woken up. The door swung open within seconds and one of the guys walked through. He was one of the ones we hadn't really had the pleasure of meeting yet. So far, he had just been a fixture among the group outside.

He was short and squatty, almost as wide as he was tall. He turned toward my dad and chucked a small, white bottle toward him. All of our hands were tied, so the bottle just hit him in the forehead and fell to the ground, rolling out of reach. Snickering, the man turned and walked out, pulling the door closed behind him.

Tony squatted down and scooped the bottle off the ground, dropping it into my lap.

"What a bunch of jerks," he said. No wonder the guy had snickered. Everyone's hands were tied behind their backs except for me. And the bottle had a childproof cap. And I'm a child. The only thing worse than having a headache and no pain reliever is having pain reliever you can't take.

"Yeah, I didn't figure it was an expression of my brother's empathetic nature."

I worked the lid off the bottle and took three of the pills over to my dad. He opened his mouth and I dropped them in. I looked up at the window and every one of them had been watching me. Their expressions were filled with disappointment as they had hoped I wouldn't be able to get the lid off. My guess was that they were looking for some comedy to break up the monotony of waiting.

The guards finally got bored of watching and went back to their wait. As did we. We sat in silence and waited. There were no clocks in the room, so the passage of time was immeasurable. Darkness surrounded the office, so there wasn't even the movement of the sun to help. We could have been in the room for one hour or five. It was impossible to know for sure.

Jacob didn't come in anymore, though. His crew would sometimes talk; sometimes, some of them would read. The short, squatty guy had a stack of girlie magazines on the barrel beside him. Every now and again, he would flip through one of them, glancing at the articles and staring at the pictures. Trip kept scribbling away on his little pad. I wasn't sure I even wanted to know what he was writing.

As for us, we could only sit and watch them. Or look up at the ceiling. Or pick at our fingernails. I almost started to wonder if they wanted to kill us with boredom. We talked some, but it was hard to maintain any conversation with interest. Our real focus was our predicament, but we had talked about it as much as was useful. Until they went to sleep, we were just talking and not doing.

Finally, it must have started to get late. A guy with dark hair and a mustache from the last decade finally got up and walked into the darkness. After a couple minutes, he emerged carrying an armload of sleeping bags.

"Darrel and Trip, you're up first," is what I think Jacob said. Even though the window was open, it was still pretty hard to hear anything. The walls were thick concrete and didn't let a lot of sound through. Before the window was open, it was like watching a silent movie. Now, it was more like someone had turned the volume way down.

"Looks like they're going to let us live till morning, at least," my mom said.

"Thank God. I wish I knew what they were waiting for, though," I said. "Do you think Jacob is waiting for someone else to come?"

"I don't know," my dad answered. "It does seem weird. I know he's got this whole control game going, but to what end?"

"I don't want to find out. I want to get out of here," Lanie added.

As I watched the group unroll their sleeping bags, it was clear that this was the opportunity we were waiting for. They had to sleep sometime, but, then again, so did we. Each of us had managed to take catnaps throughout the day; it was almost impossible not to. There was only so much ceiling staring that a person could do without falling asleep. Even still, the day had been long and stressful and had taken its toll on all of us. Our bodies wanted to recharge, but there were more important things to do than sleep.

The four of them bedded down, leaving the other two to stand guard. We had already been introduced to Trip, but I didn't know who Darrel was until the other four had climbed into their bags. He was the guy with the 70's mustache who had gotten the stuff for sleeping. He had an average build and Trip was slightly dumpy. Their sizes were suddenly a lot more important now that I was looking at going out there.

We still weren't done waiting, though. The five of us settled in for what would be the longest wait of the entire day. In reality, it was probably less than an hour, but it followed the course of the rest of the day. One hour could have been six. But the boredom of waiting was tempered with anticipation and the combination was maddening. The men on the floor shifted and turned as they tried to find comfortable positions on the hard concrete beneath them. Finally, they began to lay with open mouths, breathing or snoring softly as they slept.

"Hey," I whispered, bringing Tony's eyes into focus on me. He had been sitting with his eyes closed, but hadn't been sleeping, apparently. "Let me get your ropes undone."

Tony scooted over, being careful to stay low to keep from drawing attention. Trip had his nose buried in his notepad again and seemed oblivious. Darrel was more alert and might notice if any of us broke the plane of the window.

I worked the knot free and loosened the rope, tying it again. "What are you doing?" he asked.

"Well, I figured that it would be better if it still looked like you were tied. Don't worry though; you should be able to just pull it free."

"Let me try it," he said as he tugged at the two ends of the rope. "Nice."

I retied his rope and did the same for my dad. Just as I was about to work on my mom's hands, Tony's whisper broke the silence, drawing my attention to the window. Darrel tapped Trip on the arm. Trip looked up and Darrel whispered something before walking toward the back of the building and disappearing into the darkness.

"Time to go," I said, climbing to my feet and pulling the rope from my wrists. Instead of dropping it to the ground, I wrapped it into a coil and stuffed it into my back pocket. I had no idea what might come in handy later.

"Just to the lights," my dad said. "I saw them next to the bathrooms. Just cut the power and get your butt into the shadows. You need to guard that breaker box. Don't let them turn the power back on."

"Yes, Dad," I said, rolling my eyes a little.

"I mean it. Don't do anything crazy. They are twice your size and I don't think they'll hesitate to kill you."

"I'll be careful, Dad, I promise."

I scooted toward the window that ran along the back of the room. I hugged the wall as I rose, wriggling my body through as quietly as I could. Trip was still focusing on his notebook, but movement or the slightest sound ran the risk of catching his attention. Out of the room, I jogged as quietly as I could into the darkness, trying to keep the bottoms of my feet from slapping against the concrete. I had made it out and now I had to be extremely cautious. If they heard me, it would be the shortest escape attempt ever.

I found the back of the warehouse and turned right to make my way toward the back corner. That was where the bathroom was and, according to my dad, the main breaker box as well. In front of me, the darkness stretched out into an abyss. The light from the office area behind me quickly faded into nothing and the darkness was a solid mass. I made my way forward, keeping my hand up against the back wall for guidance. Until my eyes adjusted, it would be easy to get off track and find myself bumping into one of the large shelving units that sat to my right, running up the length of the warehouse.

A faint sliver of light streamed out from a closed door ahead of me. That must have been the bathroom. Darrel was likely still inside, completely unaware that I had left the office. My eyes were finally starting to adjust to the darkness around me and I could just make out the outline of the thin, metal door that hid the breakers controlling the power to the building. I reached up and fingered the small latch, allowing the door to swing open. I had to extend myself onto my tiptoes to find the main switch that would cut off power to the entire warehouse.

As I stood there with my fingers on the switch, I thought again of Darrel sitting in the bathroom. If I cut the power, he would come out, looking for the cause. I wondered if he would assume that the breaker had just popped over or if he would think there was a more devious cause. Like, say, a nine-year-old boy flipping the switch. In either case, he would simply reset the switch to restore power. Then the power would be on and my dad and Tony might be in the process of climbing out the window in the office. If Trip saw him, he would raise the alarm and things would get much more complicated.

I let go of the switch and pushed the door closed as quietly as I could. I was going to have to do something about Darrel. On the one hand, I could wait for him to go back to the office before I cut the power. I didn't like that approach. Getting him while he was completely unaware seemed much more strategic. But then again, my dad was right. Attacking a fully-grown man did seem more than a little foolish; if he got a hold of me, I was through. Fighting back could very well be an exercise in futility. My size gave me the best chance of getting out of the room unnoticed, but it also meant I had the least chance of overtaking our opponents.

On the other hand, I had to stop thinking of my size as a pure disadvantage. I needed to move past the limitations and look for opportunities. What was the expression? I needed to turn my lemons into lemonade. I was small and that meant I could hide. It meant I could be quick. I could use surprise to gain the upper hand. But I had to be smart. I had to be brilliant. What I couldn't do was show mercy. If I hesitated or panicked, I was done. There was no second chance once the element of surprise was gone.

My time to consider the options vanished as the toilet flushed with a whoosh. The sliver of light became a wide ribbon as Darrel opened the bathroom door. Then, just as quickly, he flicked the light switch and plunged the area into darkness. He was going to be completely blind when he stepped out. I had been in the darkness for several minutes and my eyes had adjusted. He had been sitting in the light this whole time. I felt a sudden boost of confidence as I thought back to my trip along the back of the warehouse, having to feel my way because the darkness had engulfed my vision so completely.

Darrel stepped through the doorway, cursing the darkness around him. He fumbled forward and inched past, his height towering above me. He had stood among the other men and he had seemed to be of average height. Next to me, he was a giant. My confidence faltered some as I pictured myself trying to take him down, blind or not.

I was going to have to take him low. It was the safest option. As he stepped in front of me, I swiped the blade across his Achilles tendon right at the ankle. The feeling was disgusting, reminding me of trying to slice through the cartilage and tendons on a turkey leg. The knife was sharp, so it met little resistance, but it was enough to make my stomach hurt.

He was taken by complete surprise and he dropped to the ground, clutching at his ankle. I came in with the knife before he could comprehend what was happening and scream for help. I sliced at his throat, cutting cleanly across his jugular. The blood immediately shot out in great spurts with each pump of his heart. A noise finally came from his throat, but it was only a soft gurgling sound. I wondered if I had gone deeper than I thought, cutting through his windpipe as well.

Within seconds, Darrel was lying limp at my feet, a pool of blood spreading slowly away from the gash in his neck. I watched him lay there and I couldn't believe what I had just done, what I had to do. I had never killed anyone before. I didn't know how it would feel to kill someone and I was shocked to see that I still didn't. Adrenaline coursed through my veins and my heart thumped in my chest. Looking down at the knife in my hand, I could barely see the outline of the blade shaking in the dim light.

I had to move. I knew that I couldn't stay there. Sooner or later they were going to figure out he was missing and they would come looking for him. There was only so far I could take this before I had to cut the power. I wondered how many of them I would be able to take down before that happened. One, maybe two, was my best guess. The risky part of it was that Darrel had been the exception. He was by himself and he was unaware. All of the others were grouped together by the office and that made things a lot more dangerous.

I left Darrel in a heap on the ground and worked my way back the way I came. This time was much easier since my eyes had adjusted to the darkness. Instead of seeing a solid, black mass on all sides, I could see variations in the darkness, and I could make out the distinct shapes of the shelving units as they rose toward the ceiling.

I turned left at the row of shelves just before the open gathering area where they slept. As I came up along the office, I could see my dad and Tony leaning against the far wall, doing their best to look nonchalant as they peered into the darkness. I had been gone several minutes and they were likely starting to wonder if something had gone wrong.

Outside the window, Trip had stopped writing in his book. A trail of gray smoke went up in an expanding plume from the cigarette in his hand. He watched my dad as my dad looked out into the darkness. At his feet, four men lay in sleeping bags. Everything was well as far as they knew. They had no idea that one of theirs lay in a pool of blood just a couple hundred feet away.

Both in front of and behind me, the shelves rose nearly to the ceiling. People forget to look up, I thought to myself. If I could climb the shelves and cause a small disturbance, I just might get Trip to come over and check it out. That would reduce their number by two and would make for much less of a circus when I cut out the lights. It was a risk, but it felt worth it.

I turned around and grabbed the shelf that had been behind me. Using the shelves as rungs in a ladder, I climbed up to the third shelf. That would have put me six or seven feet above the floor. Hopefully, that would be just high enough to out of their line of sight while still being able to reach out to give a passerby a very bad day.

There was just a small scattering of boxes on the shelf, some of them small and a couple of them were good sized. I slid one of the larger boxes forward so that I could create a basic blind that would protect me from being seen when he came down the aisle. Hopefully, that would grant me some additional freedom in my movement.

To my left, I found a smaller box that weighed maybe a half a pound. That should be big enough to cause a noise, but not a thunderous sound that would bring them all running. One person was all I wanted. More than one would be too dangerous. More than one could make this a much worse day than it had already been.

I lifted the box and held it out from the shelf before taking a deep breath. My heart pounded in my chest and I hesitated for a moment as I tried to gather my courage. I had been able to take Darrel by surprise. Now, I was bringing someone to me. With Darrel, I hadn't really had time to chicken out because he came out through the door. This was different. This was intentional.

I found myself wanting to bring the box back in and set it on the shelf. I wanted to climb back down and cut the power like my dad had asked. But then there would be five left instead of four. Tony and my father would have to hunt them while being hunted. They didn't have weapons and they didn't have the lay of the warehouse. They would be finding their way around at the same time they were trying to catch Jacob and his crew. And we would be outnumbered, five to three.

I knew what I had to do, but it didn't make it any easier. I held the box and waited for my heart to slow. I waited for my breathing to return to normal, but it didn't. It reminded me of a time I zip-lined over a five hundred foot gorge. I had stood on a small, wooden ledge and I had to step out into nothing. There was no calming feeling that came; there was no point where I was magically ready. In the end, I had to force myself to step off the ledge.

As I looked at the box in front of me, I knew this was my ledge. I was able to react to Darrel. He was in front of me and I had to act before the moment was lost. Trip was minding his own business, smoking a cigarette. I was going to bring him to me. There was never going to be a point where I felt ready. So, I released the box anyway, and I watched it as it fell. It smacked the concrete below, sending out an echo in all directions.

"What was that?" The short, squatty guy sat up, looking around.

"Probably just a rat. Trip, go check it out." I think that was Ray.

"Oh, come on, man. I hate rats."

"I know," he said, chuckling as he rolled over.

Rats. That was just awesome. I didn't think about rats. Few creatures on this earth are more disgusting. They are big, hairy, nasty beasts that carry fleas. Rats caused the bubonic plague that wiped out a third of Europe. And their tails. Their gross, hairless tails. I had to force myself to look at the bright side. At least he had warned me. If I had looked over to see a rat next to me on the shelf without expecting it, I might have screamed. Or fainted. Either way, it wouldn't have been good.

Trip walked away from the group, mumbling to himself as he went. Within moments, he disappeared from view and the only sign of him was the sound of his feet dragging across the concrete floor as he walked. The sound softened and then increased as he made his way toward me. I had gotten lucky. Ray had sent him to investigate and had rolled over to go back to sleep. They were still very confident in their level of control.

Below me, Trip's greasy mop came into view as he crossed out from behind the makeshift blind I had set up. It had done a great job of hiding me, but it also hid anyone who approached. Now, he stood just below me and looked down at the box between his feet. I leaned forward and extended the knife out toward the edge, but he bent down to pick up the box.

He turned it over in his hands before he stood up, placing it back on the shelf in front of him. He looked to his left and to his right, being still as he listened for the sound of any rodents or nine-year-old boys who happened to be moving around nearby. Just as I leaned forward with the knife again, he bent forward at the waist a second time. This time, he looked between the shelves for any sign of movement.

This was going to be harder than I thought. In my mind's eye, I could see him standing and working his way down the shelf as he looked for the rat. If that happened, I just might lose him. Sliding with him as he moved would bring the very real risk of bumping a box that would draw his attention upward. So, I crept forward as he knelt and I brought my legs out over the end of the shelf. I pushed out with my hands and dropped toward him, landing on his back and driving the knife into his neck from behind.

His body tensed and jumped, throwing me backwards. I gripped his hair like a horse's mane and I wrapped my legs around his waist, barely managing to keep myself from falling to the floor. He didn't even seem to notice me as he reached up, grabbing for the knife. He slapped at it and tried to pull it free, but it was too late. He sunk to his knees before slumping over onto his face. I still sat on his back and I felt his last breath go out of him. That is a feeling I never want to feel again. It is one thing to watch a man die, but feeling his last breath is altogether different. It was so much more real than Darrel. It was almost as though I experienced it with him.

From the other side of the shelves, I heard Ray's voice as he shouted into the darkness, "Keep it down over there. We're trying to sleep." He must have turned back over because his voice was much more muffled when he added, "Klutz."

I couldn't believe my luck. They were so confident in their advantage that they didn't stop to think we might have escaped the room. Even still, I sat atop Trip's back, tense and ready to flee. After Ray's outburst, there was only silence. Within moments, I could again hear the rhythmic sound of breathing as he went back to sleep.

I gripped the handle of the knife and pulled, feeling a sudden flood of panic as it wouldn't budge. It had lodged somehow and my nine-year-old arms weren't strong enough to free it. I thought about leaving it, but I climbed onto my knees and pulled as hard as I could. I used my arms, legs, and back to pull against the blade, causing it to wiggle and then begin to give. Finally, it pulled free with a thick, suction sound that brought the thick, pre-vomit saliva into my mouth.

The feeling of nausea swept over me again. It was beginning to be an all too familiar sensation. I dropped to my knees with Trip's corpse slumping next to me in the darkness. It took everything I had just to control my breathing in an attempt to keep the contents of my stomach on the inside where they belonged.

If I threw up, they would come. I knew they would hear me, and I knew they would come. I had to control myself. I had to get control of my body. As I kneeled on the concrete, I told myself I had no choice. They were going to kill us if we didn't do something. The destination of our present course was death. This was an absolute case of kill or be killed.

I didn't know how much my self-directed speech helped. It was still a couple minutes before the sound of the knife pulling free would stop playing in my head. It took a couple more before my heart rate slowed and I felt comfortable enough to begin moving again.

I climbed to my feet and crept down the aisle, rounding the corner at the end. Ahead of me, the array of sleeping bags enshrouded our enemies. There were four elongated forms, each with a head sticking out of the top. I looked to my right and could see two sets of eyes peering out at me from the office. Tony and my dad watched with fear and anticipation. I was sure they suspected I had already taken action against our adversaries, and I imagined they were terrified that I might try to take out these men while they slept.

Instead of moving forward, I turned away from the men ahead of me and made my way back toward the open window.

"What are you doing? You were supposed to shut off the lights," Tony said as I climbed through.

"I-"

"Are you trying to get yourself killed?" He cut me off.

I took a deep breath as I tried not to let my emotions get the best of me. They felt like a delicate thread that could be broken at the slightest provocation. I told myself that they were just concerned for my safety. I told myself they were on my side.

"He was in the bathroom," I said. "If I cut the lights while he was in there, he would have just come out to see what was going on. I would have had to have taken him out or waited for him to leave and just cut them out again."

"Okay, fine. What about the other guy? Did you kill him too?" Tony asked.

"Yeah. Maybe that was pushing it, I'll admit, but the idea of cutting out the lights got me worried. As soon as those lights go out, we're going to be hunting them in the dark while they're hunting us. Five of them left seemed too risky."

"All right, I see your point. But, next time, can we please come up with a plan and stick to it? We had no idea what was happening."

"Yeah. Sorry. Look, I still don't like the idea of shutting off the lights, though. I was thinking that maybe we don't have to. There are only four of them left and they're all sleeping. If we sneak out now, we can take them out before they know what hit them."

"With what? Our bare hands?" my dad asked.

"Our guns are out there. We might be able to get to them. Worst case, I have my knife."

"That just might work," my dad said.

"Uh, guys. One of them is waking up," Tony said.

"Figures," I said as I went to the window. Sure enough, one of the guys had pushed up onto an elbow and was rubbing the sleep from his eyes with his other hand. Without giving him time to register his surroundings, I raced to the open window and pulled my body through. Once one of them was awake and figured out what had happened to his partners, there was probably no getting out of the room.

"Where you guys at?" he asked the empty air around him. He flipped back the top of the sleeping bag and climbed out, wiping more sleep out of his eyes. He stood and looked around for a few moments before he moved between the rows of shelves, passing out of view. He must have found Trip's body because he popped back out from between the shelves in a hurry, a panicked look on his face. He rushed over to one of the sleeping bags and shook the still form that lay within.

"Boss, he's dead. Somebody got him."

"What? Who's dead? What are you talking about?"

"Trip. There's blood everywhere. I can't find Darrel."

Jacob slid out of the bag and jumped to his feet. He sprinted over to the office door and flung it open, surveying the room inside. My dad and Tony were standing near the window and Lanie rose into view as well. She and my mom must have woken up at the sound of the door opening.

Jacob raised the pistol toward the group and yelled, "Back against the wall. Sit down." He turned from the door and his eyes had gone completely different again. They were the eyes of a madman. Whatever sanity had been there before appeared to have finally left him. He stood with the weapon at his side, his face taut. He was too far away for me to see a lot of detail, but I could have sworn that I could see the muscles in his jaw working.

"What are you just standing there for?" he shouted at the men. They were watching him with the same horror I was. "Find him! Find Andy!"

The paralysis that had held the men in place broke its hold and they scattered. Each of them went their own way, beginning their search for me. Jacob went back inside the room, holding the pistol out in front of his body. It waved erratically as he yelled something at them. He hadn't closed the door behind him, but the cinderblock walls muted the sound to a point that I couldn't make out the words.

What I did hear was the shot. He took two steps forward and fired the weapon into the group. Immediately, a muffled scream found its way through the door and to my ears. Lanie had screamed. As soon as I heard it, I knew. Jacob had shot my dad in the head, sending blood and brains onto the wall behind him. I knew that his body had slumped over into Lanie's lap and she had screamed. My vision had become reality. In my attempt to keep us alive, I had brought about the very thing I had hoped to escape.

TWENTY

I felt like I should have been feeling despair as I watched Jacob. I expected anguish. I expected sadness and horror. Instead, I felt anger. An immeasurable rage came up from within me and projected onto the man who had just killed my father. It was as though this and all the emotions of the past several days had suddenly converted into a blinding madness that overtook everything.

All of it came forward in a rush. I remembered the fear of my dad's death and the fear that I would have to watch my mom disappear into an alcoholic depression. I remembered the loss of my wife and the overwhelming concern I had felt for Lanie and my mom. I remembered how it felt to realize I couldn't go back to my old life. And the man standing in front of the window represented all of it. No, he embodied it.

For the first time, I actually wanted my uncle to die. Before, I had wanted to escape and killing them was the only way to do that. Now, the hesitation I felt had evaporated. Gone were the feelings of remorse and regret that came from ending Trip and Darrel's lives. I was glad they were dead. And I wanted nothing more than to extinguish my uncle Jacob and the rest of them. I wanted to channel my anger into them, cleansing myself of it.

I had the sudden urge to charge the room and to plunge my knife into him. My anger had twisted my nature into a much darker version of myself. But I had to hold myself back. Rushing into the light would be suicide. The men scattered throughout the building would close on me and would take no mercy. In fact, they probably wouldn't even make it in time to do anything. My uncle would put a bullet in me before I got close enough to be a threat.

My eyes moved to a box sitting on one of the barrels by the front of the office. Jacob had dropped our guns into that box, but they might as well be a million miles away. To get to them, I would have to cross into the light. There were two things I wanted more than anything at that moment, and they were both safely within the light.

Jacob turned and walked out of the room, swinging the door closed behind him. "Andy, don't make this worse than it has to be," his voice rang out. "I wasn't actually going to kill you, you know. But you're forcing my hand. Come back before anyone else has to die."

He was lying, of course. He was never going to let us go. Even before he brought us here, he knew that we would be leaving in body bags. People like him don't understand the concept of mercy or even intimidation. He was playing for keeps. But even with that knowledge, I couldn't figure out was why he had shot my dad. Everything he had said pointed to my dad being a part of his end game. But even my vision had him shooting my dad while the rest of us watched on. It didn't make sense to me.

I twisted around and shuffled toward the rear wall, trying to move as quietly as I could. My adversaries were now fully aware that I wasn't where I was supposed to be. The slightest sound could bring them running. Sound carried fairly well in spite of the warehouse's size. I could hear some of them moving around, but I couldn't tell exactly where they were.

I reached the end of the row and turned right again, following the same general path I had several times before. I moved from row to row, being careful each time to listen for the sound of movement or of approaching footsteps. Each row was as quiet as the one before it. They hadn't worked their way this far down yet.

When I was about halfway, the lights above my head started coming on in a cascading wave. Row after row of fluorescent lights flickered on, washing the area in light. I felt naked and exposed in what had been shadows only moments before. I dropped into a crouch, trying to make myself as small a target as possible.

Looking up the aisles, I could see one guy standing by the doors where we had come in this morning. If I had to guess, that was where the bank of light switches was that had illuminated the building. I could see the short, squatty guy up the next aisle. His body was facing toward me, his head pivoting as he scanned the area. Jacob and the others were nowhere to be seen.

My only chance was to move along the end caps, ducking and dodging from row to row. For the moment, though, I couldn't move. The guy facing me was still scanning the area. If I moved from my spot, he would learn my position and would no doubt alert the others if he didn't kill me himself. I crouched and I waited as he began to walk forward, closing the distance between us. He came to a stop and did another scan before finally turning and walking in the opposite direction.

After waiting for him to move a bit farther away, I resumed my trek forward. I had to move so slowly that the trip took several minutes longer than it should have, but I finally made it to the breaker box that would bring back the protective darkness. Darrel's body laid at my feet, the blood around him now a sticky mess. I placed my legs on either side of him and grimaced at the feeling beneath my feet. It reminded me of spilled syrup.

I reached up on my tiptoes and flipped the main switch, plunging the entire building into darkness. Without the light source coming from the office area, the darkness was as thick and black as an execution hood. Even the shelves a few feet away were invisible. I had believed that the darkness would be a sanctuary, but I felt just as vulnerable in the complete darkness as I had in the light.

The feeling was confirmed when a shot exploded from somewhere behind me. Echoes from the blast ricocheted off the concrete floor and metal ceiling in a rumble that eventually dwindled into a deep silence. Within moments, the silence erupted into chaos again as several more shots fired. These shots were much smaller. They were almost tinny in comparison to the cannon blast that preceded them.

I wondered what the shooter had heard to cause such an outburst. Had Tony gotten out of the office that quickly? I hoped that he had been the shooter or at least nowhere near the shooter. But there was no way to know who was shooting, who had been shot, or even if anyone had been shot. The darkness was paralyzing. It inspired paranoia that said every noise was the enemy. Every sound was death.

I ran my hand down the series of circuits, flipping each breaker as I went. I had no idea what I was turning off, but it really didn't matter. Complete darkness was just as dangerous as being in the light, so I had to find some happy medium that was closer to the way things had been before they turned on the lights.

I left a couple of switches at the top in the on position and then lifted the main lever upward. Power returned to the building and two rows of lamps on the far end came to life. The warehouse wasn't enormous, but the lights were far enough away so that the area was almost as dark as it had been with all the lights off.

It would have to do. If I was standing here messing with the lights, that meant they had a one in two or maybe three shot of knowing exactly where I was. There were only so many places in the building that allowed you to control the lights. It might only be moments before someone came down the aisle to investigate. Or maybe just shoot blindly, hoping to hit something accidentally. Either scenario was bad for me.

I backed away from the small corner and ducked behind the first row of shelves. If I was right and they came to investigate, I would be here waiting. Even if I was wrong and they figured I left the danger area, I hoped that they would still believe their advantage was in the light. They outnumbered us and they had the firepower. If they got the lights back on, they could round us up at their leisure.

I sat and I waited, but no one came. I could only hear slight sounds of movement as they moved from spot to spot, but I got the impression that they were just as reluctant to move as I was. In this kind of environment, the advantage goes to the stationary person. Moving creates noise, no matter how quiet you try to be. And it creates changes in the shadows, giving something to see. A person hiding in the darkness can sit and wait as you approach, completely unaware of their presence. From the lack of sounds, I guessed they knew this too. That meant I either had to wait them out and hope Tony had more success, or it meant that I had to move.

Impatience finally won out and I moved, but my movement was excruciatingly slow as I made my way toward the center of the warehouse.

I stepped and I waited. I stepped again and I waited again. Each time I stopped, I held deathly still and listened for any hint of movement. And each time I stopped, I heard nothing.

I snuck forward again and froze when my foot bumped up against something in the dark. Whatever it was, it was soft and it was heavy. I was terrified as I imagined it was a person waiting in the shadows. I waited for them to stand up. I waited for the silent blast. It would be silent because you never hear the shot that kills you.

But there was nothing. I bent at the waist and looked closely at the form at my feet. It was a person, but he wouldn't be standing up ever again. He lay face down on the concrete, one arm lying neatly at his side and the other pinned under his body. It looked to be the guy who had initially raised the alarm. I wondered which shooter had gotten him, the big blast, or the flurry of smaller ones. I had to be content with wondering because there was no way I would be able to flip his large form.

I dropped to the ground and felt along the concrete near his body. There were little bits of junk, but I couldn't find what I was looking for. I was hoping he might have dropped his gun, leaving it for me to find. My bet was that it was still in his hand, tucked under his body and out of reach. I knelt down on all fours, grimacing as I tried to push my hand under his body. I could feel the wetness of his blood against my hand and arm as I forced my arm in. There was no gun that I could feel. It was either too far in or it had clattered to the ground when he fell. If that had happened, I could feel around for days without finding anything.

I moved on, changing course to get closer to the office. Trip had fallen as well and I didn't think to check him for weapons. There was also the cache of guns near the office. With any luck, no one would be guarding it and the weapons would be free for the taking. I knew better than to think that was really true, but I had to have something. I had to have hope, even if it was fleeting.

The main area around the office was surprisingly empty as far as I could tell. I snuck alongside a barrel and waited, but I was greeted only with silence. I edged forward toward the box with the guns, staying on the balls of my feet as I tried to move in silence. I could barely make out the empty sleeping bags on the floor in front of me. To my right, there was a sudden shift in the darkness. A dark shadow rose in front of me, eclipsing the meager source of light from behind it. Someone was standing in front of me.

"Hello, Andy," the man said in a low voice. It was my uncle Jacob.

My heart sank at the realization of my circumstance. He towered above me; his lower arm was outstretched toward me. Through the dim light around us, I could barely make out the silhouette of the pistol at the end of his arm.

"I have to give you credit. Nice work with the lights. You pretty much stopped us in our tracks with that one. But you didn't really think it would work out did you? I mean, you did bring a knife to a gunfight, after all."

I took a deep breath before I spoke. My knees were trembling with fear and adrenaline and I was afraid that my voice would crack and waver. I had to show confidence. One thing I had come to believe about my uncle was that fear would not draw mercy. "I thought the knife worked out fairly well. I got three of you and who knows what Tony has done. You might be the only one left." Of course, it was a lie. I had only killed two. The big guy could have been killed by his own crew for all I knew. I was stretching the truth and I hoped it would throw him off balance.

My uncle laughed at the thought. "I'm not worried about him. He's not even armed. But you should be proud of yourself for killing three."

As we faced each other, something didn't make sense. Why was he talking to me? He had shot my dad, so he shouldn't have any reason for me to live. The others and I had just been a way for Jacob to hurt my dad. Hadn't we? I started to wonder if I didn't really understand the man's motives. Maybe it was me he was after. Either way, his hesitation brought an opportunity that I couldn't afford to miss.

I swung my upper body to the left in a quick movement while bringing the knife up to my uncle's gun hand. I made a quick swipe, hoping that the blade would cut him. I couldn't see well, but I felt the knife come against resistance and there was no clank of metal against metal. I had hit flesh.

Jacob howled and the gun went off. I felt a small burst of wind as the bullet rocketed by and slammed into the barrel behind me. It had missed me by a couple inches at most, but it had missed me. Almost immediately, there was the sound of another shot from near my feet as the gun hit the ground, bounced, and skidded away.

I broke into a blind run, angling toward the corner of the office. I reached the barrel that stood at the edge of the building and fumbled around the top. I felt for the guns, but I only found some of the items Jacob's crew had used to entertain themselves. I felt Trip's notepad; I felt a couple of magazines and couple of other items I couldn't identify in the darkness. I did not feel the box that should have been there.

Behind me, Jacob either found his gun that had fallen to the floor or had reached the same conclusion I had because I heard his feet slap against the concrete as he came for me. I abandoned the search and pushed off backwards, running for the shelves where I had hidden before. I hoped that the hard turn would afford me an extra second to increase the distance.

I stretched my legs as far as I could, and I prayed that I wouldn't encounter some unseen object that would drop me to the ground. I could make out the outline of the shelves in front of me with the trace of ambient light cast by the lights from behind me. I started to dive under the bottom shelf, but I felt a hand at my back that was shoving me forward.

My feet lifted off the ground as my entire body lurched forward. I collided with the shelves, my knees smashing into the lower one and my shoulder slamming into the one above. I bounced off, turning as I fell to the ground and then smacking the back of my head against the concrete. I blinked away the dots in front of my eyes and shook my head before rolling onto my stomach. The shelves were right in front of me. If I could just get to the other side, there was the possibility I might hide.

I reached forward to pull myself under the row of shelving and I noticed the knife was no longer in my hand. I had dropped it when I collided with the shelves. Back behind me, Jacob was reaching for my legs to pull me back to him. Finding the knife was not an option.

I reached the shelf and leaned forward, kicking out to send my body under and across. I had just grabbed the far end when I felt his hand close around my ankle. He yanked me back with ease and my belly scraped across the wood of the shelf as my body slid across. Reaching the end of the shelf, I fell a couple inches onto the concrete, feeling its coolness across my belly where my shirt had pulled up.

"Help!" I called out. "Tony!"

"He can't help you, Andy! You've lost. All of you have lost!" He flipped me over and dropped his weight onto my chest. I twisted and turned as I tried to get myself free, but he pinned my forearms under his knees. He was so big and I was so small. He seemed so strong and I felt so weak. It was as though I was being held down by a monster large enough to lift cars and fling them around like toys.

The darkness kept me from seeing clearly, but I could see the evil in his face. It was as though he had become someone else. He had become *something* else. The eyes that looked back at me were devoid of humanity. I only saw the cold fierceness of a predator as he attacked. And I was his prey. It was just like the dog that attacked Lanie, only there was no one to save me.

He wrapped his fingers around my throat and squeezed. The path to my lungs choked off in an instant. It seemed like only seconds before a different darkness started creeping in from the edges. It was a soft, gray shadow that moved toward the center. It smothered everything in my vision from the outside in. Bright speckles followed that stood out in dark contrast against the darkness.

I began to feel lightheaded and giddy as he squeezed the life out of me. I was fading into the darkness that had invaded my vision and I would never emerge. But suddenly, an enormous blast assaulted my ears and the grip on my neck subsided. It seemed to be the same blast from before that echoed throughout the building in waves, but it had a different quality. It was thunderous, but it was almost far away at the same time. I wondered if my hearing was fading along with my vision.

With the pressure gone from my throat, I tried to draw in breath with a great gasp, but no air came. I tried again as I fought against the loss of consciousness, but it was in vain. Jacob still sat on my chest, slumped over so that he was almost hugging me. His hand rested on the concrete beside me and he laid still.

I struggled and I pushed to try to get his weight off me, but I could not budge him. I was stuck beneath his weight. But as I lay there, I watched as Jacob sat up and started to stand before he fell over onto his side, releasing the compression on my lungs. The air came into my lungs in heaves, slowly pushing the darkness away from my vision. I sucked in breath and savored it. Rich oxygen was slowly vanquishing the dizziness that had swelled with suffocation.

In front of me, there was a darker darkness just as there had been when Jacob stood up. It had no shape; it was only one shadow across a backdrop of more shadow. I felt a hand close around my wrist and pull, bringing me to my feet.

"Are you okay?" It was my dad's voice. But it couldn't be.

"Tony? Is that you?" I rejected the idea that it was my father as soon as the thought came into my head. That was a hope I couldn't allow to be crushed, so I kept it from becoming a hope in the first place.

"It's me, son. Are you hurt?"

Again, it was my father's voice. Even in his reassurance, I was afraid to believe it.

"How? He shot you. I watched him," I croaked, drawing my hand up to my throat. I never realized how much it hurt to be strangled.

"Whoa, try not to talk. He shot Tony. In the foot of all places. I don't know how, but you called it."

"There's two-" The fire in my throat made me stop, but I forced myself to continue. "Two more." I tried to step around him to see. There was only darkness behind him, but I suddenly felt very exposed.

My dad gripped my arm, holding me in place. "It's okay, Andy. I got them. It's over. We're safe."

EPILOGUE

"Who's ready for a burger?" Tony asks. He stands at the grill, a spatula in one hand and the handle of his cane in the other. My dad had volunteered to do the burgers, but Tony wouldn't have it. He was tired of sitting around not doing anything. The bullet had gone through his foot without doing irreparable damage, but it had still taken its toll. He'd likely be using the cane for at least the next several weeks, if not longer.

The group answers his call in a chorus. He piles the burgers onto a cookie sheet, making an odd, meat pyramid decorated with various cheeses. Some are covered with Swiss or jack, while others sport delicious layers of cheddar. He lowers the sheet to the table, being careful to keep too much weight from bearing down on his foot. He says it doesn't hurt much anymore, but we catch him wincing more often than he would like to admit.

Things aren't quite getting back to normal, but they are a little better. Three weeks isn't quite enough time for too many miracles to happen. But I am at least sleeping through the night without seeing ghosts from the past. It has been at least a week since I've seen myself killing Trip or Darrel in my dreams. I have no idea whether the dreams are gone for good, but I can hope.

Then again, I guess normal is still relative. I'm still trying to get a good grasp of what normal really is. Normal used to be spending each day with Sarah. We might have gone to a movie or out to eat or maybe just stayed home. What was important was that we were together. Now, there is no Sarah and that is still the hardest thing to get used to. I don't know if I'll ever get used to it.

"What kind of cheese do you want, babe?" my mom asks as she pulls a bun from the clear, plastic packaging on the table.

"Don't worry about it, mom. I can get it."

"Shush. You may have had fifteen or twenty years to get used to you being an adult, but I've only had three weeks. Don't you take all of it away at once," she says, pointing the bun toward me.

"Fine, mom. Cheddar," I say, rolling my eyes in mock annoyance. The truth is that I can only imagine how hard it might be for a mom to have her child suddenly be an adult without the gradual process that normally takes close to two decades. To her, the change was overnight and dramatic.

Tony, Lisa, Lanie, and my mom stand at the table, dressing their burgers. My dad sits at the far end of the table sipping a light beer. I can't see how he can drink that stuff. He has the sophisticated palette of a chef and he's drinking light beer. Even still, I resist the urge to lick my lips. The sun was warm today and a freezing cold beer sounded awesome. Unfortunately, that is another area where my mom still draws a line. "You aren't 21. It's not legal," she said when I mentioned something about wanting one a couple weeks ago.

Although, I guess that's better than the reality from my alternate past. She hasn't really drunk much since the night she was upset about Lanie. She's had a glass of wine with dinner a couple of times, but she's always been able to stop there. That is one of the positives from this whole experience. I actually have my mom back. In fact, I'm building relationships with both my parents that I've never had before.

My mom fills three plates with burgers, potato salad, baked beans, and chips. She sits one plate in front of my dad and the other in front of me. My mouth instantly begins to water as I look down at the backyard feast in front of me. The rest of the gang loads their plates as well and each takes their place around the table.

Tony lifts his burger to his mouth, but doesn't take a bite. "So, Joe," he asks. "You figure out what you're going to tell your dad?" As soon as the question was out, he sinks his teeth into the burger, taking a big bite.

"No. Yes. I don't know," he says as he takes his own bite of burger.

"I'm pretty sure you have to pick from one of those, not use all of them. It kind of sends a mixed message, don't you think?" Lisa teases.

"Very funny." My dad pitches a potato chip at her. It bounces off her neck and catches in her blouse instead of falling to the table. "I'm just not sure I have a choice now. Jacob is dead and there is no heir without me."

"We do need an heir," Tony says. "If we don't have a leader, we won't know where to go, who to guide. How about you, Andy? You want the job?" He smiles as he takes another bite.

"Oh, no. Not me. I wouldn't even know what to do. I'm not even sure I know how to be a nine-year-old boy."

"But you'll be ten in a week," my dad says with a smirk. "Nah, I couldn't do that to him. Anyway, it's my job. Plus, I don't have the reason anymore that I don't want them to have to know about it. Maybe it's time I accepted what's mine. We don't always get to pick the situations we find ourselves in." My dad points the end of his beer toward me as he says that last part.

He's right: we don't get to pick it. Luckily, though, human beings are very adaptable creatures. We can get used to just about anything. I'm finally starting to get used to this idea of being a kid. Or at least I'm not doing a double take every time I see myself in the mirror anymore. What is weird about it is that I don't really feel like a kid or an adult. It's almost as though I'm trapped somewhere in between. Even my parents see it. My mom said that she wasn't sure how many candles to put on my birthday cake – ten or thirty-six.

She meant it as a joke, but it is a real question for me. When this mess started, my body belonged to a kid and my brain belonged to an adult. There isn't such a clear distinction anymore. Things are different now. My grandpa said I wouldn't forget and, so far, he's been right. All my memories are intact and I still know how to do everything I knew how to do a month ago. I still look like a nine-year-old who is going to be ten in a week. But it's more than that.

The way I see things is changing; everyone is getting *older*. At first, my mom's youthfulness was striking. Some of it had to do with a comparison to the mom I had left in the future, but it wasn't just that.

Tony and Lisa were young; my dad was young. Lanie was a *baby*. She was young enough to be my own daughter.

But then, I started noticing the lines in my parents' faces. The signs of age became more pronounced. It was subtle at first, but it was more and more noticeable each day. They seemed to gain years for each week that passed. And it's the same with Lanie. She is getting closer to me. My parents and Lanie's parents are getting farther away and she is getting closer. I wondered how long it would be before we intersected and she began to move away again, only in the opposite direction.

That's really the key, I think. Lanie still looks twelve. My parents and her parents look like they are in their thirties. I am the one who is changing. I am seeing them relative to me. This change is a comfort because I am not feeling as alien in this new world, at least as far as appearances go. But it is also alarming because I don't know what impact all of this will have on my relationships. When I see kids who are the same physical age as me, I feel a sort of kinship. As soon as I talk to them, though, that feeling vanishes as quickly as it comes.

I still lack the spirit of a child. Children have a sense of wonder because so much of what they experience is new. They have an immaturity because they have not yet lived a life full of the experiences that will forge them into adults. That difference still worries me. I worry that the next several years of my life might be without any deep relationships. I cannot build relationships with adults because they see me as a child. I can't develop strong friendships with kids because I still see them as children. I feel like I lack common ground to build on.

I worry about the effect this might have when I do finally meet Sarah in this life. Will I see her as a child and be unable to wait for her? We grew together in our first life. In this second one, I have done the growing and she is still at the starting point. I don't know how this will change things and it scares me.

As I look across the table at Lanie, I think to myself that she is still the only child I can really relate to. She is still a child and there are limits to our relationship. There are limits to what we can talk about because there are limits to what she can understand. Like other children, she lacks the wisdom, experience, and maturity that comes from age.

At the same time, she has lost part of her innocence. She is a different child than she was before. She still smiles and she still laughs, but there is a new seriousness about her. I think she has found that there are no limits to the evil that people can bring to the world around us. She doesn't see the world with the same naiveté she did a month ago. She sees that there is real danger that should be feared.

We finish our meal and we sit well into the night. We talk and we laugh. We watch the stars as the day transitions into darkness. The crickets and other creatures of the night came to life, keeping us company as we sit together. We talk about life and we talk about death. We talk about Timekeepers and the threat of Jacob's attempt at a coup.

As we sit, my mind often returns to the idea of second chances. This ordeal has been scary and it has been stressful. I have spent a good deal of it wishing to go home. I have never wished for anything the way I wished for Sarah to be at my side again. But my uncle's words have echoed in my head since he said them. There is nothing to go back to. I left a shell of a body behind and it is without life. It is without a future. The cosmic mishap that allowed me to follow a time rip back to my youth gave me a second chance at life.

Finally, we give our hugs and we say our goodbyes for the night. My parents and I take the short walk home and say our own goodnights. Climbing into bed, I am finally confident that the ghosts of the past might leave me in peace. I hope I will no longer feel the need to chase what might have been. Instead, I hope to embrace my life as it now is. I am ready for a new future, even if it is uncertain. Because it is, at least, a future.

(Not) The End

ACKNOWLEDGEMENTS

Most endeavors of any size require much more than the efforts of a single person to pull off. This book is not an exception. The contributions of several people have helped make this book much better than I would have been able to do on my own.

First, I would like to thank all of my friends who offered encouragement as I began the long process of committing this story to paper. Writing a first novel can be daunting, but my good friends offered a lot of support as I worked through it. There are too many to name here, but they know who they are. Or at least I hope they do.

Next, I want to thank my faithful beta readers. These brave souls slogged through early drafts, pointing out unanswered questions and areas for improvement. Mindy Barrett, Greg and Denise Coleman, Nicki Redes, Sarah Aisling, Maeghan Thomas, and Cassy Miller offered up their time and talent to help make this book better.

Finally, I want to express a special thanks to my wife, Cassy. Thank you for being the inspiration for Sarah Meyers. Thank you for being my number one encourager and supporter through this whole process. Thank you for being you. I couldn't have done this without you.

About the Author

Mike E. Miller makes his home in a small suburb on the southern edge of Kansas City, MO. He lives with his lovely wife, his two phenomenal boys, a neurotic German shepherd, and a tuxedo cat who believes he owns the place.

Mike loves to hear from his readers. You can contact him at MikeEMillerBooks@gmail.com.

www.ingramcontent.com/pod-product-compliance
Lightning Source LLC
Chambersburg PA
CBHW070816120626
46556CB00002B/524